Praise for *The Apprentice Witch*

An Amazon Best Book of 2017
A Summer 2017 Indie Next List Selection
A Barnes & Noble Best Books for Young Readers Pick

"*The Apprentice Witch* will at once open a new and imaginative world and feel like the book you have loved forever. I couldn't turn the pages fast enough!"
—Jennifer A. Nielsen, author of *The False Prince*

"*The Apprentice Witch* is entirely more charming, adventurous, and full of heart than a book has any right to be. Make no mistake: There's magic afoot."
—Trenton Lee Stewart, author of *The Mysterious Benedict Society*

"[*The Apprentice Witch*] takes readers on a pleasant trip back to a simpler age. . . . Arianwyn is a likeable hero, with well-drawn struggles—both professional and personal." —*The New York Times Book Review*

"There is something in the air of its world that causes a reader to breathe deeply and be immersed. Its characters feel known to us, its forests trodden by our feet. . . . One of the delightful aspects of *The Apprentice Witch* is the effortless and natural feel to the worldbuilding."
—Kenny Brechner for *Publishers Weekly's ShelfTalker*

"With brisk pacing and sophisticated writing, this book is one of those rare, unputdownable gems. This tale is somewhat reminiscent of J.K. Rowling's *Fantastic Beasts and Where to Find Them*, and fans of magical fantasy will be enthralled with the details of this fascinating world." —*School Library Journal*

"While adorned with funny and charming details, Arianwyn's story is primarily one of personal growth and discovery that will gratify fantasy readers." —*Booklist*

"Feeling at once fresh and familiar, James Nicol's enchanting debut will charm fans of Jennifer Nielsen, J.K. Rowling and Eva Ibbotson. The world of *The Apprentice Witch* is comfortable, funny, and well-imagined. Underneath all the magic, fey creatures and monsters, Arianwyn's struggles with self-doubt will ring true with readers." —*Shelf Awareness*

"An insecure young witch comes into her own in this pleasantly old-fashioned fantasy debut. . . . This one is as cozy as a teapot and as comfy as old slippers." —*Kirkus Reviews*

"These believable and engaging characters appreciate each other's talents and collaborate to annihilate their demon foes. Readers who enjoy fantasy and challenging predicaments will appreciate Arianwyn's transformation from a failure to a competent and valued sorcerer." —*School Library Connection*

"Magical. . . . Readers will love this fast-paced fantasy read and won't be able to put it down." —*B&N Kids Blog*

"In Nicol's charming debut novel, failed witch Arianwyn Gribble learns of the power that comes with knowing one's self-worth and conquering the darkness within." —*Publishers Weekly*

"A middle grade fantasy novel with all the charm of Harry Potter, but a magic all its own." —*Portland Book Review*

"Nicol's debut offers a fresh take on the genre. . . . Infused with mystery, adventure, and bundles of charm." —Fiona Noble, *The Bookseller*

"The plot moves along at a steady pace that gives the reader just enough time to enjoy the magical details that debut author, James Nicol, has seamlessly woven into the story . . . [and] quickens dramatically as we reach the cinematic climax when the book becomes impossible to put down." —*The Bookbag* (UK)

"A charming tale of magic, bravery and friendship, reminiscent of Diana Wynne Jones." —*Guardian* (UK)

THE APPRENTICE WITCH

THE APPRENTICE WITCH

JAMES NICOL

Chicken House

SCHOLASTIC INC.

ISBN 978-1-338-11860-5

10 9 8 7 6 5 4 3 2 1   18 19 20 21 22

Printed in the U.S.A. 40

This edition first printing 2018

Book design by Maeve Norton

Grandmothers are the best but
mine *really* is magic!

For Mollie Rose Serella—with love.

Witches have always used magical symbols known as glyphs to harness, control, and utilize the magic around us. There are four cardinal glyphs and two secondary glyphs. Imagine that magic is like thread and glyphs like a needle. One without the other is of limited use. A witch will use one or more glyphs to pull magic toward her, and as the magic and glyphs connect, a spell is formed. Despite all witches using the same set of glyphs, the individual skill of the witch, and the natural deposits of magic used, makes every spell entirely unique to the caster.

CHAPTER ONE

THE CIVIL WITCHCRAFT AUTHORITY

itches of Hylund, the poster declared, *your country needs you! Join up TODAY!* Arianwyn stared up at the elegant woman gazing proudly from the poster. The woman's hair was golden and flowing, her lips bright red. She wore the dark navy uniform and the silver star of a fully trained witch. Arianwyn glanced down at her coat and the space that her own star would soon occupy.

Far-off bells sounded the hour, cutting through the noise of busy morning traffic rushing past, horns screaming out across the bustling street. She would be late if she stood daydreaming much longer. Grabbing her bag, she skipped between the crush of passersby through tall wrought-iron gates, following the signs for registration. Steps led through an open doorway and into a long, gleaming corridor.

Other witches rushed past—some now proudly displaying bright new stars and broad grins—as did administrative staff carrying stacks of files or clutching clipboards. The air was full of excited chatter and the tang of damp wool coats and antiseptic cleaners. Arianwyn's wet shoes squeaked across the polished floor.

She joined one of several haphazard lines and suddenly wished she hadn't. Gimma Alverston was handing over her identity card at the desk, surrounded as ever by a small group of other young witches.

Gimma looked just like the witch on the poster outside, all flowing golden hair and bright smile. Arianwyn patted nervously at her own messy curls and tried to shrink back into the line. But she was too late—and too tall. One of the other girls—a neatly dressed witch who Arianwyn recognized as Polly Walden—nudged Gimma and pointed in her direction. Gimma glanced over, offered a mean, tight smile, and whispered something to the others. The corridor rang with cruel giggling and Arianwyn went red. *This is all I need*, she thought. *What did I ever do to her?*

Gimma was cruel and a snob, and you were either with her or against her. She'd been like this since they first met at school five years ago. As they had been the only witches in their year, everyone had assumed they would get along, but Gimma had made it quite clear she didn't want to be friends with Arianwyn, and that was that.

"Oh, look, it's Arianwyn 'Dribble'!" Gimma called out as she retrieved her card from the young man at the desk and tucked it away in the silly tiny beaded bag that she always carried with her. "Ready for your evaluation?" More laughter. Gimma moved slowly down the line until she reached Arianwyn. "I've already been offered a position as a private witch for a family in Highbridge, you know," she said smugly. "I wouldn't be seen dead dealing with some old lady's pixie infestation, or making charms for a bunch of country bumpkins. What do you think you'll be doing, Dribble, if you pass?"

The other girls crowded around Arianwyn, smirking. Gimma flicked her mane of shiny hair. "I *do* hope they find you something you can cope with, nothing too taxing! Not everyone has the luxury of the training my family provided for me. Who trained *you*, Arianwyn?" she asked, even though everybody already knew.

Arianwyn didn't reply, her cheeks burning.

"I heard it was her *grandmother*," Polly whispered nastily.

She wished more than anything that she had the nerve to do something, say something. But she looked away, as she had so many times before, finding a spot on the wall to focus on even as tears pricked at her eyes. This was the usual way she dealt with Gimma's taunts.

Ignore her and she'll get bored.

"Er . . . name, please? Miss? Hello?"

Arianwyn had reached the front of the line and hadn't noticed. Gimma and her group had wandered off. A harassed young man, about her age, smiled politely at her as he fumbled with piles of folders, a typewriter, and various notes. His dark hair flopped across his face and he tried to blow it out of his eyes.

"Sorry. I'm Arianwyn Gribble." She smiled.

"And do you have your identity card, please, Miss . . . Gribble? Oh, here you are!" He yanked a brown card folder from the bottom of a precarious pile, which wobbled threateningly. He blushed as Arianwyn handed over her witch's identity card, clearly stamped with a large blue *UA* for Unevaluated Apprentice. As the young man reached forward, the column of paperwork shifted, quivered, and slowly started to slide toward the floor. As quick as a blink, Arianwyn leaned forward and with her index finger sketched a tiny symbol onto the desk.

Briå, the air glyph.

It glowed with a soft blue light that only a witch could see. The papers and folders not only righted themselves but also started to slide into the correct order on the desk.

The boy smiled again. "Thank you!"

"*What* is going on here?"

A voice, raspy and indignant, cut through the hubbub of the room. A shriveled, spidery woman in a severe gray suit that didn't fit entirely well stood glaring at them both over the top of some very thick spectacles.

"Oh, Miss Newam, sorry! I was just about to fetch you. This is Miss Gribble, here for the eleven o'clock evaluation ceremony."

Miss Newam continued to stare, as if waiting for further explanation.

"Well, you see," the boy continued hopelessly. "There are so many files, and they were all getting in a muddle with so many witches coming and going and suddenly— whoosh! They're all falling onto the floor. And Miss Gribble here was *amazing*! She just tapped something on the desk and they all zipped back into place. Look—good as new!" He gestured to the orderly pile of folders.

The woman's eyes narrowed to two tiny slits. "Colin, I am neither interested nor concerned with what Miss Gribble did or did not do with your folders. It is your job simply to ensure the apprentice witches are put through for their evaluations as soon as possible, not to engage them in performing little . . . tricks!"

Colin glanced at Arianwyn and shrugged.

Miss Newam hadn't quite finished. "If it's not too inconvenient, perhaps you could go and fetch the files I need from my office. I'll deal with Miss Gribble."

Colin gave Arianwyn a gentle smile, his cheeks flushed, and jogged off down the corridor, dodging the tide of oncoming apprentices.

"Miss Newam, it's really not his fault . . ." Arianwyn attempted to explain, but fell silent as Miss Newam's full attention turned on her.

"Miss Gribble, we don't want to keep everyone waiting. I have two more evaluation ceremonies to get through today. What with war work claiming some of our most experienced witches and the recent increase in dark spirits, every village and hamlet from Goldham to Vellingstone has suddenly decided it needs a witch. We simply can't keep up with the demand, even when we take on young ones such as yourself."

"Yes, I see," Arianwyn said.

"Do you have any family with you?"

"No, I'm on my own," she replied, feeling guilty about slipping out of the apartment so early and hiding the letter with the details of the evaluation from her grandmother. Miss Newam shot her a suspicious glance and opened the brown file on the desk, flicking through some of the papers.

"Ah, I see you've been an apprentice for only two years?"

"Yes," Arianwyn replied. "But I wanted to—"

"And you were trained by?"

"Maria Stronelli . . . my grandmother."

Miss Newam gazed over the top of her spectacles again. "I see. And now you are apprenticed to?"

Arianwyn blushed, recalling Polly's taunts. "My grandmother."

"Well, that's rather . . . old-fashioned." Miss Newam stared hard at her, then back at the paperwork, as if she were trying to figure something out. Then her face lit up. "Oh, Madam Stronelli is on the Council of Elders." She peered closer at Arianwyn through the soda-bottle spectacles and smiled. But it was bitter and tight, not really a smile at all.

A knot of anxiety twisted in Arianwyn's stomach. She could see Miss Newam was about to say more when a tinny voice crackled out from a speaker fixed high up on the wall.

"Could all apprentices for the eleven o'clock evaluation ceremony please proceed to the central courtyard. That's the central courtyard for the eleven o'clock evaluation. Thank you."

CHAPTER TWO

THE EVALUATION GAUGE

A small group of other apprentices waited in the freezing, rain-drenched courtyard, surrounded by well-wishers. Gimma was there with her parents. Her mother wore an expensive fur-collared jacket and an elegant skirt, and fussed over her daughter's uniform. Her father chatted jovially with several men who were dressed in the robes of the Royal Senate. Gimma glanced coolly at Arianwyn.

"Quickly now!" Miss Newam barked, ushering the fifteen young witches onto the platform. All wore navy dresses and smart navy coats, their shoes polished and their hair sleek, but all identically damp. Arianwyn caught sight of her reflection in a window: a head taller than all the other girls, hair already frizzing in the rain.

She sighed. Whoever thought it was a good idea to hold a ceremony outside on a wet and cold January morning was crazy or sadistic. *It was probably Miss Newam.*

The air buzzed with excitement but Arianwyn just couldn't muster the enthusiasm; a sense of dread had been creeping over her all morning. She couldn't shake it off.

A peal of giggles from farther along the line drew her attention and she quickly glanced at Gimma. How did she manage to look so perfect even in this downpour, when Arianwyn looked so messy? Gimma turned just in time to catch Arianwyn staring at her again.

Jinxing-jiggery!

"Eyes front, Miss Gribble!" Miss Newam prowled the line of apprentices, adjusting collars and snatching hands from pockets.

Arianwyn felt uneasy. Something was wrong, off balance. She ought to be excited, she thought. Soon, she would realize her dream: All she had wanted since she could first remember was to serve the kingdom, just like her mother and grandmother had, and like her brave father still did . . . and yet that sense of dread lurked.

There was a quiet commotion as elegant doors were flung open and August Coot, the director of Thaumaturgy and head of the Civil Witchcraft Authority, appeared. A gramophone burbled into life, the slow stirring sounds of the national anthem echoed around the courtyard, and everyone immediately stood a little straighter.

"Honor the magic. Serve the kingdom. Honor the king. Serve the magic."

The apprentices spoke as one as the music faded and the director stepped up to the lectern and began his speech.

"Good morning, everyone, and thank you for attending this evaluation ceremony. The evaluation today will be carried out by Miss Hortensia Newam, in full consideration of the Civil Witchcraft Authority's policies and procedures." He shuffled his papers and cleared his throat.

"These young witches are about to embark on wonderful careers serving their country. They will hold positions of honor among their new communities at this difficult time of war on the continent. As you will be aware, numbers of spirit creatures and, indeed, dark spirits have increased by more than ten percent in the last five years alone, and the Royal Senate has requested action. Our new witches will play a vital role as the Civil Witchcraft Authority embarks on our first ever mission to catalog the various types of spirit creature present in the Four Kingdoms!"

There were a few murmurs of interest from the crowd, but clearly not the response Director Coot had been hoping for. He coughed and glanced quickly at the speech laid out before him before continuing.

But through the pouring rain and the chattering of her teeth, Arianwyn could barely concentrate. She was thankful when the speech eventually came to its groaning end and there was a small clatter of applause. The director moved to one side as Miss Newam approached the first apprentice, a cheery-looking girl in glasses. The young man, Colin, appeared on the stage. He carried what seemed to be a moderately sized dark wooden box with a large electric lightbulb on the top and several switches, buttons, and recording dials on one side. The evaluation gauge!

Miss Newam set about unraveling the twisted cream wire that was attached to a slender metal wand ending in a perfect shiny sphere.

Next, she unrolled a small chart that displayed the cardinal glyphs. "Focus on all four glyphs at once," she said to the waiting apprentices curtly. "We wouldn't want any *actual* spells forming, would we?"

She flicked the switch on the evaluation gauge and it hummed into life. The first girl offered her palm to Miss Newam and the silver wand was lowered.

The assembled crowd held its breath as the seconds ticked past. After a long minute the evaluation gauge sputtered to life, the light pulsed, and a thin curl of paper spewed from its side. Miss Newam pulled the readout free.

"Pass!" she called after a moment.

There was a ripple of applause from the other witches and well-wishers. Miss Newam tucked the reading into a folder and moved on. The cheery girl blushed with excitement and waved happily to someone in the crowd.

Arianwyn shuffled impatiently as one witch after the other was tested, the gauge whirring and churning out its thin ribbon of paper. It took a different amount of time for each witch. Polly's evaluation was over within a matter of seconds, but then Gimma's took an agonizing five minutes, which Arianwyn was secretly pleased about. Still, each time Miss Newam announced "Pass!" and the courtyard echoed with the same applause and loving calls of support.

And then eventually, Director Coot, Miss Newam, and Colin were standing right in front of her, the last witch in the line.

Miss Newam arched an eyebrow, reached back for the evaluation gauge, and flipped the switch. It hummed slightly. She stretched toward Arianwyn with the silver probe wand and Arianwyn took a deep but shaky breath.

"Please focus on the glyphs," Miss Newam commanded. She held up the poster with the cardinal glyphs printed on it.

BRIÅ

ALUNA

ERTE

ÅRDRA

Arianwyn closed her eyes, breathing deeply and steadily, and pictured the glyphs all together.

There was a very faint pull of magic from somewhere nearby. It flowed toward her and she felt the softest tingle as magic brushed against her skin.

The cool metal of the wand pressed into her palm.

She could hear Miss Newam breathing in and out through her nose with the tiniest whistling sound.

She kept the glyphs focused in her mind.

Briå: air, flight, transformation.

A small surge of power zipped through Arianwyn as the flow of energy connected with her.

Aluna: water, healing, divination.

The sensation was like cold pins and needles. She felt dizzy.

Erte: earth, strength, protection, life.

The glyphs formed and died in the darkness like rare flowers.

Ärdra: fire, energy, defense.

And then she saw it, hanging there, blooming in her mind among the other glyphs.

Not now! Arianwyn thought, and tried to blink it away.

It was an impossible glyph. One that didn't really exist except in her imagination. Its shape was strange and yet familiar. She could feel its power pulling on the flow of magic that lingered around the square. She tried not to focus on it, but it was larger and bolder than the other four, although it didn't glow in the same way. It was dark and seemed to suck light toward it.

Stop it!

This hadn't happened for ages. Typical that it should happen today of all days.

The last time she had seen it this clearly it had ended so badly . . . no, she wouldn't think about that now.

She had kept it a secret, telling nobody, not even Grandmother. And yet something drew her to the strangeness of its shape, and before she knew what she was doing or why, she was reaching toward it with her mind.

It bristled with energy. But it felt cool, distant. Not warm and vibrant like the real glyphs.

Arianwyn felt the connection and now it was too late to stop. It felt as though all the energy nearby was suddenly doubled and rushing toward her, slamming into her with a jolt.

Her eyes flew open and she stumbled back on the platform. The gloomy day seemed somehow darker than it had only seconds ago. The shadows thicker, blacker. The evaluation gauge whirred and then several loud popping sounds echoed around the courtyard. The lights in the offices blinked out. The watchers gasped. Miss Newam gave a small cry of dismay as a thin column of smoke twisted steadily from the evaluation gauge.

"Is it broken?" Colin asked, peering over the top of the smoking device.

Miss Newam glared at him. "No . . . I don't think so. A power surge has interrupted the recording, that's all!" She flicked switches, twisted dials.

Nothing!

Arianwyn's heart quickened. What had just happened? She glanced down at her hands. Tiny bright sparks of energy flew from her palms and fingertips. The dizzy sensation passed over her again and she struggled to focus.

Miss Newam repeated her frantic switch flicking and this time the ribbon of paper unwound slowly from the slot at the base of the gauge. She tugged it free and held it so that the pale light caught the reading. A moment's hesitation played across the woman's features and then a small look of triumph replaced it as she turned back to Arianwyn.

"I regret to inform you, Miss Gribble, that your result is 'ungraded.'" She seemed unable to hide the joy in her voice.

There was a gasp from someone in the audience, followed by excited whispering.

Miss Newam thrust the recording forward for Arianwyn to see. She took it with shaking hands, thankful that the sparks had now vanished. It was full of small markings and a squiggling red line. It meant nothing to her.

She was sure she was going to be sick; she could feel every pair of eyes in the courtyard on her. All she wanted to do was run, run away as fast as she could. But she couldn't move.

"I think we shall take a moment just to deal with this," the director said in a mock cheery voice, and he indicated for Arianwyn and Miss Newam to follow him. Colin trailed after them, the evaluation gauge still smoking in his arms.

As they crossed the courtyard Arianwyn saw someone moving at the back of the watchers: a tall, elegant figure draped in a dark coat, with a bright sunshine-yellow shawl flicking in the wind, her face partly hidden under a large-brimmed hat.

Grandmother!

Arianwyn's heart sank through the floor. She had been here the whole time, had witnessed everything. Things couldn't possibly get any worse!

"Director Coot!" Her grandmother stepped out of the crowd. "Might I have a word, please?"

Arianwyn looked away. Her cheeks felt as though they were alight. She sensed every pair of eyes in the courtyard shift back and forth between her grandmother and the director.

"Elder Stronelli, what an . . . honor." The director glanced around at Miss Newam, Colin, and Arianwyn, as if unsure exactly how to proceed. But there was no way Grandmother was going to take no for an answer. She scowled at the director, a look that could turn Arianwyn's blood to ice.

"It would be my great pleasure, of course." He smiled.

The director led them into a small office off the court-yard. As the door clicked shut the director turned to Miss Newam. "Well?" he demanded. "What is this all about? I've been director here for twenty years now and never seen an apprentice fail an evaluation test like this before. What on earth is going on?"

Arianwyn could feel her legs wobbling, suddenly unable to hold her up. She steadied herself against the wall, still unable to meet her grandmother's gaze. She really thought she might be sick.

Miss Newam stepped forward, wafting the reading from the gauge. "Ungraded means that the evaluation device has been unsuccessful in picking up a required level of energy."

"And that means?" the director pressed, his cheeks red, his eyes wide.

"It means!" Miss Newam snapped, and then, clearly thinking better of it, said more calmly, "It means, Director Coot, that while Miss Gribble should be able to perform the majority of simple tasks, she is unlikely to be able to deal with more specialized problems, or ever develop beyond basic spell craft."

Arianwyn felt everything slowly start to slip away from her—all she had ever hoped for, all she had ever wanted to do.

"But what about the power surge?" Colin asked. "That might have affected the reading."

"The evaluation gauge got a clear reading before the surge," Miss Newam replied shortly.

No, this couldn't be happening, there had to have been some sort of mistake.

"Can't we test her again?" Director Coot asked. Arianwyn felt a flutter of hope.

"That's *quite* out of the question: We have a sufficient reading." Miss Newam moved to stand in front of the director, and there was a hurried whispered conversation that came to an abrupt halt when Grandmother coughed loudly.

"Perhaps, Director Coot, we might have our discussion now?" She glanced at Miss Newam. "In *private*?"

It was not a request.

"Very well," the director said, fanning his red face with a folder.

"This is ridiculous!" Miss Newam protested. "The council has no authority in these matters—"

"Thank you, Miss Newam!" the director said firmly. Then in a softer voice, "Perhaps you would all be so good as to wait outside for a few moments, please?"

Arianwyn followed Miss Newam and Colin out into the dim corridor and the door shut gently behind them. The corridor rang with silence.

A few minutes later Grandmother emerged. Director Coot followed, his stumpy legs struggling to keep up with the older woman's elegant stride down the corridor.

"Well, come along, then," he barked at Arianwyn, Colin, and Miss Newam. "Back to the courtyard, if you please!"

Outside, everyone had returned to the platform. The other witches scowled at Arianwyn as she rejoined the end of the line. Rain still fell steadily and those few people who had bothered to remain were looking decidedly soggy. Arianwyn had no idea what to expect next. She risked a quick glance at her grandmother, who stood still and calm at the back of the crowd.

Colin stood shivering to one side of the platform. He gave Arianwyn a cheery thumbs-up but she couldn't meet his beaming smile. Why was he being so nice?

Miss Newam and Director Coot were embroiled in a furious whispered conversation. Miss Newam pointed angrily at the director, who turned beet-red and responded in very hushed but definite tones.

After a few moments, the director seemed to win the silent argument. Slowly they started to make their way along the line onstage, pinning brilliant silver stars to the coats of all the other witches.

Arianwyn, terrified of what would happen when they reached her, stared straight ahead. She could feel everyone else just waiting for her turn, too.

"Ah, Miss Gribble," beamed the director as they finally reached her. "Despite your poor result, this doesn't completely prevent you from becoming a fully fledged witch at some point . . ."

The director held out his hand.

Miss Newam placed a small velvet box into it, just like she had for all the other witches. She smiled, but it looked wrong on her pinched face. Was this some cruel joke? Had there been a mistake? A thousand thoughts flashed through Arianwyn's mind.

The director fiddled with the clasp, and then he lifted his hand up to pin something onto Arianwyn's coat. There was a halting, stunned round of applause. Arianwyn glanced down. There was no bright silver star pinned to her coat, just a dull bronze disk.

CHAPTER THREE

HEADING HOME

The bronze brooch nestled against the dark of Arianwyn's coat. What had just happened?

The director turned to the waiting crowd.

"Ladies and gentlemen, despite her ungraded evaluation, we are delighted to award Miss Gribble the honor of the moon brooch. The moon brooch is awarded to an apprentice witch who displays potential but has not yet reached the full maturity of her powers. The Civil Witchcraft Authority is under immense pressure and we have a position that would have remained vacant otherwise."

Arianwyn's cheeks burned. What had happened in that office? She looked over at her grandmother again, but her face was hidden in shadow.

What had she done?

There was a faltering ripple of applause, dying as quickly as it started. Miss Newam moved a little closer and spoke to Arianwyn directly. "Evidently the director cares more for keeping on the good side of the Council of Elders than he does for procedure and protocol." Miss Newam threw a sour look in Grandmother's direction and then continued. "There is a small town, just a large village really, a back country sort of place, you know. I am sure they can be persuaded to take you on as an apprentice witch. You'll get on famously there. I have no doubt." She spat the last words, and her eyes flashed with malice as she jabbed the moon brooch with a spindly finger.

Arianwyn looked across at her grandmother. Her face was as white as bone and the rain on her cheeks looked just like tears.

Arianwyn huddled under an umbrella outside the Civil Witchcraft Authority buildings. She pretended to be reading a poster entitled "Everyday Spirit Creature Identification for You & Me," but secretly she watched as the newly qualified witches were whisked away by families and friends to celebrate with fancy lunches or rich afternoon teas at Kingsport's finest hotels and restaurants. Grandmother had stopped to talk with an old friend inside. The gutters ran heavy with water, overflowing onto the sidewalk.

Arianwyn felt a light tap on her shoulder and turned to see Colin. He clutched a large brown envelope. "Congratulations!" he said, indicating Arianwyn's badge.

"Thanks," she mumbled, trying desperately to hide it beneath the collar of her coat.

"Look, I know this isn't the result you were hoping for, but at least you've been given an assignment!" He smiled cheerfully and held out the envelope. "And," he whispered, "you can request a reevaluation in six months; the forms are inside." He shook the envelope encouragingly.

Arianwyn could see he was trying desperately to be helpful but she just couldn't stop herself. She snatched the envelope from Colin's hand. "That's wonderful! I'm over-joyed. No doubt being sent to the middle-of-nowhere's next-door neighbor, as an *apprentice* witch, will be a real hoot! Don't you have any idea how humiliating this all is?"

Colin stepped back quickly, obviously stung by her words, and started to mumble an apology.

"I think I'd rather just be on my own." Arianwyn turned away from him and came face-to-face with her grandmother. The old woman's eyes were narrow, her lips a thin line. Arianwyn knew that look. She was in trouble. She heard Colin's footsteps retreating into the building.

Sighing, she looked away, avoiding Grandmother's angry stare.

"Get in!" Grandmother said, her voice quiet and tired. She gestured to a gleaming Kingsport taxi that waited at the curb. Gleaming black, its bright lights shone in the gloom.

Inside, Grandmother issued the address and snapped shut the glass window that separated them from the driver. The taxi pulled away and the Civil Witchcraft building was swallowed up by the city and the dank afternoon gloom.

Arianwyn picked nervously at her soggy dress. Grand-mother fidgeted with her gloves. They glanced at each other, accusing, expectant. The taxi turned onto the Royal Circle and straight into the middle of a monstrous traffic jam. Muffled honks and toots from other cars reached them. The soft golden light of the Royal Palace shone through the rain.

"Say it! I know what you're thinking!" Arianwyn burst out, unable to wait a moment longer for the lecture she knew was coming.

"What do you want me to say?" Grandmother asked, her voice steady and calm.

"Something . . . anything! About this!" She pulled at the badge. "Or the evaluation. Or about how humiliated or angry you are, how I've let you down . . ." Arianwyn's voice broke, but she was determined not to cry. "Or how about what you said to the director in that office?"

Grandmother reached for Arianwyn's hand. "I had to. It was for the best."

Arianwyn snatched her hand away and scowled. "No way. You just didn't want to be embarrassed in front of your friends."

"Behaving like a spoiled child is not going to help the situation," Grandmother warned, her voice rising slightly.

"What? But I haven't—"

"And neither was picking on that poor young man at the CWA. No matter how upset you are, that's no excuse for being rude to others," Grandmother continued.

"I can't believe this," Arianwyn mumbled.

Grandmother reached out her hand again. "Perhaps it was too soon to ask for your evaluation. Most witches wouldn't end their apprenticeship until they were older, in my day."

"Oh for heaven's sake, Grandma, it's the modern world, not a hundred years ago. I'm ready to help. I want to help now! There's so much going on in the world, which you might be aware of if you ventured out from the bookstore more than twice a year!" She regretted the words as soon as she said them.

"Now you listen to me!" Grandmother pointed a finger in warning as she spoke. Arianwyn knew she had gone too far. "Despite my *advanced* years, I was not actually alive a hundred years ago and I am well aware of what is going on beyond the walls of the bookstore, maybe even more than you think. Perhaps it *is* too soon to end your apprenticeship if you can't behave like an adult. But . . ." She paused, searching for her next words. "If this was some sort of attempt to impress your father, then you have no business being a witch."

The sudden mention of her father startled Arianwyn more than the jolt from the evaluation gauge had. She could almost feel the rough green uniform under her hands as she clung to her father on the docks in Kingsport, before he left to join his unit. "It'll not be for long, love," he had said, blinking back his own tears. That had been when she was five and she had seen him only a handful of times since. A few days' leave here or there. Sporadic letters and even rarer phone calls from mysterious-sounding places thousands of miles away. And last time she had heard from him he was heading for the border towns of Veersland to protect the Veerish people against the Urisian attacks that had been growing more and more frequent and terrible.

"That's not it," Arianwyn said defiantly, but it felt like a lie. "I put my heart into this!"

"Well, perhaps that's the problem, then. You should have been thinking with your head."

Arianwyn sat in silence, glowering.

The taxi moved again, clearing the traffic and turning off the Royal Circle. They sat for a few more minutes in rumbling silence, the only sound the engine and other motorcars on the street.

Eventually the taxi came to a halt outside Stronelli's Bookstore, Grandmother's bookshop and the place Arianwyn had called home since her mother had died and her father, drowning in his own grief, had returned to the army.

CHAPTER FOUR

THE UNWANTED GIFT

Arianwyn jumped out of the taxi and ran straight to the door. She fumbled for the key in her pocket, wanting to get inside and away from her grandmother as quickly as possible. The shop was in darkness and a sign had been placed in the window of the door: *Closed for family celebrations.*

Arianwyn felt her heart sink again.

As she pushed the door open, a charm sang out through the store, and Arianwyn felt a wave of magic as the six bells on bright red ribbons danced overhead. An ancient Grunnean charm against dark magic. Charms had been her grandmother's specialty, before she had all but given up magic to look after Arianwyn, buying this bookstore and stepping back from her official duties on the Council of Elders.

Arianwyn walked briskly through the dark shop. She knew the place so well she could move between the towering bookcases blindfolded, negotiating precarious stacks of books piled on the dark floorboards and rugs.

The bells on the door rang again and the lights snapped on. "Shall we carry on our argument down here or would you rather go upstairs and have a cup of tea?" Grand-mother asked, walking slowly to the back of the shop and her huge desk, also piled high with books. "Well, we can't go on like this," she said, her voice softening.

"Perhaps you should tell me what you said to Director Coot," Arianwyn said. "You made him give me that position, didn't you?"

Grandmother started to rearrange the pile of paper-work on her desk, humming to herself.

"Grandma!" Arianwyn pushed. "What did you say to him?"

There was another long moment of silence, and then Grandmother sighed and looked up at Arianwyn. Her face was sad, careworn, and pale in the light from overhead. Her hair was damp and hung in loose strands around her face.

"I *may* have suggested that he would be shortsighted if he didn't ensure you were given a position, given the demand for witches we currently have."

"Oh, Gran . . . you didn't. Tell me you didn't!" She clenched her fists. "Everyone will know that it was you—that I only got a position because of *you*!" Boiling with rage, she pulled at the moon brooch until it ripped free from her coat and she hurled it across the room. It skittered across the floor and came to a halt against Grandmother's shoe.

Grandmother turned away and noisily lined up a stack of books that were close to hand. "I know you've had a hard day but you are starting to behave like one of those spoiled Highbridge brats," she said angrily. "Like that Alverston girl!"

Arianwyn considered retaliating but instead she sank into a large battered armchair and buried her head in her hands.

"I'm sorry . . . ," Arianwyn mumbled eventually, through her fingers.

"I beg your pardon?" Grandmother asked. Her voice was lighter now.

"I'm . . . sorry, Grandma."

There was a long silence, then just Grandmother's footsteps moving across the store. When Arianwyn peeked from behind her hands she saw her grandmother standing in the middle of the shop, her coat and scarf removed, her long dark dress sweeping the dusty floorboards. Grandmother smiled.

"Do you remember the first time you selected a book?" she asked.

The memory was as crisp as if it had been only moments ago. It was the day her father had headed off to rejoin the army, leaving her behind with Grandmother.

"I couldn't sleep . . . ," Arianwyn muttered. "I was scared. You brought me down into the shop. I was wrapped in a thick blanket and you told me to close my eyes and select a book. I didn't know what you meant." All the walls had been lined with books; books were tucked under windows and over doorways, piled and stacked on chairs, tables, and the floor. Just like today.

Arianwyn remembered almost everything: standing still, her eyes closed so tight! Thinking of the most wonderful thing she could imagine. And then the magic had happened.

"Why don't you try it now?" Grandmother suggested gently.

She closed her eyes once more and tried to let the memories of the day slip away. The evaluation, Miss Newam, Gimma, the moon brooch. Instead she conjured up her parents, young and carefree. The beautiful young witch and the handsome soldier; their arms wrapped gently around each other. It was the image from the wedding photograph that sat beside Arianwyn's bed. It was still her wonderful thought.

The image melted away slowly, her mind blank and dark. And then there was a faint glow. She reached out for it, stepping forward blindly. Blobs and smudges of color floated behind her eyelids, dancing and flickering.

"Don't rush," Grandmother's voice cautioned.

She waited and allowed her breathing to slow. After a few moments there was a flash of light; it pulsed like a heartbeat. She reached out her hands toward the light and made another step forward. Another pulse of light and another step, and so on.

She could feel the closeness of the shelves. The musty smell of the books filled her nose, warm and familiar. She stopped. Her hands reached out. There was a rush of air; her skin fizzed, and then she felt something solid and cool slide into her waiting hands. She grasped the book tightly. It was thick and heavy, not fairy tales this time, she guessed.

She opened her eyes and looked down.

The Apprentice Witch's Handbook

It was a rather unremarkable book really. A faded green cover displaying a symbol that looked like a star, a broom, and a glyph, twined together. It wasn't a book Arianwyn had ever seen—it wasn't on the set reading lists for apprentice witches, certainly not one approved by the CWA. Was it some sort of cruel joke meant to teach her one last lesson? She was suddenly hot and angry all over again.

She lifted the book to show her grandmother. "Well, that's a clear message, I think." Her eyes swam with tears; she didn't want to be standing in the bookshop with this stupid book a second longer. She let it slip from her hands and ran.

All she heard was the thud of the book hitting the floorboards.

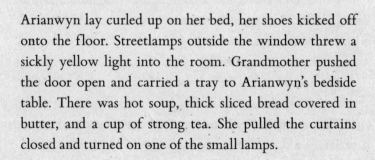

Arianwyn lay curled up on her bed, her shoes kicked off onto the floor. Streetlamps outside the window threw a sickly yellow light into the room. Grandmother pushed the door open and carried a tray to Arianwyn's bedside table. There was hot soup, thick sliced bread covered in butter, and a cup of strong tea. She pulled the curtains closed and turned on one of the small lamps.

"Was it all a dream . . . or a nightmare?" Arianwyn asked, shifting on her bed. She spotted the green book on the tea tray. "I guess not!"

Grandmother took her hands and said firmly but gently, "Arianwyn Gribble, you are my granddaughter . . ."

"Please, Gran, I'm not sure I can take a motivational speech right now. I feel like I've let you down. All I ever wanted was to be a witch like you. Like Mom. I thought it was the only thing I was any good at and I'm not. I failed!" For a brief second she thought about telling her grandmother about the strange glyph. She had tried to tell her so many times before and always backed down at the last second. Grandmother would, no doubt, only take it as another sign that Arianwyn wasn't truly ready for the responsibilities of a fully fledged witch.

"Sometimes we appreciate something more when we've struggled for it," Grandmother said. "Do you think all the other witches who have had assignments handed to them on a plate will be better than you, just because a machine said so? No. They will not, because they won't try to be better. They won't push themselves or work hard, and you will. I know you will, because you always have." She paused. "We must never shy away from where fate has brought us. If you are to remain an apprentice witch for a while longer, then so be it. But you'll be the best you possibly can be, as you have *always* been."

"But haven't I had *my* assignment handed to me on a plate?"

"Oh, it's not like that, I promise you!" Grandmother folded her into a hug. She smelled of summery perfume and dusty books.

"Everyone will be judging me now, more than ever," Arianwyn mumbled.

"Ridiculous! I know more than that daft woman from the CWA. I don't care how many gadgets say otherwise. You will be a great witch one day, I have no doubt. But the road is going to be less straightforward for you than for most. And don't think that just because I had words with that silly little man, your job will be any easier for it!"

"And what about that?" Arianwyn asked, moving her head in the direction of the book.

Grandmother glanced at it again. "*That* is a very old training manual. It hasn't been used for years. Not since the Civil Witchcraft Authority was set up. They no doubt thought it was too 'arcane.'" She wafted her hands around her head and rolled her eyes theatrically.

Arianwyn gave a half smile and then flicked the book open.

The pages were thick and brown, marked with small, careful illustrations. There were chapters on brooms, herb gardens, use of the cardinal glyphs, and many other things that Arianwyn already knew. Some pages folded out to double or triple the original size, revealing complex diagrams of spell combinations. She flicked back through, about to close it, but paused. On the title page in small tidy handwriting was her grandmother's name.

"It was yours?"

Grandmother gave a little chuckle. "It was required reading back in my day, a *hundred* years ago. I haven't seen it in decades. But it came to you for a reason. Called to you and you alone in all the years it's been on the shelves here. So keep it handy if you know what's good for you!" She winked, and Arianwyn was sure they were friends once more and the worst of the day was behind them. She pulled the book close to her chest. Knowing it was Grandmother's made it feel different, special.

"And what about this?" Grandmother asked, passing the brown envelope to Arianwyn. "Don't you want to find out about your new position?"

"I don't think I do. Don't you know already, though?" Arianwyn said. She shivered as though an icy draft had filled the room. Was it excitement or fear?

"I have no idea. Honestly!" Grandmother smiled.

Taking a deep breath, Arianwyn ripped the envelope open, spilling the contents onto the bright quilt. The first was a certificate, signed by August Coot. It stated her "grade" and continuing status as "Apprentice Witch."

The next item was the form for requesting a reevaluation. A note was clipped to it from Colin. It simply said *Good luck*. Arianwyn felt another pang of regret as she thought of how unkind she had been.

The last item was a brief, typed letter:

Dear Miss Gribble,

Following your recent evaluation and in light of national developments, the Civil Witchcraft Authority will be placing you as an Apprentice Witch for the town of Lull and the surrounding area.

You will take up your post on March 8th and should report to the mayor of Lull, the Honorable Josiah Belcher, on that date.

We wish you every success in your new position.

Yours sincerely,
C. J. Alberias
Assignments & Placements Dpt
Civil Witchcraft Authority, Kingsport

She handed all this to her grandmother and went over to her bookcase. She scanned the spines, searching for the atlas her father had given her on her birthday one year. She had never heard of Lull before, which wasn't a promising sign.

"I think it's south of Undle somewhere," Grandmother offered, "near the Great Wood."

Arianwyn laid the atlas on the bed, opening it to the pages that displayed the island nation of Hylund. It rested in an expanse of blue, safe and solitary, cocooned in a ring of seas and oceans. Arianwyn's fingers traced the mainland kingdoms, Dannis, Grunnea, and Veersland, that framed the page to the top and right. The Uris lay beyond this page, north of Veersland, where her father was fighting. It was as though her father and the war were happening in some make-believe country.

Her eyes skimmed down the island, taking in rivers, towns, and cities she knew or had visited. And there, almost at the bottom of Hylund, right at the very edge of the Great Wood, was a small dot next to the word *Lull*. Arianwyn let her finger rest there. She wondered what sort of a place it might be. The Great Wood itself was a shaded, foggy expanse reaching to the south coast—a dangerous and remote place, full of seams of magic. There were legends about the Great Wood, about ancient spirits that retreated there to escape the intrusion of the human world. A few expeditions had been launched to chart the wood, but none had been successful and the Great Wood clung tightly still to all its secrets.

Despite everything, she felt a little thrill at the idea of being so close to so much magic.

Grandmother came to stand beside her, wrapping a reassuring arm around Arianwyn's shoulders. They both gazed down at the map.

THE APPRENTICE WITCH'S HANDBOOK

✦ ✦ ✦

Those who are born with the ability to control the natural flow of magic around them are commonly known within the Four Kingdoms as witches. A witch's training begins from the age of four, with basic glyph craft. As they get older a witch usually takes up his or her apprenticeship, under the guidance of an elder witch. Apprenticeships last for up to three years, at the end of which the apprentice would undergo the three trials, although more modern methods of gauging a witch's skill are becoming increasingly commonplace.

CHAPTER FIVE

THE BUS RIDE

laxsham station was rainswept and empty. Arianwyn stood alone, surrounded by luggage, her broom lashed to the top of her largest trunk. The hooting call of a train sounded in the distance. The smell of coal dust and hot metal lingered in the air.

It was late afternoon. She had been on the train since sunrise, crammed in among men, women, and children traveling to the four corners of Hylund. She stretched her aching muscles and checked the station clock; her connecting train was due any minute. For the tenth time that day she pulled out the letter from her satchel that had arrived a few days ago. She read it just once more, checking all the details.

Dear Miss Gribble,

On behalf of the Town Council of Lull, may I congratulate you on your appointment.

We have been without a witch for many years and are so glad to have at last been allocated one.

The south of Hylund, as you are no
doubt aware, is rich in natural magic,
though we are generally untroubled by
dark spirits. Despite our proximity to
the Great Wood, Lull has always been a
quiet and pleasant town to live in.

Despite my reluctance regarding your
continuing apprenticeship status, the
CWA has persuaded me that you are
ready to face the challenge, and that
with support from the CWA district
supervisor, Miss Jucasta Delafield,
you will be able to fulfill your role
without incident.

We hope you will be a useful addition
to our community.

                              Yours sincerely,
                              Josiah Belcher
                              Mayor of Lull

The minutes passed, but no train arrived.

"Excuse me?" Arianwyn called to the stationmaster as he appeared from his office carrying a huge steaming mug. "Is the train for Lull late?"

"Canceled, I'm afraid, miss—all the Lull trains have been. Damage to the tracks over the winter." He was merrily dunking cookies into his tea and swallowing them in one gulp. "There's a bus running, parked up around the corner."

Arianwyn smiled and was about to thank the man when she realized he was staring straight at her stupid badge. She quickly pulled her scarf to cover it, and went in search of the bus.

Thankfully she found it just in time and, with lots of help from the driver, Mr. Thorn, was able to get all her luggage into or on top of the bus. Mr. Thorn was a tiny man, with a snow-white mustache and glinting cheerful eyes. "Whole town's been waiting for you, miss." He smiled. "Be my honor to take you the rest of the way in old Beryl." He patted the bus and grinned.

"Beryl" was clearly Mr. Thorn's pride and joy. She was green and silver and polished till she shone like a rare jewel. Arianwyn made sure she said several times what a beautiful bus Beryl was and Mr. Thorn beamed like a proud father.

But sadly Beryl was about as comfortable as a tea tray, and Arianwyn soon discovered that each small bump—and there were lots and lots—turned into a sheer drop and Beryl crashed down with all the elegance of an avalanche. As long as she kept concentrating on the road ahead she *probably* wouldn't be sick. She felt her stomach flip-flop.

The one blessing was that her two fellow passengers had so far ignored her. One, an older gentleman, whom Mr. Thorn had called Grimms, climbed on, took his seat, and fell immediately into a deep, snore-filled sleep.

The other was a young girl about Arianwyn's age, dressed in an impossibly glamorous but old and faded red coat and hat. She had only just gotten on the bus when it pulled away from the station; she greeted Mr. Thorn kindly, asking after his wife. Then she glanced briefly at Arianwyn, took her seat, and burst into tears. She had been quietly sobbing into her handkerchief for the last fifteen miles or so.

The bus jolted over another pothole, throwing Arianwyn forward in her seat, queasiness washing over her again.

"How much farther is it, Mr. Thorn?" Arianwyn shouted over Beryl's roar. But Mr. Thorn was absorbed in his driving, peering over the steering wheel, and didn't hear.

The sobbing girl looked up from her soggy handkerchief. "Another half hour," she said, "it'll probably be dark before we get to Lull." The girl looked at Arianwyn carefully, as though she was studying her, and then she burst out with "*Oh*. You're the new witch! Miss . . . Gravel? No, Grapple? No . . ."

Arianwyn gave a small laugh. She smiled warmly and extended her hand. "Gribble. Arianwyn Gribble."

"Oh my! Everyone will be so jealous that I met you first. You're all anyone's been able to talk about for weeks and weeks—Miss Gribble this and Miss Gribble that."

"Really?" Arianwyn blushed.

"Oh, don't feel bad, there's not *usually* that much going on in Lull. You've given us all something to talk about. I'm Salle Bowen."

"Very pleased to meet you. Do you live in Lull?"

"Yes." Salle smiled. "But I've just been to an audition at the Palace Theater this afternoon. I'm an actress . . . well, I *want* to be one but I don't seem to be able to get any of the parts . . . except for the town play, and that really doesn't count." She suddenly fell quiet and then she blew her nose into the already soaked handkerchief. Tears welled in her eyes and then tumbled down her cheeks.

Seeing Salle so obviously heartbroken took Arianwyn back to her evaluation and how wretched she had felt after that. "It's awful when things don't quite go according to plan, isn't it?" Arianwyn said, and she gestured to her badge. "You could sort of say I failed my audition too!" She grinned at Salle, who seemed to brighten for a moment. Before she knew what she was doing, Arianwyn was pouring out the whole story as the bus rattled along and the darkening world whistled past the windows.

"Your parents must be so proud of you, though," Salle said.

Arianwyn fell silent; she reached into her satchel and pulled out the photograph of her parents, offering it to Salle. "My dad's in the army. He's stationed up in the north of Veersland, helping the Veerish guard against the Urisian attacks." Salle nodded knowingly. Arianwyn carried on, "I wrote to him weeks ago, but I don't know if he even got the letter. We don't hear from him very often these days. And my mom, well . . . she died when I was little. My grandma is the one who raised me."

Salle's hand reached out tentatively and rested on Arianwyn's. "Both my parents died when I was a baby. It was the ruby fever," she said quietly. "I don't even remember them. Aunt Grace and Uncle Mathieu have been my parents, really. They run the inn in Lull, the Blue Ox. What happened to your mom? Was she a witch too?" Salle didn't seem to dwell at all on the tragedy of not having even one parent.

Arianwyn nodded. She didn't like to think about it, but the memory was as fresh and raw as though it had only been that morning. "She was hit by a delivery van in Kingsport," Arianwyn said quietly. "We'd been to the bakery to get fresh bread and some cakes for dinner." She gazed past Salle, out across the darkening countryside. "We'd just crossed the street. Someone shouted for help. A little boy had wandered into the road and the van was coming at him, so fast. Mum just ran straight into the road. She didn't think twice about it. She must have known they wouldn't both get clear. She hurled a spell at the boy, threw him out of the way, but . . ."

Arianwyn looked at Salle. The girl's hand covered her mouth, her eyes huge and wet once more. "Grandmother tried every spell she knew, but nothing worked."

They looked at each other for a few moments. Arianwyn thought of telling Salle that just before this had happened she had seen the unknown glyph for the first time.

It had formed on the pages of a book of glyphs for young witches, emerging among the cardinal glyphs, dark and brooding, a twisting strange shape that didn't belong.

It vanished as quickly as it had appeared. Terrified, she had thrown the book across the room and run screaming to her mother.

"Whatever is it, darling?" her mother had asked, placing a soothing hand on Arianwyn's forehead and staring deep into her eyes. To calm her she had suggested a visit to the bakery and Arianwyn had always thought the accident was her fault. But she had never told anyone any of this. And of course the strange glyph had appeared every now and again ever since that day, forming in the mist on a window or a mirror, or among shadows—and afterward, every time, something bad had happened.

"I'm so sorry, Arianwyn," Salle said, offering a fresh handkerchief from her pocket and pulling Arianwyn out of her reverie.

The bus continued to bounce along, Mr. Thorn whistling a little tune quietly to himself. Mr. Grimms slept on.

Outside, Arianwyn could see a line of trees in the distance. They must be on the road to Lull at long last, she thought. "Is that the Great Wood?" she asked, pointing to the trees.

Salle laughed lightly. "Heavens, no. That's only Clover Hollow. The Great Wood technically doesn't begin until after Lull. We dip down into the valley and in the daylight you can see the Great Wood really well from up here, but it's too dark now. We're nearly home, though, can't wait for you to meet Aunt Grace and Uncle Mathieu— you'll love them, I just know it." Salle beamed.

There was a sudden screeching of the brakes and Salle and Arianwyn both fell forward in their seats. Beryl shuddered to a halt.

"Good grief, what a day." Mr. Thorn sighed. "The road's flooded; we'll never get through this way. We'll have to go on the old track. Sorry, ladies, it's a bit of a bumpy ride!"

"Not that you can tell the difference," Salle whispered.

Mr. Thorn turned the bus off the main road and onto a dirt track, but it was decidedly more dirt than track and only just wider than Beryl. The trees of Clover Hollow grew right up to the very edge of the track here; their branches, bare and bone white, reached out toward the bus, and dark brooding pines kept the fading light at bay.

"I hope we make it back before curfew," Salle said.

"Curfew?" Arianwyn asked. The mayor hadn't mentioned anything about a curfew in his letter.

"Oh, didn't you know? We've had a spate of dark spirit sightings this winter; nobody knows why, though. So the town council set a curfew and issued us all with these." She held aloft her bag; a small charm dangled from it.

Arianwyn didn't have the heart to inform Salle that it was a charm for fishermen.

Mr. Thorn called over his shoulder, "And I got a nasty infestation of grindlesmudgers. Can't go in our spare room now it's so dark, even with two lamps! My wife's been nagging me about it for weeks."

"I promise I'll come and visit you as soon as I can, Mr. Thorn, and sort out your grindlesmudgers." Arianwyn beamed.

"Look out!" Salle shouted. She pointed at the windshield of the bus. A large tree blocked the track.

"Well, that's a devil," Mr. Thorn sighed, hitting the brakes. "How'll we get around that?"

CHAPTER SIX

THE DEMON OF CLOVER HOLLOW

D amp air surged around Arianwyn as she climbed down from the bus. Above her, the sky was scudded with storm clouds and the first sprinkling of stars could be seen in between them, against the velvety blue. The only sound was the empty whisper of the wind through the bare branches and the crunch of stones beneath her boots.

"I think I can move it," Arianwyn said confidently. There was a rich seam of magic, strong and urgent, in the ground beneath her feet and in the air around her. She stood at its center. In the dying light she could just detect its faint shimmer, invisible to Salle and Mr. Thorn.

Crouching down, she began to sketch the glyph she required into the dirt of the track.

Erte, the glyph of earth. It was a rich dark green color that flashed as she made the last curl of its shape.

The magic energy began to flow toward her and the

glyph; Arianwyn drew on it, focusing on the tree ahead of her on the track. Her hands tingled. The spell was ready. She raised her right hand, flexing her fingers slowly, and the huge trunk quivered for a second and then lay still.

She could feel Salle and Mr. Thorn watching her from the bus. Slowly she repeated the gesture and this time the trunk turned gradually in place. Branches crunched and cracked against the stones on the rough road. She felt her grip on the trunk strengthen and slowly used the spell to drag it to one side, off the track and into the tangle of trees by the roadside.

That was when she noticed the base of the trunk. It was neither a clean cut nor a torn or jagged piece of wood you might expect to see from a tree that had fallen of its own accord. It was as though huge claws had ripped through the wood, shearing it in two.

This was a bad sign. A *very* bad sign indeed.

Mr. Thorn and Salle were moving some of the smaller branches, and as Salle moved to the edge of the track she let out a little gasp of fear.

"What's the matter?" Mr. Thorn called.

Arianwyn looked over at once and followed the direction of Salle's outstretched arm, pointing into the darkness of the wood. "There's something there."

"Can't see nothing," Mr. Thorn replied, and carried on moving the branches, but Salle stayed rooted to the spot, gazing into the never-ending trees.

Then something moved. A huge black shadow that set the trees swaying.

"I told you!" Salle's voice came out in a nervous whisper; she took a few hurried steps backward.

As the earth spell faded, Arianwyn's senses picked up another pull of magic. There *was* something in the wood. A very large, very dangerous something.

She was just about to suggest they move back to the bus when the inky black of Clover Hollow spat forth a huge dark beast.

It was, unmistakably, a crawler.

No, no, no! Arianwyn thought. *This can't be happening, not today! I haven't even arrived in town yet!* Instinctively, she put herself between the crawler and Salle and Mr. Thorn.

The crawler paused by the side of the track, sniffing the air, then emitted a gurgling roar that ripped through the trees.

"What is it?" Salle whimpered. "What do we do?"

"Keep still," Arianwyn whispered as quietly as she could. "It's just a crawler . . . a low-level dark spirit creature. They have very poor eyesight, but excellent hearing and sense of smell."

And it could kill them without breaking a sweat, she thought, nervously.

The crawler's face was scrunched up, shrunken inward, as though it was collapsing in on itself. It stood as high as the bus, its skin gray and leathery. It lifted its head, large ears twitching in the cool air.

"Back. To. The. Bus," Arianwyn whispered. "On my signal. Ready?"

Salle and Mr. Thorne nodded.

"Run!" she hissed.

As Salle and Mr. Thorn rushed toward the bus, the crawler swiveled in their direction, growling. Arianwyn raised her arm. "Årdra!" she called, breathing the fire glyph into the air.

A shivering, crackling ball of red-hot flame formed just above her hand. She hurled it at the crawler.

It hit the creature full in the face, blinding and confusing it. Salle and Mr. Thorne made it to the bus, Arianwyn close on their heels.

Mr. Thorn started the engine, but with the track still strewn with large branches, they were trapped in the hollow. Arianwyn racked her brain trying to think of what she could do. What were the main points in dealing with a crawler?

She suddenly remembered the handbook, rifled through her bag, and pulled it free, her hands shaking as she flipped quickly through its pages.

Crawlers are easily distracted and will follow whatever moves the quickest or makes the most noise. The best defense is distraction.

"Pass me my broom!" Arianwyn said urgently to Salle. "I'll draw it off while you clear the last few branches, okay?"

Salle passed the broom reluctantly, her face pale and frightened. "It'll be all right," Arianwyn said, though she wasn't at all sure it would be.

A moment later Arianwyn tucked the broom beneath herself and kicked off from the steps of the bus. She zipped skyward. She wobbled more than she would have liked, but this wasn't a time for fancy flying, which was just as well as she had always been rather bad on her broom. She skimmed past the crawler's head and reached into the pocket of her coat, pulling free her standard-issue brass whistle on a long chain. She clamped it between her teeth and blew hard. The piercing scream of the whistle did the trick. The crawler wasted no time in swinging one of its long sinewy arms at her, its clawed, twisted hand swiping the air inches from her face.

Arianwyn willed the broom faster and she shot off, the icy air whipping past her. She swooped to the right and circled high, out of the creature's reach. She blew hard on the whistle again, circling down. The trick worked; the crawler was soon following, away from the bus, slashing and screeching wildly.

A long claw sliced past the side of her face, too close for comfort. Arianwyn banked to the left sharply and for a moment feared she might slip off, but the broom responded and she flew forward, the crawler close behind. One quick glance and she was relieved to see the road cleared and

Mr. Thorn and Salle heading back to Beryl as fast as their legs would carry them.

But then Arianwyn's blood turned to ice as Salle stumbled and fell on the track, crying out as she fell with a squelch into a muddy puddle. The crawler turned in a split second, bored of Arianwyn, and headed straight for Salle. It roared with triumph as it dragged itself toward the bus.

Arianwyn wrapped her arms around the broom handle as she spun around. Icy tears blurred her vision as *she* now chased the crawler. The ground rushed beneath her and she overtook the demon just as it was reaching out its clawlike hands toward Salle.

In desperation Arianwyn jumped off the broom, landing on the ground between Salle and the crawler. She stumbled, falling to her knees. The broom clattered beside her. The crawler's hot, rank breath blasted in her face.

Her fingertips pressed into the cold wet earth of the woodland track as she started to trace the banishing glyph, L'ier.

But the other glyph—the dark glyph—flashed before her eyes, the jumbled, tangled shape of her nightmares. She froze. Her mind went blank.

Totally blank.

She scrubbed out the marks and tried again. The crawler stretched one of its long sinewy arms toward Salle, snorting with anticipation.

Arianwyn stilled her thoughts as she had been trained to do, feeling for the flow of magic. But it was difficult to feel anything except the overpowering presence of the crawler.

Taking a deep breath, she closed her eyes and started to trace the glyph again, the damp earth slick beneath her fingers; she needed to open a rift to banish the creature back to the void.

"Arianwyn!" Salle's cry jolted her back to her senses.

Her eyes flew open just in time to see the demon's massive arm swing down toward her. It batted her to one side and she flew through the air, landing in a knot of branches and brambles at the edge of the hollow. Stunned and breathless, she couldn't move. She watched as the demon crouched low over Salle, its claws glinting like knives as it reached for her.

Arianwyn tried to cry out but she had no breath, her lungs empty and raw.

And then a flash of silver and green whizzed past. Beryl was hurtling at top speed along the track, headed straight for the demon.

She heard the horn sing out through the wood, followed by the sickening crunch of bones and metal. The crawler was flying through the air now, smashing through the trees of Clover Hollow. The bus screeched to a halt just yards from Arianwyn. Arianwyn snatched her broom up from the ground as the bus doors opened and Mr. Thorn helped Salle and Arianwyn inside.

"Quick! Before it comes around!" Arianwyn said urgently.

Mr. Thorn slammed his foot against the accelerator and Beryl shot forward. "But we killed it, didn't we?" Salle asked.

"I think we probably just knocked it out, and annoyed it!" Arianwyn sighed as she slumped back onto the floor of the bus, Mr. Thorn and Salle staring at her in disbelief.

That had not gone according to plan.

CHAPTER SEVEN

WELCOME TO LULL

S alle gave a whoop of excitement and relieved delight as the bus hurtled along the track once more. Arianwyn watched, alert, as the beams of brilliant light from the headlights revealed portions of tree trunks and the bright eyes of animals and other creatures hiding in the dark. Drops of heavy rain splashed against the windows.

"Did the spell work? Did the rift open?" Arianwyn asked.

"I didn't see anything," Salle said. "It probably came from the Great Wood. Maybe it went back there?"

Had the rift opened? Had her spell worked? She thought she had seen a flash just before the bus hit the crawler but she couldn't be sure. If she had left a rift spell open in the wood, anything could get through from the void. Rule number one: Never leave a banishing spell half formed or unattended. Otherwise anything lurking in the darkness of the void could come *into* the world . . .

She slumped in her seat. *How much more pathetic can I get?* Arianwyn wondered wearily.

As the bus emerged from the confinement of the trees, Arianwyn felt relief wash over her. She could see the bright lights of Lull clustered in a shallow valley below them. The town sat cozily behind a high wall, towers and roofs standing proud. Thin curls of smoke wafted up into the purple night sky. In the distance, cresting the top of low hills, was the dark shape that must be the Great Wood.

The bus slowed and they bumped over an ancient bridge and through a large gateway. The walls were strung with a collection of archaic-looking charms, and Arianwyn felt the faint energy of the old spells. She hoped they were strong enough to keep the crawler at bay.

The streets were narrow, houses and shops clustered against the twisting roads and lanes. Here and there a lit window or welcoming lamp by a front door were the only indications that the town was inhabited. The streets seemed to be deserted. They were late for curfew.

Arianwyn glanced over at Mr. Grimms. He slept on, appearing not to have moved or even been aware that the bus had been under attack and they had all been in mortal peril. Arianwyn was amazed: Surely nobody could have slept through all of that? Just then, as the bus hit a particularly large pothole, he jumped awake, eyes bleary and confused as he took in his surroundings. "Aren't we home yet?" he moaned, and then promptly fell back to sleep.

Mr. Thorn executed an elegant loop with Beryl into what Arianwyn thought must be the town square. The windshield wipers cut back and forth through the driving rain as the cobbles of the square shone in the bright glow of Beryl's headlights. All the buildings around the edge of the square were shuttered and in darkness, locking out the night and anyone crazy enough to be out in it, Arianwyn thought.

Bunting, which would have been bright and cheery in daylight, hung around the square, slapping damply in the wind and rain. A large sign strung across the front of the town hall had sagged and torn. Arianwyn could just make out *Welcome to Lull*, but then a sudden gust sent it swinging and flapping free from its ties before it wrapped itself wetly around one of the stone columns that guarded the town hall.

"So much for a warm welcome," Salle sighed, peering out through the dark, rain-streaked windows.

Pulling her coat tightly around her, Arianwyn climbed out into the stormy night.

The only sign of life came from far across the town from a tall, grand building with soaring columns and long elegant windows, some of which were bright with warm light. The flag of Hylund snapped and twisted at the end of a long flagpole that protruded from a high balcony.

"It wasn't really supposed to be like this," Salle said, following her. "There was supposed to be more of a welcome." She gestured to the wet, empty square.

"Oh, it doesn't really matter—" Arianwyn began, but a movement in the shadows made her stop dead. In the darkness behind the tall marble colonnade something was watching; something was waiting.

Instinctively, Arianwyn pulled Salle backward, her fingers twitching in the cold night air as a ball of fire formed easily in her hand. Was it the crawler? Had it followed them and somehow gotten into town?

"I was beginning to think you were not going to arrive at all." A deep voice boomed from the shadows. Arianwyn shifted and saw a large, round man come forward out of the gloom. He was dressed for the night in a dark raincoat, and his round face, which Arianwyn thought should have been jolly, looked pinched and tired.

"Mayor Belcher?" she asked, quickly extinguishing the spell with a flick of her hand. It shimmered briefly and drifted away in the rain.

The man nodded.

CHAPTER EIGHT

MAYOR BELCHER

Miss Gribble, I was growing very anxious. We had expected you much earlier than this. I was worried we might have to assemble a search party, and after curfew!" Something in his voice made Arianwyn think he was more concerned about arranging the search than the fact that Arianwyn and three townspeople might be in danger.

"We did have quite a gathering of people to welcome you." He gestured at the soggy bunting. "But it grew dark and then this terrible wind and rain started up so I sent everyone home." He sounded tired and a little angry.

He peered at them through the blustering rain. Arianwyn noticed his expression change slowly from irritation to something else—was it concern? She turned to Salle. She had a thin red scratch across her cheek and her clothes were muddy. Her faded red coat sported a large rip near the pocket: clear signs of their adventures.

Arianwyn wondered what she looked like and reached up to feel a large collection of twigs and leaves trapped in her hair. She glanced down at herself—her knees were scraped and her fine blue coat was streaked with mud.

"What on earth has happened?" the mayor asked in hushed and horrified tones.

"We were attacked on the way into town, just as we came into Clover Hollow," Salle said quickly, and went on to explain the incident with the crawler. Mayor Belcher listened intently, his mouth open in shock. Arianwyn was surprised at the liberties Salle took with some of the details—the crawler tripled in size—and Mr. Thorn, who had joined them, was agreeing with everything she said.

"But you managed to banish the creature?" the mayor asked, looking carefully at Arianwyn.

"Um . . ." Arianwyn faltered, unsure exactly what to say. "No, Mr. Thorn hit it with his bus and scared it away!"

"That's a rather unusual method of dealing with a dark spirit creature, isn't it?" Mayor Belcher asked.

Arianwyn chewed on her lip. "I lost control of my banishing spell as well . . . there may be a rift open in the wood . . ."

The mayor stared hard, his eyes narrow, his full lips pursed. "Well, this is not the best of starts, is it? Might I suggest we keep the crawler information between ourselves? We don't wish to cause panic among the townspeople . . ."

"Of course," Arianwyn replied quietly.

"Mr. Thorn, will you take Miss Gribble's luggage to the Blue Ox?" The mayor turned to Arianwyn. "Just for tonight. We can get you settled into the Spellorium tomorrow, after we've gone to check on the rift." The mayor moved off to one side with Mr. Thorn, issuing further instructions.

"I knew you wouldn't get rid of me that easily!" Salle beamed, and Arianwyn felt relieved that she wouldn't be spending her first night in town in a strange place *and* all alone.

"Now then," the mayor said, "we'd best be out of this awful weather." He led them up the steps of the town hall and out of the miserable night. Arianwyn turned and waved to Mr. Thorn as Beryl rattled across the cobbles.

The mayor took them into a dark hall with a wide sweeping staircase and gleaming tiles. Oil paintings and gilt-edged mirrors hung on the walls. He pulled off his heavy raincoat to reveal a fancy suit with a long-tailed jacket and a regal sash of purple silk. An official golden crest the size of a small dinner plate was attached to it, which he adjusted in a huge mirror. Around his neck he wore a charm, which Arianwyn thought might be the kind used by farmers to keep their cows calm.

He caught Arianwyn looking. "Better to be safe than sorry, and we have had such a winter for sightings of dark spirits. Very unusual for us, Miss Gribble, I assure you. I feel I must say that we hadn't really expected to be allocated a witch at all, so I suppose we should be thankful we have you, even if you are still . . . an apprentice."

Arianwyn, unsure how to answer him, simply smiled.

He glared at her badge intently. "I suppose you are able to do all the usual things . . ."

"Mayor Belcher!" Salle exclaimed in horror. "She's a witch—of course she can do *things*."

Arianwyn wasn't so sure after the recent adventure.

"Heavens, yes, where are my manners? I do apologize, Miss Gribble." He was flustered, his eyes widening. He turned away and pretended to rearrange an ornate flower display in a massive vase.

"Well, I think we should be getting back to the inn," Salle said quickly. "Arianwyn has had a long day and could no doubt do with some warm food and a nice bath." She wrapped a protective arm around Arianwyn.

"Of course. I shall see you tomorrow." The mayor bowed low.p

Wrapping themselves up against the cold, Arianwyn and Salle emerged onto the town square. The Blue Ox inn stood on the far side of the square and it seemed like miles to Arianwyn as they trudged wearily through the wind and icy rain, which still fell in torrents. Salle took her through the huge archway that led to a back courtyard and then through a small door half hidden in the dark.

A cozy sitting room waited. A tall lamp in the corner cast a soft light over everything. A man dozed in a worn green velvet armchair beside the cheery fire. A radio crackled softly, the crisp voice of the announcer reading the day's news. "The king has passed a decree through the Royal Senate today, pledging further support for the destabilized area in the Urisian and Veersland border towns . . ."

A beautiful woman, her hair the same color as Salle's, sat knitting by the light of the lamp. She glanced up as the door squeaked and, seeing Arianwyn and Salle, she leapt up, casting the knitting aside. "Where on earth have you been, Salle Bowen? It's past curfew, you know!"

Salle flushed and started to explain, but Arianwyn stepped forward. "I'm so sorry, it's my fault."

The fire popped and the radio news ended. The Hylund national anthem began playing as the day's programs came to a close. The man jumped awake, startled from his dreams. He blinked bleary-eyed at the scene in front of him. "Evening, Sal. Who's your friend?"

"This is Wyn—um, Arianwyn Gribble, our new witch!" Salle said, beaming. "Wyn, this is my aunt, Grace Archer, and that's Uncle Mathieu."

"Everyone calls me Mat, though," he said, and shook Arianwyn's hand enthusiastically.

"We're very pleased to meet you, Arianwyn," said Aunt Grace. "We've got your room all ready. Would you like something to eat before you go up? Or a cup of tea?"

Arianwyn shook her head. "Thank you, but I'm so tired, I think I'd just like to go to bed. It's been a rather long day."

"Oh yes," Mat said. "Old Thorny told us all about the crawler!"

Arianwyn caught sight of Salle gesturing frantically for Uncle Mat to shut up. *Oh, wonderful*, she thought. *The whole town will know by morning!*

"Well, I'm sure that story can wait until morning," Grace Archer cut in. "Let's get you up to bed, shall we?" She wrapped an arm tightly around Arianwyn's shoulders and guided her out of the parlor. She smelled of soap and baking and warm fresh linen.

Arianwyn was never so grateful to see a bed as she was that night, her trunk, suitcases, and other luggage all stacked neatly in the corner of the small whitewashed room. A huge wooden bed filled the space. It was covered with a thick pink eiderdown comforter and several cozy-looking blankets. A dressing table stood against one wall and Arianwyn caught a glimpse of herself in the mirror, pale and tired.

"There's a bath next door, and you can have a nice long sleep-in tomorrow, love. I'll get you breakfast whenever you want it," Aunt Grace said, moving to draw the curtains. Then she stopped. She peered out into the night. "Will you look at that?" she said, her hand rising to her mouth.

Arianwyn crossed to stand beside her. Her bedroom window looked out over the rooftops of Lull, out across the shallow valley. The storm clouds had parted slightly to reveal a slice of the moon, and in the distance she could see a thick dark patch against the stormy night sky, which Arianwyn thought must be the edge of the Great Wood. Several little bright lights danced through the trees just briefly and then vanished.

"What was that?" Arianwyn asked.

"I was hoping you would know—you're the witch! We've been seeing them every now and then all winter." Aunt Grace smiled warmly and winked.

"*Apprentice* witch," Arianwyn mumbled, and indicated her badge.

"Not for long, I'm sure!" Aunt Grace said firmly. "Good night, love!"

The door clicked quietly behind her and Arianwyn was alone. She pulled on a nightdress and padded back to the window, watching the dancing lights. They whizzed in and out of the distant trees before vanishing, only to reappear a few moments later. *Probably just sprites*, she thought, before letting the curtain fall back across the window.

She rummaged through her bag and pulled out the handbook, then clambered onto the bed. It was as soft as a cloud. She leafed through the book's pages, searching for anything to do with lights and woodland, but after only a few minutes the book had slipped from her hands and tumbled to the floor.

THE APPRENTICE WITCH'S HANDBOOK

❖ ❖ ❖

Like other natural resources, magic exists within seams, pockets, or deposits, which can be present in the earth, air, or water. Magic is more abundant and plentiful in the wildest, most natural regions, and scarcest in the cities and built-up areas. The Four Kingdoms are naturally rich in magic and it is believed that some magical disaster resulted in the Uris being depleted of its magic many hundreds of years ago.

CHAPTER NINE

BRIGHT AND EARLY

Arianwyn woke with a start. Salle stood over her, her hair wild from sleep. "Get up," she said, giving her a gentle shake. "The mayor's waiting for you downstairs!" She moved to the window and pulled back the curtains. Pale light flooded the room.

"Ouch!" Arianwyn blinked and squinted. "What?" she mumbled, still half asleep.

Salle poured steaming water into a bowl on a stand near the window; most of it slopped onto the rug. "Hurry up; you may have gathered he's not that patient at the best of times!" She grinned.

Arianwyn slid out of bed, picking up the handbook from where it had fallen and shuffling over to the wash-stand. She caught a glimpse of herself in the mirror on the dressing table. Her hair was a wild jangle of curls; she looked as if she had been electrocuted. She quickly splashed warm water over her face and tried to tame her hair before pulling on her crumpled and still-muddy uniform. She followed Salle downstairs, yawning as she went.

They emerged in the main room of the inn; it was

bright and warm, a fire crackling merrily in the grate. The huge flagstone floor was damp and glistened from the busy mop of Aunt Grace. She smiled warmly and pointed into the far corner.

Josiah Belcher, looking quite out of place and rather uncomfortable, was squeezed behind a table tucked into a recess in the thick stone wall.

"Ah, Miss Gribble! Good morning, good morning." The mayor rose to his feet, the table wobbling enthusiastically. "I thought I should let you sleep in after your long day traveling."

Arianwyn glanced at the huge clock above the fireplace. It was just seven thirty.

"Thank you," she muttered.

The mayor reached inside his coat and pulled out a shiny pocket watch, which he clicked open and checked against the clock on the wall. "Now, despite my incredibly busy schedule, I thought it best to give you a tour of the town and the surrounding area myself."

"Now?" Arianwyn said.

"Unless you would like to arrange for this yourself . . . ?" The mayor pursed his lips and snapped the pocket watch shut.

"Oh no, now would be lovely." She yawned. "Very kind of you, Mayor Belcher."

The mayor frowned and his eyes drifted to Arianwyn's badge once again. "I'll give you a brief history of the town as well; you may find it useful in your work."

Arianwyn stifled another yawn and looked briefly away. Then she recalled the rift spell that she had summoned in Clover Hollow the night before.

"Please can we go to Clover Hollow to check if the rift spell took or not? An open rift to the void could be more trouble than we want to deal with!"

The mayor looked uncertain, swallowed hard, and glanced about the inn. "Um . . . yes, of course. Well, shall we get on, then? I do have other things to do today." He sniffed.

It was market day in Lull and the town square outside the inn was bustling despite the chill and early hour. Excited chatter filled the air as people caught up with the latest gossip and news, and judging from the curious looks as she and the mayor crossed the busy square, most of it seemed to be about Arianwyn.

Once or twice she heard her name in whispered conversations. A few people hesitantly waved hello and she waved back or nodded a friendly greeting as she kept pace with Mayor Belcher. She noticed that lots of people wore some sort of charm either around their neck or tied to their clothes in some way. The charms were all old and as useless as the one Salle had on her bag. She'd never be able to keep up with demand, she thought.

They passed market stalls where the vendors were calling out cheerfully to every passerby.

"Fresh fila cakes from Galus!" The smell of warm pastries filled her nose as they passed one stall and her stomach rumbled.

"Finest leather boots from St. Ovel in Veersland!" The mention of these faraway places made Arianwyn think suddenly of her father. She should write to him that evening and let him know about her first day in Lull.

"Market day is our busiest day of the week. We have traders from all across the Four Kingdoms coming into town and it brings in everyone from the smaller villages and hamlets between here and Flaxsham," Mayor Belcher said, waving regally at people as they passed.

They had reached the far side of the town square. "Most people live within the town walls, although there are farms and a few other houses outside Lull. There are also some orchards on the edge of the wood where the famous Lull apples come from—you've no doubt tried them in Kingsport?" Mayor Belcher smiled proudly.

Arianwyn shook her head.

"Really?" The mayor looked as though he couldn't quite believe it and quickly whisked out a small black notebook and started to jot something down.

"Well, come along, then!" he said briskly. "Let's get on!" He set off at breakneck speed into the crowd. Arianwyn scrambled to keep pace, dodging around busy shoppers getting on with their day.

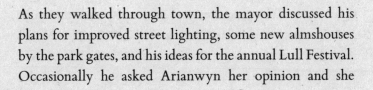

As they walked through town, the mayor discussed his plans for improved street lighting, some new almshouses by the park gates, and his ideas for the annual Lull Festival. Occasionally he asked Arianwyn her opinion and she quickly realized that if she didn't agree with him his expression turned sour and he pulled out his little black notebook, scribbling something down.

Eventually she decided simply to nod and say as little as possible.

"And this is the town school," Mayor Belcher said as they came to a brief stop by high metal railings. A bell rang from within the building, and seconds later a swarm of excited and noisy children poured from the doors.

There were suddenly eager faces gazing at Arianwyn through the green bars of the fence. "It's the new witch!" she heard a small girl whisper, and immediately there were even more smiles, while welcoming hands waved and reached through the fence. Arianwyn waved shyly back.

"There's a little more to being town witch than being a celebrity, you know!" The mayor huffed and reached for his notebook once more.

Arianwyn sighed and followed as the mayor walked briskly on.

They walked along Old Town Road in uncomfortable silence. The gate they had passed through the night before opened before them now. "This is the North Gate," the mayor said as they passed through. "The town has four gates. The West Gate is the main road in and out of town usually . . ." But Arianwyn wasn't really listening as she caught her first daylight glimpse of the land beyond Lull.

A wide but gentle river wound close to the town and then out across the meadows and farmland to the east and disappeared into the thick line of trees of the Great Wood. The wood seemed to circle the town entirely, covering the rolling hills and stretching on as far as Arianwyn could see. There was only a small break, where the old track wound up and past a solitary bunch of trees that must be Clover Hollow, so close it was almost a part of the Great Wood.

They carried on over the bridge, past an old abandoned building with boarded-up windows. The faded yellow sign above the tall doors read *Kurtis Mill*. The road became the track across the meadows and was full of puddles. The mayor stepped carefully around these, which slowed them a little. Arianwyn wondered if he was doing it on purpose.

"Thankfully, we are not usually plagued with too many problems with creatures from the wood, but this winter we've had more sightings than I've ever known and several attacks on animals on the local farms. Luckily we are used to dealing with things on our own." He gestured to his charm.

"Um, about these charms, Mayor Belcher. I'm not sure they will work very well against any creatures . . . unless you're attacked by a herd of cows!" Arianwyn couldn't believe the words had flown out of her mouth. She stared at him.

"Well, really!" The mayor went crimson and pulled out his little notebook once more.

They walked the rest of the way in silence.

As Clover Hollow loomed into view, Arianwyn paused for a moment. She reached out with her senses, waiting for the feeling of a creature nearby.

The wood emitted a huge amount of magical power. Listening for the creature was like trying to hear a whisper over an orchestra. They would have to go farther to be sure that the crawler had disappeared. As the trees closed in, Arianwyn felt increasingly anxious. Something niggled at her and she shivered.

"Is it much farther, Miss Gribble?" the mayor asked, huffing and panting to keep up with Arianwyn's stride along the track.

She saw a crumpled patch of trees at the edge of the track just a little way ahead. "There, look! That's where we were!" She moved on quickly, hoping against hope that the rift spell had never really formed.

The track was churned up from Beryl's wheels, and the surrounding wood lay in quiet ruin, trees snapped and bushes trampled where the crawler had landed. No birds sang and the air was full of stale dark magic.

Retracing her steps, Arianwyn crouched at the side of the road where she had been last night, where she had summoned the banishing glyph. She searched around, gazing into the shadow of the trees.

"Can you see anything?" the mayor asked as he finally caught up with her. "My goodness," he panted. "What a mess."

Everything was silent as she scanned the road and the edge of the trees for any sign of a rift. Mayor Belcher crouched at her side to peer as well. Then there was a rustling noise from close by and a small bush started to shake violently. Arianwyn moved forward carefully. "What are you doing, Miss Gribble?" Mayor Belcher gasped.

Arianwyn took a few more steps. The sound of chattering filled their ears. "Oh, good heavens, what is that?" Mayor Belcher squeaked. "Is it that thing—that crawler?" he shrieked.

"I doubt it, Mayor Belcher." She parted the leaves of the bush and peered inside. A swarm of doris sprites scuttled over the branches of the bush, chattering madly as they went. They were tiny, each one no larger than a moth, their miniature bodies dark as tree bark but their small wings a blaze of blues and reds. Seeing Arianwyn, they paused for a moment before taking up their call again and moving at twice the speed.

"It's fine—it's just sprites. Look."

Arianwyn reached inside and a nearby sprite clambered happily onto her hand. She turned to reassure Mayor Belcher but he leapt back suddenly as though he was going to run away. "No, don't let it near me, please, Miss Gribble!" He grabbed his cow charm and rattled it fiercely at Arianwyn and the sprite while staggering backward. He wasn't looking where he was going, though, and the mayor caught his foot on a twisted root and tripped.

He crashed down hard on the ground and gave a loud, sharp yelp of pain. Startled, the sprite flew from Arianwyn's hand and disappeared back into the bushes.

"Oh, Mayor Belcher, are you okay?" Arianwyn dashed to help him to his feet.

"I'm fine!" he snapped, all manners and courtesy fled. He pulled his jacket straight. It was smeared with mud and grit. "I really think we should be heading back into town now, Miss Gribble. I have plenty to be getting on with today." He looked as if he might be about to cry.

"Yes, of course," Arianwyn said quietly. She was happy to head back, although she wished it had been in better circumstances. It seemed she hadn't opened a rift, after all— and the crawler was long gone, probably vanished deeper into the Great Wood.

They'd gone just a few yards when the mayor gave a loud shriek. "My ankle!"

"Oh no, what is it?" Arianwyn asked rushing forward to take his arm.

"I think I've broken it!" he growled through gritted teeth, hopping from foot to foot, dancing around in a wobbly circle.

"Are you sure?" Arianwyn asked. She didn't know anything about broken ankles, but didn't think you would be able to stand on one, let alone hop around like a crazed chicken.

He glared at her again.

"Here, let me help you." Arianwyn looped the mayor's arm over her shoulder and very, very slowly helped him to limp back to Lull.

CHAPTER TEN

KETTLE LANE

The walk back to town seemed to take forever, as the mayor seemed to need to stop and wince every few steps. The wind had risen and brought occasional flurries of rain and wet snow.

"Oh, you're just in time!" Salle called out as they walked into the Blue Ox. It was bustling with shoppers and market vendors crowding in for the warm fire. "By the look of you, you've had an eventful morning," she said.

Arianwyn rolled her eyes.

The mayor groaned and slumped into the first chair he saw, alarming a lady in a very large hat whose minuscule dog yapped threateningly. "I'll get Mayor Belcher something to eat; there's someone on the telephone for you." Salle gestured to a narrow corridor half hidden behind a curtain.

"Hello?" Arianwyn said, lifting the heavy black receiver. The line crackled and hissed. "Hello?"

"Miss Gribble? Is that you? Can you hear me?"

The muffled voice sounded familiar but distant. "It's Colin. Colin Twine from the Civil Witchcraft Authority."

"Oh, hello!" Arianwyn replied, unable to mask the surprise in her voice.

"I just wondered how your first morning had been. We've been asked to check on all the new witches on their first day."

"Really?" Arianwyn asked.

"Um, no. Not really. Look, the truth is there has been a report of a crawler spotted near Lull and we just wondered if you had seen it or not."

"Ah, I see." She felt a little deflated that Colin hadn't called to check how she was. "Yes, I saw the crawler on my way into town yesterday. It attacked the bus I was on."

"Was anyone hurt?" Colin asked quickly.

"Just a few scrapes, thankfully," Arianwyn said.

"And what happened after that?"

Arianwyn could hear the scratch of a pencil on paper; Colin was obviously filling in a form.

"It disappeared back into the Great Wood, I think."

"Thank heavens you weren't hurt, I mean *no one* was hurt. Everything else okay?"

"Well, I don't think the mayor likes me very much," Arianwyn said, and then laughed at the daftness of it. She realized it was the first time she had smiled that day.

"Have you been to the Spellorium yet?" Colin asked.

"Not yet, the mayor . . . twisted his ankle on our walk and we had to come back early."

"Oh, sounds like you've been busy! Well, I've mailed some forms and things to you there and also the spirit lantern should be arriving in the next few weeks, if everything goes smoothly. It's the new model, with Doctor Bandora's triple-aperture design . . . I just wanted to let you know."

"Thank you," Arianwyn said quietly. It was so nice to hear a friendly voice.

She heard a muffled sound, like a shout, from the other end of the line and the noise of a hand quickly covering the receiver. "Hello?" Arianwyn said, worried they had been disconnected.

"Look, I have to go, Miss Newam's on the warpath . . . again! Cheerio!" Colin said.

"Bye!" Arianwyn said, but all she heard was a click and then the line was dead.

The inn was still bustling as Arianwyn emerged. The warm, cozy smell of stew mingled in the air with the soft woodsmoke from the fire. Salle was just placing a large steaming bowl in front of the mayor. Arianwyn's stomach rumbled. "What did your friend want?" Salle asked, her eyes twinkling.

"He works for the CWA," Arianwyn explained. She raised her voice to be heard over the hubbub. "He just wanted to check some details about the crawler we saw last night."

"About what?" Salle asked distractedly, handing out two more bowls of yummy-smelling stew.

"The crawler!" Arianwyn said louder, without thinking.

The inn fell miraculously quiet at just that moment, of course, except for the clattering of someone's fork against the tabletop. Everyone turned and looked at Arianwyn. The mayor scowled.

"There's a crawler nearby?" someone asked.

"Will it attack the town?" another worried voice called. Nervous chatter spread around the inn.

The mayor pursed his lips. He dropped his spoon into his bowl with an angry clank and got to his feet. When he spoke his voice was full and commanding. "Ladies and gentlemen. Miss Gribble did indeed encounter a crawler last night on her way into town."

The chatter intensified and everyone was asking questions at once.

The mayor held his hand up for silence. "But Miss Gribble has just been in communication with the Civil Witchcraft Authority in Kingsport, and there is no need for alarm. The curfew will remain in place for a another two weeks and it would be advisable for nobody to venture into the Great Wood unaccompanied until further notice."

Arianwyn was impressed. Everyone seemed happy with the mayor's explanation, even though it wasn't exactly true. They all slowly returned to their food and conversation, though Arianwyn noticed a few furtive glances in their direction.

"Sorry," she whispered to the mayor.

A look of displeasure clouded his face again. He turned to Salle. "Miss Bowen, I have a very busy afternoon, on top of which I now also need to see the doctor about my injury." He pointed to his ankle. "I wonder if you would be so kind as to take Miss Gribble and show her the Spellorium."

He reached into his pocket and withdrew a large brass key, handing it to Arianwyn. It was dull with age, a battered label tied to it. "It has been years since the last witch occupied it; I'm not sure what state you will find it in."

"Thank you," Arianwyn said quietly, and slipped the heavy key into her own coat pocket.

"It's not far, just down Kettle Lane," Salle reassured her when they set out a while later. Arianwyn had eaten a bowl of stew and dumplings and felt revived and warmed after the morning's escapades. They crossed the town square and turned into a bright, twisting lane that was crammed with shops and cottages. People glanced curiously in their direction. Salle greeted a few of them as they passed, while Arianwyn smiled shyly and hurried to keep up.

"There it is!" Salle said, and pointed to a narrow building tucked in and slightly back from the lane. It was taller than its neighbors, an empty-looking house to its right and a boutique on the left, its window full of bright hats that looked like bouquets of exotic blooms.

The Spellorium had a huge bay window that took up most of the front of the ground floor, the glass thick and smudged with grime and age. A sign hung over the door, squeaking rhythmically in the wintry wind that whistled along the lane. The paint, which must once have been brilliant, was faded and peeling. The silver star was nothing more than a ghostly outline.

Arianwyn mounted the three steep steps leading to the door and fished out the heavy key from her pocket.

Her hand shook slightly as she slid the key into the lock. She paused and took a deep steadying breath. The key clicked loudly in the lock and Arianwyn pushed the door wide.

The Spellorium seemed to heave a dusty sigh of relief, as though it had been holding its breath, waiting for this moment.

CHAPTER ELEVEN

THE SPELLORIUM

A rianwyn took a few hesitant steps into the room, not wanting to disturb anything, trying to hold the moment in her mind and take it all in.

Everything was painted white, except for the dark floorboards, the curving wooden counter, which swept out from the wall into the middle of the room, and a small round potbellied stove. There was a warm musty smell, a bit like a shed or a greenhouse. Tumbles of thick dust whispered across the floor.

Arianwyn ran her hand over the shelves that took up the wall on the left of the room. They were full of charms and potion bottles—their contents dried and useless—and stacked with books and pieces of equipment. All hidden under layers of gray cobwebs and dust.

Salle peered through the long glass doors at the back of the room, rubbing at one of the crusted panes of glass with her gloved hand.

Arianwyn moved behind the counter. She saw row upon row of tiny drawers, each with a brass handle and faded label. Inside the first row she found collections of tiny feathers, pebbles, and curls of paper. Below those were leaves and small flowers (mostly now dry and brittle). Another row contained beads of glass and stone and hoops of silver, iron, and gold.

Everything she needed for preparing charms.

She smiled.

Arianwyn knew charms; she had inherited her grandmother's skill, she could construct them with her eyes closed. She sat staring happily into the drawers for a while, lost in thought, letting items fall through her fingers. She loved the way her mind became totally absorbed in the task. The work was delicate and precise: selecting the perfect small glass holder, adding the right collection of objects and spells to create a host of charms for all eventualities. Charms to ward off dark spirits or offer inspiration or comfort, charms to help find a lost object or protect a ship on a voyage, even to protect you from an angry herd of cows!

"What's through here, do you think?" Salle called, pushing against the door at the back of the room. It gave way noisily, revealing nothing more than a dark storeroom with a wooden bench and large stone sink, complete with rusty dripping tap.

"Can we look upstairs now?" Salle asked, unable to hide the excitement in her voice. Arianwyn nodded and they raced up the twisting metal stairs that wobbled a little too enthusiastically. They emerged into another large whitewashed room full of light.

Two long windows looked out on Kettle Lane, and Arianwyn could just see over the rooftops of the buildings opposite and into the town square beyond. Another wood-burning stove stood against one wall with two neat but worn-looking armchairs in front of it. Over one of them lay a faded yellow dress—beautiful but rather old-fashioned—as though the wearer had only just placed it there and might return any moment.

A deep alcove housed a large metal-framed bed piled high with flowery duvets and blankets, and there was a huge wardrobe against the wall.

"Oh, look!" Salle gasped, pulling open the wardrobe door, revealing a rail of long formal dresses and a much older style of witch's uniform. As Salle rummaged, she dislodged something in the bottom of the wardrobe and a pile of papers tumbled onto the floor.

A photograph caught Arianwyn's eye and she bent down to pick it up. It showed a young witch, probably slightly older than Arianwyn, standing proudly in her uniform, her hair pinned up in a style she recognized from old photos of Grandmother. Beside her was a much younger girl, about seven or eight years old. She was rather gangly, as though she had just had a sudden growth spurt, her hair in two thick braids. She gazed adoringly at the witch. Arianwyn felt certain they must be related—sisters, perhaps?

She shuddered suddenly. She felt as though she was intruding and yet at the same time it felt as if she had been here before. She gathered the papers and placed them carefully back into the wardrobe, moving on to explore the rest of the apartment.

Near the tall windows were another stone sink and a rickety kitchen cupboard next to it. A round table, set for tea, with three mismatching chairs stood close by.

The only other room revealed a claw-footed bath that looked as if it would need several spells to remove the rusty ginger stain from its bottom. It smelled bad, and Salle quickly threw open the sash window to let in some fresh air. It was Arianwyn's first glimpse of a small yard below, where large clay pots mostly lay empty and some old cane furniture was stacked in a corner.

"Looks like you've got your work cut out for you, Wyn!" Salle said as they made their way back downstairs. "Are you okay? You're very quiet."

Arianwyn turned slowly, taking in the room again. "It's odd. Everything looks as though she just went out moments ago, but I don't feel anything of her here, no residual magic or lingering spell work . . . it's as if it's been abandoned for centuries . . . it's a bit creepy."

She suddenly remembered a small parcel her grandmother had forced into her hand at the train station in Kingsport. "Don't open it until you arrive at your new home!" she had said.

Pulling it free from her bag, Arianwyn tore open the paper.

It was the old door charm from the bookstore. It had been packed carefully, so that the tiny brass bells were silent. Arianwyn lifted it free of its wrapping and the six bells rang brightly in the quiet store.

"How beautiful!" Salle said.

Arianwyn reached up and hung it onto a small hook on the door, so that it would sing out just as it had done in the bookstore in Kingsport. She felt a sudden longing to see her grandmother. It had only been a day, but she missed her so much. They had been together every day for all those years and now she wouldn't see her for months.

"I'll help you clear out all the old stuff if you like. We'll soon get it feeling like home for you!" Salle offered gently.

"Thanks," Arianwyn said, smiling.

A few minutes later, Arianwyn had locked the front door and was tucking the key safely in her pocket. She stared up at the building.

"Hello, Miss Gribble," a bright voice called. A large woman dressed in a frothy pink outfit smiled and waved at them from next door. The sign above the window read *Caruthers' Boutique*—it was the hat shop she'd spotted earlier.

Arianwyn smiled and raised a hand in greeting.

"Getting all settled in, are you? I'm Millicent Caruthers. Just you drop by if there is anything you need, anything at all."

"Thank you." Arianwyn smiled.

"I've just had in a new shipment of hats from Kingsport, Salle. All the latest fashions! Want to pop in and have a look?"

Salle nodded. "Oh yes, please. You coming too, Wyn?"

"No, you go ahead, I'm going to have a look farther down the lane," Arianwyn replied.

Salle went into the boutique and Arianwyn turned once more to look at the Spellorium.

This was her new home, the place where she would prove herself as a witch. She looked at her moon badge. The crawler, Mayor Belcher, and the evaluation gauge flashed through her mind. She felt a pang of hopelessness. She really didn't know what she was doing. She'd not gotten off to the best start, but things were going to change from now, she decided.

There was a sudden noise from behind her, the clatter of an overturned trash can. She turned quickly. Kettle Lane was empty. But then she saw movement in the shadowy alleyway opposite.

"Hello?" she called, taking a step forward. There was a sound of hurried shuffling footsteps and then nothing.

Suddenly she didn't want to be alone outside anymore. She crossed the lane again toward the boutique, glancing at the Spellorium on her way.

"Cast the protection spell!" She heard Grandmother's warning words in her head.

For years, witches had cast protection spells over their homes or places of work. Protection for themselves, and for those who lived or worked nearby. Checking the street was still empty, Arianwyn raised her hand, feeling for the flow of magic around her. It was strong, but clustered at the far end of the lane, around a tree.

For a protection spell it was normal just to summon Erte, but Grandmother had always taught her to add another glyph to the spell. As Arianwyn drew the shape of the glyph in the air in front of her, she also called out "Oru!" summoning the glyph of light.

It was not one of the cardinal glyphs, and its properties often proved unstable or insubstantial, but this was an old family spell and Arianwyn wouldn't consider using any other.

The glyphs flashed in the air for a moment and magic flowed toward them. She repeated the glyphs, adding these to the spell, and then they began to multiply on their own, expanding and growing, invisible to any non-witches who might be watching.

One final blinding flash and Arianwyn felt the magic rush toward her. She raised her hands, sending it toward the Spellorium, and began to form the protection barrier.

Now, as the actual spell formed, it glistened briefly, illuminating Kettle Lane with a magical glow that could be seen by anyone. Arianwyn saw a few eager faces peering from windows and doorways, drawn by the light of the spell.

And then it was set.

The visible part of the magic faded from view, but Arianwyn could feel the energy thudding and humming around the building.

It was a strong spell; she had done well.

At last.

Witches have always held an important role within the communities of the Four Kingdoms. In ancient times they were sought for their powers of divination, cures to treat illness, and to help protect against dark spirits, particularly by the crafting of charms.

Charms can be effective protection against a variety of dark spirits and come in various forms, the most common being those created in small glass spheres containing natural objects and bound or activated with a series of glyphs.

CHAPTER TWELVE

THE DISTRICT SUPERVISOR

Soapy, filthy water splashed across the cobbles of Kettle Lane and swirled down into the drain near the Spellorium. Arianwyn paused for a moment and glanced along the lane. She had been in Lull for a week and was busy cleaning the Spellorium and the apartment above, from top to bottom. She paused for a moment and watched people coming and going busily in and out of the shops.

She wiped the back of her hand across her forehead, picked up her bucket, and turned to go back into the Spellorium to carry on cleaning. But then the shrill call of a motorcar horn rang along the lane and a huge silvery-green vehicle came charging over the cobbles. It was a shiny open-topped car that seemed to fill the whole lane. Shoppers threw themselves out of its path.

Arianwyn leapt back onto the steps of the Spellorium just as the car pulled up right next to the door. The driver peered straight at her through bright green driving goggles. Massive froggy eyes blinked and a trumpet-loud voice rang out: "You Arianwyn Gribble, then?"

Arianwyn nodded and clung tighter to her bucket.

"MARVELOUS!"

A tall, broad figure swathed in a long trench coat unfolded itself from the vehicle, swinging a large satchel over one shoulder. The figure had leather driving gloves that reached right up to the elbow. A bright silver star shone from the right-hand side of the coat.

"I'm Jucasta Delafield, dear. Your district supervisor!" She thrust a gloved hand toward Arianwyn.

"Oh, of course. Mayor Belcher said you would be coming!" Arianwyn fumbled with the bucket, which fell with a clang against the cobbles. She blushed and reached for the older witch's hand. "It's good to meet you."

Miss Delafield's eyebrows rose over the top of her driving goggles. She paused for a moment and glanced up at the Spellorium as though she was expecting to see someone at the window. Then she seemed to take a deep breath and strode past Arianwyn inside. There was the definite sound of a tut as she passed.

Retrieving the bucket, Arianwyn noticed a few people had stopped to watch the goings-on. She flushed some more and turned quickly to follow her supervisor inside.

Miss Delafield had stopped dead in the doorway, and stood gazing straight ahead.

"Would you like a cup of tea?" Arianwyn asked carefully, glancing toward the little potbellied stove. Bright warm flames danced in the window of the door.

"Oh no, dear, that's fine. Thank you," Miss Delafield replied, as if coming out of a dream. "I have my own with me." She reached into her satchel and pulled out a large thermos and a slender cocktail glass. Arianwyn was surprised it hadn't been smashed to pieces in the bag. Unscrewing the lid of the flask, Miss Delafield proceeded to pour herself a drink. It was bright blue and had a very pungent odor.

"Would you care for some, dear?" Miss Delafield raised a quizzical eyebrow. "It does wonders for the complexion."

Arianwyn stared at the blue drink for a few seconds and then caught a whiff of something really quite foul. "No, that's all right." She smiled. "I think I'll stick with tea!"

"Now then, my girl," Miss Delafield said, placing her glass down carefully on the counter and pouring some more of the blue liquid, "how are you settling in? Do you like the old place?" She shrugged off her coat and stood solidly by the desk, examining Arianwyn's cleaning efforts.

"Yes, it's great. It's in quite a state, though. I've been staying at the inn since I arrived." Arianwyn swung the bucket gently as she spoke. "The last witch seems to have left everything behind—do you know who she was?"

"Umm . . . no idea!" Miss Delafield said eventually. "I could check the register and see, but certainly Lull has been without a witch since before I was supervisor. We've dealt with the bulk of problems from Flaxsham but the CWA seemed to think we needed somebody here on the ground! No doubt some interfering busybody who ought to keep their nose out of other people's business!"

Miss Delafield's voice had risen sharply and her cheeks were flushed.

Arianwyn felt her insides twist with shame as Miss Delafield's gaze fell on the moon badge. Arianwyn instinctively started to move her hand to cover it, and there was an uneasy silence as Miss Delafield worked out the connection.

"Oh. I see, dear. Well—yes. Of course your grandmother is very well respected within the witching community . . ."

"I know exactly what you're thinking and I feel the same way," Arianwyn said. She felt suddenly and unusually bold. "But I've vowed to do my work and I promise to try my hardest to serve Lull to the best of my abilities. I don't know what happened at the evaluation but—" For a second she considered telling Miss Delafield all about the unknown glyph, but the moment passed quickly.

Miss Delafield half smiled and said in her business-like voice, "Anyway, dear, you're here now, which will be a great help, I'm sure. How has it been going so far?"

"It's all been quite quiet, but . . ." She trailed off.

Miss Delafield was gazing at Arianwyn levelly. She clearly knew more than she was letting on. "And how are you getting along with the mayor? Frightful old snob in my opinion, but best not to get on his bad side."

"He's been very . . . helpful."

"Ha! I'm sure he has!" Miss Delafield winked and pulled open her huge satchel, the straps and buckles jangling.

From its depths she dragged out a huge leather-bound book. Tall and narrow, its red cover looked very official and was stamped with a large silver star. Miss Delafield placed the book reverently on the counter. "This is your ledger. You'll record all of your appointments and work in here, please, and then when I visit I will check against the work you have completed, for my district report to the CWA."

She flipped the ledger open and ran a gloved hand across the blank pages that were faintly marked with red and green lines. "Date here, nature of problem. Resolution in this box and date here. Please leave this area blank for my comments." She prodded the page firmly.

Arianwyn stood mutely staring at her, fiddling with the bucket briefly before muttering, "Yes, of course." It felt suddenly very real to her.

"Beg pardon, dear?" Miss Delafield asked loudly.

"Sorry. I said, yes, of course," Arianwyn said more firmly.

"Are you going to pop that bucket down, dear?" Miss Delafield asked, a small smile playing across her lips.

Arianwyn felt her cheeks warm and she quickly placed the bucket down on the shining dark floorboards.

Miss Delafield reached once more into the satchel and this time she took out a sheaf of papers, different sizes and colors. She dropped them onto the ledger. "These are the outstanding appointments that will require your attention sooner rather than later."

Arianwyn peered at the papers and her stomach wobbled nervously. She gulped.

"And of course you'll have your cataloging duties once the spirit lantern arrives." Miss Delafield sounded less than impressed. "Oh, and this is the most recent CWA newsletter." She tossed a flimsy magazine down onto the counter.

"New Witches off to a Flying Start," it said on the front in huge bold letters. Arianwyn peered closer and came face-to-face with a photograph of Gimma Alverston. She gazed perfectly out of the newsletter, laughing and waving. Arianwyn groaned and flipped it over. She'd throw it in the trash as soon as Miss Delafield had left.

Arianwyn heard raised voices from the street and Miss Delafield turned just as the door burst open. A boy not more than ten years old staggered in, the bell charm jangling wildly. "Miss. Miss? Miss . . . Witch?"

He was out of breath as he skidded to a stop just in front of Arianwyn. "Me mam's sent for you, says you're to come straightaway," the boy said breathlessly.

"What's the matter?" Arianwyn asked.

"She's found a snotling nest in the under-stairs cupboard and wants you to come and sort it out right now."

"Right!" Arianwyn said, struggling for a moment to think things through.

"Do you need me to come with you, dear?" Miss Delafield asked, watching Arianwyn carefully.

"No. It's all right, I think I can manage a few snotlings," Arianwyn replied.

"Well, I'd best not keep you when you have plenty to be doing. Off you go!" she beamed.

Arianwyn smiled at Miss Delafield and then at the young boy as he hopped from foot to foot. Then she grabbed up her coat and followed him as he raced out of the Spellorium.

CHAPTER THIRTEEN

THE SNOTLING NEST

The boy disappeared through an arch and down a narrow alleyway. Arianwyn followed and found herself at the back of the churchyard beside a short row of dilapidated cottages. The church loomed over everything.

Damp clothing flapped limply in the icy breeze, the lines zigzagging the lane. Arianwyn ducked beneath the laundry and followed the boy to the shabbiest-looking house in the row.

The boy kicked on the door and yelled "Mam! Witch is here!" Then he ran off to join a small group of children playing a game at the end of the row.

Arianwyn was just about to knock on the worn door when it swung open. A shower of rotten wood fell down from the lintel.

"Yes, what is it?" The woman balanced a fat baby on one hip. Her apron was splattered and smeared with various stains. She bore a floury smudge across her red cheeks, with more dusting her frizzing hair.

"What?" she demanded, glaring at Arianwyn.

"Er . . . ," Arianwyn stammered, "I'm Arianwyn

Gribble, the new witch. I've come to deal with your snot-ling problem."

The woman's face relaxed. "Oh, thank heavens. Pesky little rascals have been driving us up the wall." She peered out into the street. "Where's that boy gotten to? CYRIL!" She looked up and down the row quickly, then boomed, "Cyril Myddleton, get home this instant!"

The only answer was the sound of laughter and quick feet on cobbles. The woman frowned at Arianwyn. "Well, you going to come in?"

The door swung wide, with another shower of rotten wood, revealing a cluttered kitchen dominated by a massive table that seemed to be almost entirely covered with stuff.

Clothing hung from a drying rack over a hulking stove that smoked profusely; the kettle was whistling away to itself, billowing clouds of steam up toward the ceiling. The sink was piled high with pans and dishes in various states of cleanliness. On the table, Arianwyn could now make out an assortment of mixing bowls, cans and jars of flour, dried fruits and sugar. Eggshells were spread across an open cookbook and some had fallen to the floor. Two vast baskets were stacked high with yet more laundry.

Playing on a rug near the stove sat two chubby, rosy-cheeked toddlers, probably no more than two years old. They looked like fat little cherubs in paintings, Arianwyn thought, just as one raised the building block he had been playing with and brought it crashing down on the other's head. The other child started to wail and lifted his arms toward his mother.

"Caspar! Naughty!" the woman scolded without any real enthusiasm. "You don't hit Jaspar like that!" She hefted the baby farther up on her hip. "All I do is cook, clean, and wash." She sighed. "I'm Blanche, by the way, Blanche Myddleton."

Arianwyn shook the woman's floury hand.

"Where's the nest?" Arianwyn asked.

"This way!" Mrs. Myddleton led her through a door and into a small gloomy hallway, the only light coming from a tiny window at the top of the staircase.

"There, in the under-stairs cupboard." Mrs. Myddleton gestured to the small door.

"How many are there?" Arianwyn asked, shrugging off her coat and rolling up her sleeves. It was strange for snotlings to be awake at this time of the year; usually they preferred to hibernate until the warmer months.

"I'm not sure really; maybe three of them. I saw them stealing cake from the bread bin this morning!"

Three. That was okay. Arianwyn was sure she could easily deal with three half-awake snotlings. A simple stunning spell and then banishing, she just needed something as bait . . .

"Could I have those eggshells?"

As Mrs. Myddleton went off to fetch them, Arianwyn pulled open the cupboard door.

In the darkness, she could just make out the shape of the snotling nest tucked into the corner of the cupboard, half hidden behind a pile of shoes and a broom. It looked like a matted ball of rags with a small hole near the top. The snotlings had most likely shredded up a few coats and scarves from the cupboard with their sharp needle teeth, possibly a bit of carpet or rug, to make the nest.

Arianwyn crawled into the space, minding the snotling droppings that littered the floor, wrinkling her nose at the pungent stench. Carefully shoving the shoes and broom to one side, she suddenly pulled back. The nest was larger than she had imagined, much larger indeed!

"I think you might have a few more than three," Arianwyn called over her shoulder.

Mrs. Myddleton came hurrying back with the eggshells cupped in her hands; she gave a quick gasp when she saw the size of the nest. "You going to be all right dealing with them all on your own?" she asked, looking skeptically at Arianwyn.

"It'll be fine. But can you keep the children in the kitchen? Snotlings aren't that dangerous, but they've got really sharp teeth."

Mrs. Myddleton nodded and wandered back to her various jobs in the kitchen. Arianwyn noticed the two toddlers peering around the door before a sharp call from their mother sent them scampering away again.

Scattering the slimy, sticky pieces of eggshell onto the floor, Arianwyn gave the nest a quick shake and reversed quickly out of the cupboard.

She didn't have to wait too long before the nest started to quiver ever so slightly and then from the small hole at the top a snotling emerged. He was about as tall as a school ruler and a sickly green color, but not particularly slimy (which was the curious thing about snotlings). He did have a few short and sharp-looking spines growing on his shoulders, though.

The tiny little beast was bleary-eyed and groggy. He tumbled down the side of the nest, shuffling sleepily across the floor of the cupboard and following the scent of the eggshell.

He didn't get far. Arianwyn cast her stunning spell at him, sending him falling backward onto the floor with a soft thud.

Reaching into the cupboard, she dragged his limp body quickly out into the hall and left it to one side, waiting for the next one to emerge from the nest.

CHAPTER FOURTEEN

SPLAT!

I t was so easy. Snotlings were not the cleverest of creatures and were easily lured by the aroma of the eggshells piled on the floor of the cupboard. After half an hour there was a pile of four snotlings in the hallway and it had been quite some time since the fourth one had emerged. Crawling back into the cupboard, Arianwyn gave the nest one final vigorous shake, but nothing happened. After another quick jab and still no movement, she was satisfied all was well. She would just need to raise the banishing spell and return them to the void.

"I think that's it!" she called as she backed out of the cupboard, relieved to have completed her first official task without any trouble. She gave a huge sigh of relief, unaware she had been holding her breath.

But as she emerged back into the hallway she saw the Myddleton twins dragging two of the stunned snotlings off into the kitchen like a pair of rag dolls. That was bad enough, but things took a sudden turn for the worse when a high-pitched growl, something like an angry cat, sounded from behind her.

Turning, she saw another three snotlings had crawled from the nest, and one of them had a huge thick crest of brown spines. It was a female, a she-snotling, and females were always more vicious and dangerous than the males. And she had just seen Jaspar and Caspar dragging her nest mates away!

"Oh, rune-rot!" Arianwyn groaned, and as quickly as she could she hurled a spell orb at the new snotlings in an attempt to stun them.

She missed. The spell bounced into the cupboard, exploding the nest with a loud dusty whoosh. Bits of nesting material—scraps of old coats, twigs, a sock, even bits of shoe—were blown out into the hallway.

The snotlings scattered and, as fast as lightning, scrambled into the kitchen in search of their nest mates. Arianwyn was on her feet as an earsplitting scream came from the kitchen.

The scene that greeted her would have been funny, if it had not been so terribly and seriously awful.

Caspar had abandoned his stunned snotling, but Jaspar was hugging his as though it were his most precious toy. Mrs. Myddleton stood on the kitchen table with one of the snotlings dangling from her apron, snapping its angry jaws. She was screaming as if she were actually being murdered while the baby laughed and gurgled with obvious delight at his mother's predicament.

The other male snotling was skipping around the kitchen emitting high-pitched shrieks and hisses.

Summoning the glyphs again, Arianwyn spelled two

bursts of energy at the snotlings, but missed once more. The smell of scorched magic mingled with the damp clothing and cooking odors in the kitchen.

At that moment the door swung wide open and Cyril appeared, bouncing a large ball.

"Close the door!" Arianwyn shouted. But it was already too late: The two male snotlings had skipped out between Cyril's legs and through the open door as the boy gazed in amazement.

Arianwyn took a deep breath, brushing stray curls from her face. "This can't possibly get any—"

She turned and froze in horror. Caspar had seen the she-snotling and had obviously decided that an awake snotling was far more exciting than the limp, clammy thing he had discarded. Arianwyn could see what would happen and she was powerless to do anything about it. If she tried to stun the snotling now, she could hit Caspar.

The she-snotling was moving forward slowly, wary of the toddler. She was trying to get back to the nest! But Caspar lunged forward, grasping the she-snotling around the throat with his chubby little fingers.

Shocked, the she-snotling did nothing, except give a slightly choked whimper. But, as Caspar reached out with his other hand to pet his new toy, the she-snotling's mouth gaped wide, revealing spiny sharp teeth, which she clamped down into the pudgy flesh of the child's hand.

He screamed at once. Thick tears tumbled down his cheeks, now pale with fear. He shook his arm, trying to throw the creature off, but she held fast.

"My babies! MY BABIES!" Mrs. Myddleton screamed, hovering between rushing forward to help and clambering back up onto the table.

The she-snotling was flailing about in the air, Caspar still wailing in terror and pain. In a split second, Arianwyn saw her one and only chance.

Drawing on a deposit of magic that had clustered around the kettle, Arianwyn summoned the glyphs speedily and hurled a stunning orb once again. It soared across the kitchen like a fiery comet, but something wasn't quite right. The ball of energy was the wrong color, far too big, far too bright, and far too fast.

Thwump!

Splat!

It found its mark. But, instead of simply stunning the snotling, the spell exploded it. There was a burst of stinking, slimy green gloop that splattered and splashed across the walls, floor, and Caspar's chubby face.

Everyone froze. Everything was quiet except for the drip, drip of snotling goo.

The spell had been too strong. Arianwyn looked at Mrs. Myddleton, unsure how to explain exactly what had happened. Mrs. Myddleton half sat, half collapsed into a chair, the baby still happily gurgling in her arms. She raised a hand, pointing back to Caspar. "My b-b-baby . . . ," she whimpered.

Caspar, for all of his screaming, was recovering quite quickly and sat poking the head of the snotling (which was all that had survived the spell) as it wobbled on the kitchen floor amid puddles of green slime.

"Blimey!" Cyril said, a broad grin on his face. "That was awesome, miss! Do it again!"

"Don't you stand there gawping," his mother snapped. "Get off with you and go fetch the doctor, poor Caspar's been bitten by one of those little beasts."

Arianwyn was on her feet. "I'm so sorry, Mrs. Myddleton; I didn't know there were so many of them—" But the woman wasn't listening; she pushed past Arianwyn, dashing to Caspar's side. She kicked the she-snotling head and it rolled across the kitchen floor, bumping against Arianwyn's boot.

"I'd better banish the stunned ones before the spell wears off . . . ," Arianwyn said to Mrs. Myddleton's back, desperate to be out of the cottage. There was no reply.

She moved quickly through the cottage, retrieving the stunned snotlings, and then escaped back into the yard. There was no sign of the two males that had gotten away—they could be anywhere by now. She took a deep breath.

The sky was growing dark, a few stars just visible. Arianwyn knelt on the cold ground, her breath misting in front of her.

L'ier, the banishing glyph. It curled like black smoke on the stones of the lane; then a tiny rift opened. Arianwyn felt the chilly pull of the void. Dust swirled around the opening and disappeared inside like water down a drain.

She glanced across at the house. She could still hear Mrs. Myddleton's shrieks from within.

And that was when Arianwyn noticed a dark patch on the wall near the window. It couldn't be, could it? Keeping a careful eye on the rift, she moved quickly back to the house.

"No, no, no!" she mumbled. She bent forward to peer closer. Thick ridges of black mold bloomed against the stone of the house.

But this wasn't any ordinary mold.

She heard hurried footsteps and saw Cyril returning with the doctor, who carried a large leather bag.

"Ah, Miss Gribble, I'm Doctor Cadbury. I gather you've had trouble with some snotlings," the old man said kindly. He was a little out of breath.

"There were more of them than I thought." She gestured to the still bodies at her feet. "I don't think Caspar was hurt too badly, but the she-snotling gave him a nasty bite." She knotted her fingers nervously.

"Not to worry, my dear, I'm sure all will be well . . . I say, is that . . . ?" The old man stepped closer.

"It's hex," Arianwyn replied, her voice steady and certain.

"Goodness, we've not seen any hex in Lull since I was a boy—nasty stuff, eh?" Dr. Cadbury asked. He stroked his chin and leaned a little closer.

"What is it?" Cyril asked, reaching out a grubby hand toward the black patch.

"Don't touch it!" Arianwyn said quickly, and grabbed his hand. "It's dangerous; it could make you ill . . . or worse! It's caused by dark magic or stale spells. It's like a fungus or a mold. Hex plagues have wiped out whole villages, you know."

"Wow!" Cyril replied, and gazed even more.

"Well, best get rid of it if you can, eh?" Dr. Cadbury smiled and went into the house after Cyril, who still craned to see the hex patch. There were more wails from Mrs. Myddleton.

It really wasn't a terribly thick patch, though it was dangerous all the same. Arianwyn took a deep breath and summoned Årdra, the fire glyph. Quickly she pressed her palm close to the dark patch of hex. Bright red flames sparked under her fingers. She counted to twenty and then pulled her hand away.

The black patch was gone. There was only a faint ring of darkness on the wall now. She hoped there were no more. She made a mental note to tell Miss Delafield about it as soon as possible and went back to the rift.

Kneeling again on the cobbles, Arianwyn reached forward and scooped the stunned remaining creatures closer to the rift.

"Return to the void. Your spirits must not linger here. Go in peace. Return to the darkness."

She whispered the binding words, a ritual as ancient as the spell itself, and watched as the snotling bodies dissolved into light, shimmering fragments that swirled away into the air. All that remained were minuscule dark whirls of magic, their spirits, and these floated down through the rift and returned to the void.

She heard a movement from behind her, turned, and saw Mrs. Myddleton emerge from her house. She was pulling a woolen scarf around her shoulders. She cast a filthy glance at Arianwyn and then bustled off between the lines of laundry as fast as her feet would carry her.

From the distance she heard the chattering laugh of the surviving snotlings, followed by shouts and screams.

"Oh, I'm going to be in so much trouble," Arianwyn groaned.

CHAPTER FIFTEEN

THE DISAGREEMENT

Arianwyn trudged slowly back to the store, replaying everything in her mind. How had the spell gone so wrong? She wandered up and down streets, along alleys and lanes, avoiding as many people as possible.

On the corner of the town square she passed the telephone booth and felt a sudden need to hear her grandmother's voice.

Her coin dropped with a clang into the slot and she lifted the receiver, giving the operator the number of the bookstore back in Kingsport.

"Connecting you, one moment please!" came the operator's bright reply. Then a click and the sound of the phone ringing.

"Hello, Stronelli's Bookstore!"

The voice was not her grandmother's.

"Mr. Lomax? Is that you?" Arianwyn asked. Mr. Lomax was their neighbor in Kingsport and had occasionally watched the shop when her grandmother was away.

"Yes, Arianwyn, are you all right? How is it going in . . . where have they sent you again?"

"Is my grandmother there?" She felt a lump in her throat, sudden and unexpected.

"No, dear . . . did you not know? She's gone off on a trip, west coast somewhere, I think . . ."

Gone? Without mentioning it at all? How long has she been planning a trip away?

Arianwyn clumsily replaced the receiver, cutting off Mr. Lomax's words. Then she rested her head against the side of the phone booth and cried.

It was entirely dark when she eventually turned into Kettle Lane, and she felt a moment's cheer as she saw the bright welcoming lights shining from the Spellorium's huge bay window.

Salle was there, propped up against the counter and flipping idly through a magazine. The cover was filled with glamorous photographs of film stars. She turned at the sound of the door and the bell charm. She looked up, smiling. "How did it go?"

"Not according to plan!"

"What happened?" Salle asked.

Arianwyn slumped into a chair and let the whole story tumble out.

"I shouldn't have let Caspar get bitten," she said, sliding lower into her seat.

"Don't be silly. It's not your fault, Wyn," Salle reassured her. "I'll get you some hot chocolate."

Arianwyn leaned forward and rested her head in her

hands. It was only a second or two and then the bell charm sang out and she looked up quickly. Mayor Belcher and Miss Delafield stood in the doorway. Mayor Belcher looked very unhappy. Very unhappy indeed.

News clearly traveled fast. *Just as well I haven't unpacked everything*, Arianwyn thought.

"You've had an interesting afternoon, I gather," the mayor said.

Arianwyn shook her head, not sure what she could say to make things better. Salle returned, carrying a mug of hot chocolate. She immediately came to stand beside Arianwyn and said, "It's not Wyn's fault: That stupid Mrs. Myddleton didn't pay any attention—"

Miss Delafield raised a hand. "Yes. Thank you, Miss Bowen. But I should like to hear Miss Gribble's version of the events, if you don't mind."

Arianwyn swallowed. She saw Mayor Belcher take out his little black notebook and flip through some pages. "Now then," he began. "Mrs. Myddleton came to see me. She seems very upset about your visit. She claims you allowed her children to be attacked by a swarm of"—he checked the notebook—"snotters?"

"Snot*lings*!" Arianwyn and Miss Delafield said at the same time.

Arianwyn thought she might burst into tears again. She took a deep breath, and with a faltering, hushed voice, she started to explain. "Well, first things first, it wasn't a swarm: There were seven of them . . ."

A while later, Arianwyn had recounted her story and

Mayor Belcher and Miss Delafield had asked endless questions: Where she had been standing? How large were the snotlings? What type of spell did she use?

There was a long pause as Mayor Belcher read back through his notes. She was careful not to mention that the last stunning spell had been too strong and she didn't know why.

"I think we can all see that Miss Gribble wasn't entirely at fault here, if at all," Miss Delafield said gently.

"Perhaps," the mayor grumbled. "Nonetheless I have a duty to report this to the Civil Witchcraft Authority."

"But—" Arianwyn began. Something like this could end up on her record for years, and that was all she needed!

"I don't think that's necessary!" Miss Delafield protested.

"Miss Delafield, we must follow the correct procedure. Miss Gribble's actions have resulted in an injury to a small child."

"A very minor injury!" Salle butted in. Three pairs of eyes turned on her quickly. "I'm just saying . . . ," she mumbled.

"That is not the point. The child has been injured, minorly or otherwise, and it is a result of Miss Gribble's carelessness . . ."

Arianwyn really could feel the tears forming as the older witch and Mayor Belcher continued their argument.

"I think we have made a very grave mistake in taking on such an inexperienced young witch." Mayor Belcher paced the floor. "I don't think this is going to work!" His voice was low and threatening.

"Don't be ridiculous!" Miss Delafield said. "She's been here five minutes; you've given her no chance to settle in."

"I have to think of the safety of the town and the people who live here! I think it would be best if Miss Gribble returns to Kingsport as soon as possible and we ask for a replacement. And a fully trained witch this time. No more accommodating the demands of the CWA," the mayor muttered, glaring at Miss Delafield.

Arianwyn glanced down at her moon brooch. Snotling goo had dried on it.

"No!" Miss Delafield said, her voice raised. "You're not being fair, Josiah. Arianwyn has explained and Mrs. Myddleton should accept the responsibility for this. She was warned about the snotlings and did nothing to help herself. Dr. Cadbury said it was little more than a nip to the child's skin and there are no lasting effects." Miss Delafield moved forward, placing herself slightly between the mayor and Arianwyn. "We're not sending Miss Gribble back to Kingsport. She is our witch and she stays here in Lull! It's my responsibility, Josiah. *My* responsibility as district supervisor, thank you very much indeed! And we will offer her our *full* support in the future."

They glared at each other.

"Excuse me?" a soft voice called. Arianwyn, Mayor Belcher, and Miss Delafield turned to see a small elderly gentleman standing by the open door, nervously twisting his cap in his hands.

"Oh, Mr. Turvy, is everything all right? Come in out of the cold," Salle said, scowling at Mayor Belcher as she passed and leading the little man to the counter.

"Now, what can we do for you?" she asked gently.

The old man raised his head. He had kind, bright blue eyes and a soft warm face. "I heard the new witch had arrived and I wondered if she could repair a charm for me." He looked at Arianwyn. "Only if it's not too much trouble. You must be very busy."

Arianwyn looked at Miss Delafield, who glared at Mayor Belcher.

After a second or two he nodded.

CHAPTER SIXTEEN

A CHARM FOR MR. TURVY

C ould I see the charm, Mr. Turvy?" Arianwyn asked.

He held out his hand. Half a silver chain, a small, cracked glass orb, and a collection of beads, metal rings, and a silver locket rested in his palm. It looked to Arianwyn like a standard personal protection charm to ward off dark spirit creatures.

"Such times we live in. Every day the newspapers are full of sad tales from the Uris and now all these things in the Great Wood . . . I'm not ashamed to tell you, it scares me."

Are things in the Great Wood so bad? She glanced at Mayor Belcher and Miss Delafield briefly, then reached out a hand of reassurance. It shook just a little. "I know. Of course I'll help."

"Mr. Turvy lives in Orchard Cottage, on the edge of the Great Wood," Salle said quietly to Arianwyn.

He gave a shy little smile and emptied the remains of the charm onto the countertop, which Arianwyn noticed had been polished to a high shine—Salle must've been hard at work. He laid the locket down carefully and it flicked open. Two bright faces stared up at her, a man and woman captured forever in the faded sepia portraits. The young woman's hair was braided and coiled atop her head and she wore a high lace collar. The man wore a military uniform, his cap displaying a regimental badge. There was no mistaking the gentle look of Mr. Turvy in the young man.

"My beautiful Rose," he said, stroking the locket gently with a fingertip. "Married fifty-three years, we were, before she passed away."

Arianwyn wasn't sure what to say, so she patted the man's hand gently. "You look like you were very happy."

"We were." Mr. Turvy sniffed.

Arianwyn quickly pulled open several drawers under the counter, fishing out the components she would need to repair the charm.

She saw Mayor Belcher and Miss Delafield studying her carefully and realized this might be more than just a reworking of a charm. It might be a test! She felt a moment's hesitation, worried she might muddle the charm spell or explode Mr. Turvy's precious locket.

Just concentrate and stay calm, she told herself.

She pulled a fine silver chain from a low drawer and gracefully but quickly began to thread on the correct items for a personal charm. One gold hoop and two silver and a bead of amber. Next came the small glass container, which held a few dried lavender flowers and daisy petals. Lastly the open locket. She smiled again at the photograph.

She was nearly there. Taking a steadying breath, she began to sketch a repeated pattern of glyphs onto the counter: Briå, Oru, Briå, Oru, over and over until the new charm was surrounded by the glyphs for air and light.

The circle complete, the spell formed a ring of light that glowed against the dark wood. It grew brighter and brighter. Mr. Turvy, Salle, and Mayor Belcher shielded their eyes, but Arianwyn was able to stare into it and watch the energy tumble and pour into the charm. Out of the corner of her eye she could see Miss Delafield watching closely too. A smile half formed on her lips.

This was the moment it could all go horribly wrong. She felt the flow of magic around her, surging over her. It was too much, the spell was too strong—*again*. She panicked.

What could she do? She racked her brain. The charm quivered and rattled on the countertop. She saw the worried glance from Mr. Turvy and the satisfied look from Mayor Belcher. Hurriedly, without really knowing what she was doing, she re-sketched the glyphs for the spell, but this time in the air above the locket.

The combination of the two spell circles seemed to slow the stream of magic just enough and the charm stopped its jittering dance.

The light began to fade, growing fainter and fainter as the spell set.

Salle was already clapping loudly and glaring at Mayor Belcher.

Arianwyn lifted the charm, handing it carefully back across the counter. "There we go, Mr. Turvy. Good as new!"

Mr. Turvy held it briefly in his hand, gazing at the pictures in the locket, before tucking it safely into his pocket once more.

"Thank you so much, young lady. It was very kind of you to help me."

"It was my pleasure, Mr. Turvy."

He headed for the door, but just before he stepped out into Kettle Lane he turned and said loudly, "I think you have done a fine job with this witch, Mayor Belcher. I say she's a real credit to the town!"

The door closed quietly. The store was silent for a while.

"I think Miss Gribble has proved herself more than adequate. Don't you, Josiah?" Miss Delafield asked. Arianwyn glanced at the mayor.

He mumbled and stared hard at Arianwyn. "I think it's safe to assume you did all that you could to help Mrs. Myddleton, and that on this occasion you were unlucky. A little extra care would be advisable in the future."

Arianwyn felt a flood of relief. "Yes, of course. I won't let you down again."

"Be sure you do not. I shall be watching your progress carefully, Miss Gribble." And with that the mayor turned on his heels and left the Spellorium.

"Well, what a day! Any more of the hot chocolate

going, young Salle, dear? Could you pop some in my thermos?" Miss Delafield asked. Salle took the flask and scampered upstairs.

When she was gone, Miss Delafield stood close to Arianwyn and said in a hushed voice, "Be cautious, Arianwyn. I have no doubt Mrs. Myddleton will be telling her tale of woe to anyone who might listen. And Mayor Belcher has been won over this time, but—Ah, here's Salle with that hot chocolate. Thank you, dear. You girls have a good evening!"

Miss Delafield waved a gloved hand as she left the store and Arianwyn closed the door behind her. The silver-and-green car roared off into the night. Headlights flashed along the shops and houses on Kettle Lane.

"Looks like you have a fan there!" Salle beamed.

"Hmm, it's just as well. I think I might need all the help I can get!"

"You have to come and see what wonders I've done upstairs!" Salle said, jumping on the spot and clasping her hands together. "Come on!"

Arianwyn followed Salle upstairs to the apartment, *her* apartment.

Salle had indeed worked miracles. Everywhere was clean and dusted, fresh blankets on the bed and a warm delicious smell coming from the oven. "One of Aunt Grace's pies!" Salle smiled. "And I've packed all those old clothes and bits of paper and things away in a suitcase; it's in the wardrobe if you need it."

Arianwyn thought briefly about the photo of the witch and the young girl. Perhaps she should show it to Miss Delafield next time she saw her.

She felt so tired. She sank slowly into one of the armchairs next to the stove and gave a long, weary, and relieved sigh.

THE APPRENTICE WITCH'S HANDBOOK

✦ ✦ ✦

Legends tell us that at the dawn of time
great spirits separated darkness from light,
forming our realm—the world of spirits,
witches, and humans—and the void. Those
great spirits still guard over their creation
to this day. Great spirits are naturally
incredibly polite and follow a very intricate
set of rules, which can be incredibly confusing to the uninitiated.

CHAPTER SEVENTEEN

THE SPIRIT LANTERN

It was more than a week later, early one morning, when Miss Delafield appeared with a large wooden crate.

"It's one of those blasted spirit lantern contraptions!" she puffed. *FRAGILE* was stamped in large red letters across the sides and top of the box. "Well, let's have a look at it, shall we?"

Mrs. Delafield reached into her cavernous satchel and pulled out a crowbar. She set about opening the crate and within seconds the floor of the store was littered with a drift of wood shavings and the sides of the crate. A small square leather case nestled among the curls of wood. A long strap curved around it like a tail.

"Well, there you go, then!" Miss Delafield beamed. "That's for you and all this cataloging you're supposed to be doing!" She pulled a face. "Rotten waste of money and time, if you ask me. Not that anybody ever does." She laughed.

Arianwyn smiled, but she was excited at the prospect of using the lantern to capture better images of the various spirit creatures. The best she had ever seen were some blurry photographs from a normal camera or line drawings in books. She stepped cautiously forward and lifted the case onto the counter. Pulling it open, she reached in and lifted the spirit lantern free. She had seen one only once before and it had been huge, standing on a vast workbench with three long brass tubes, like telescopes, protruding from the front.

She held in her hands its double, in miniature. The main body was polished wood; it was a compact rectangular box. And from its front protruded three brass-encased lenses. On its side were several switches and dials. Lifting it to her face, she peered through the viewing aperture at the back. Everything was blurred.

"Can you see anything?" Miss Delafield asked.

"Not really," Arianwyn replied.

"Is it broken?"

"No. I just think I might need to look at the instruction pamphlet first," Arianwyn answered.

"Well, best be quick about it, then, dear!" Miss Delafield smiled, handing over the flimsy white pamphlet that she had just plucked from the case. "We're off to the Great Wood to get started on your project! Now!"

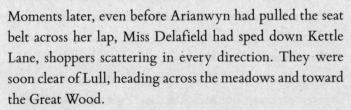

Moments later, even before Arianwyn had pulled the seat belt across her lap, Miss Delafield had sped down Kettle Lane, shoppers scattering in every direction. They were soon clear of Lull, heading across the meadows and toward the Great Wood.

"I didn't think there were any roads through the Great

Wood anymore!" Arianwyn called over the engine's roar and the wind rushing through her hair.

"Yes, that's quite right, dear!" Miss Delafield shouted back. The car was jolting across the meadow, Arianwyn leaping from her seat at every rut and bump.

"Then how are we going to drive into the wood?" Arianwyn yelled, gripping the seat and the spirit lantern case tightly, her knuckles white.

"There's still the odd pathway and track that hasn't entirely grown over. Watch yourself, dear!"

Branches whipped over Arianwyn's head and passed her face as the car rumbled from the grass and under the first thick line of trees and into the Great Wood.

Birds scattered at the sudden disturbance, and a few startled deer hurried away just in time.

"Won't this scare away any spirits?" Arianwyn asked, feeling slightly foolish for even mentioning it to the district supervisor.

"Nonsense, dear. The spirits all live much deeper in the wood than this. We shan't disturb anything for a while yet—except for the odd sprite, perhaps! That's why it's quicker to drive . . . it'd take hours to reach the—"

Arianwyn could hear the sound of earth spraying behind them as Miss Delafield slammed her foot hard on the brake. The car screeched to a halt.

Arianwyn rocked forward, still clutching the leather case tightly for fear of damaging it. "What on earth—" she started to say, but Miss Delafield's gloved hand slipped speedily over her mouth.

"Ssssh!"

With her free hand, she pointed ahead to where the trees parted briefly, forming a small clearing that was filled with rich sunlight and dappled shade. And something else.

That was when Arianwyn felt the tingle of magic. A spirit creature. She leaned farther forward in her seat. The shadows and light moved and she heard the snapping of twigs.

There in the clearing was a stagget, a huge spirit creature that guarded the woodland. It looked like a massive deer; its body almost as big as Miss Delafield's car, it stood twice as high as a tall man. It had large silver antlers that branched out like trees, spiraling high above its head. It grazed calmly in the clearing.

"Oh my! What a beauty!" Miss Delafield breathed. "Well, are you going to . . . take its picture? Or whatever it is you do with that thing?" She gestured to the spirit lantern.

Arianwyn didn't dare to move. She had only ever seen a sketch of a stagget; there was one in her handbook but it didn't do the creature justice. She slowly pulled the case open and let her hand slip inside to grip the lantern. All the while she kept watch on the spirit creature.

It returned to its clump of grass, ears flicking and twisting, alert. Then its head came gracefully up again and it peered out through the trees straight at Miss Delafield and Arianwyn, its silver eyes shining in the gloom of the wood.

"I've never seen one this close to a town before, amazing!" Miss Delafield sighed. "Ready with that yet?"

Arianwyn was just lifting the lens caps free and was about to get the lantern into position when the stagget became rigid, still as stone, and looked back into the wood. Something had disturbed it.

A low sound, deep and echoing, vibrated from the earth. Arianwyn looked at Miss Delafield. "It's the call of the stagget!" Miss Delafield whispered. "Oh, we're very lucky to hear them, dear."

The sound stopped as suddenly as it had started, and then the stagget bounded out of the clearing, swallowed suddenly by the shadows of the trees. Miss Delafield smiled and clapped her hands together. "Did you get anything?" she gestured to the lantern.

Arianwyn shook her head—but then a rumbling sound filled her ears and seconds later a small herd of staggets bounded through the clearing following the trail of the buck. She lifted the lantern free at once, holding the viewer to her right eye. The wood blurred before her but this time there was a brilliant white-and-gold light that flashed across the scene, just for a second. She pressed the button on the top of the case.

CLICK!

The herd disappeared into the blurred wood.

"I got it!" Arianwyn beamed. "I saw the staggets in the spirit lantern. All white and gold! I got the image . . . I think."

"Excellent! But I wonder what it was that disturbed them. Shall we go on a bit farther into the wood?" Miss Delafield grinned and, without waiting for an answer, she pulled her driving goggles down over her eyes, revved the engine, and the car was charging through the trees once more.

Arianwyn caught occasional glimpses of rushing streams, still pools, and more clearings, some small and dark, some vast and meadowlike. Every now and then the trees would open up, revealing great swaths of wintry blue sky high above them. And then they emerged into a vast clearing swaying with wild brown-and-golden grasses.

CHAPTER EIGHTEEN

THE MOON HARE

M arvelous!" Miss Delafield grinned, pulling her goggles back over her head and taking a deep breath.

Arianwyn climbed shakily from the car. It felt good to have solid ground beneath her feet at last. She rested the spirit lantern against the wheel and stepped away to take in the meadow and the wood beyond.

"Shall we have a cup of tea, dear?" Miss Delafield delved into the trunk and extracted a large wicker picnic hamper and a small gas stove. She busied herself setting things up as Arianwyn moved away from the car, taking in more of her surroundings.

It was so quiet, a silence broken only by the murmuring of the wind and the trees, the occasional call of birds and the sounds of Miss Delafield's small kettle beginning to bubble away. A shiver curled along Arianwyn's spine. There was magic nearby. But not just a pocket of magic this time—something else. Something shifting, something moving.

Another spirit creature.

Quickly and quietly she moved back to the car and

picked up the spirit lantern. Loosening the straps and then freeing it from the case, she quickly popped off the lens caps on the three aperture tubes.

She lifted the lantern high so that she could gaze through the viewer, and then she turned slowly, letting the lantern sweep across the meadow that opened out before her.

The familiar blurry image filled her vision as she turned slowly on the spot.

Nothing.

Then there was a terrible screaming noise, like a child or animal, or somewhere between the two. Something scared and hurt.

Miss Delafield had heard it too and glanced up briefly from the kettle, staring at Arianwyn. "What on earth . . . ," she breathed.

Arianwyn was still sweeping the meadow and trees with the spirit lantern, but still nothing appeared. And then, on the far side of the clearing, hidden behind a tangle of bushes and grasses, was the faintest flicker of white light. A spirit creature.

The gentle sounds of the meadow were disturbed as a large black wood hawk swooped down into the grass before soaring skyward again. It was hunting! The spirit creature still hidden among the grasses screamed, its fear and panic flooding across the meadow—it must be injured. Arianwyn felt the tug of magic and without thinking she was running toward it, the lantern abandoned on the grass and Miss Delafield calling from the side of the car, "Where are you going, dear?"

Running as fast as she could, she watched the hawk diving straight down toward the ground again, wings tucked in close to its body as it dropped like a stone. It looked as though it would plow straight through the earth! But just at the last second it spread its wings wide, slowing. Its claws, spikes of acid yellow, flicked open and it dropped into the long grass.

The terrible cry of pain rang out once more.

Arianwyn's feet pounded across the earth and she could hear Miss Delafield close behind, the tea things abandoned. Closer and closer, she could see the wood hawk swooping into the air before falling on the spirit creature curled in the grass. The cry had stopped; now the only sound was the hawk's triumphant caw.

"No!" Arianwyn screamed, skidding to a halt a few yards from the hawk. Spots of red marked its yellow claws. After a few seconds, Miss Delafield caught up. "What are you doing?" she asked. But Arianwyn was too focused on the hawk and whatever it was attacking to answer.

Without thinking about it, Arianwyn called Årdra, and a small bright spell orb crackled in the air just above the palm of her right hand. She threw it straight at the hawk and there was a small explosion of sparks, bright yellow flame, and black feathers as the spell found its mark.

It was the hawk's turn to scream, but after a second it continued to attack.

"I. Said. No!" Arianwyn growled. She summoned Oru, the light glyph.

A spell formed in the air in front of her, crackling with

angry energy. She hurled it skyward and watched as it exploded in a shower of noise and light like a firework, but a thousand times brighter.

The hawk wheeled away, screeching loudly in anger as it caught a breeze and flew off, finally defeated.

Arianwyn started forward.

"Wait!" Miss Delafield's strong hand wrapped quickly around her wrist, holding her back. "Be careful. You've no idea what it might be, dear!" Arianwyn nodded but continued to cross the few yards to where the grass was now shaking slightly. Whatever was there was trying to move, to get up, get away!

Crouching slightly, Arianwyn edged toward the shape in the grass. She saw a flash of white and heard a soft but definite growl.

Her skin fizzed from the flow of magic that swirled around her. Whatever it was, it was incredibly powerful.

And then she could see it. Curled against a large pile of stones was a creature so white it looked like a piece of moonlight made whole. It was roughly the size and shape of a hare but its glimmering ears were much, much longer. Around its neck, chest, and shoulders it was covered in fine, iridescent, pearl-white scales that shimmered in the dappled light.

"You're an odd little creature, aren't you?" Arianwyn reached out, only to be met with a fearsome growl. Its hackles rose, brilliant white fur along its spine bristled. It lashed out with its front feet.

She saw a gash on its leg; the hawk had indeed found its mark. She inched closer, extending her hand toward the creature. It sniffed at her and relaxed, then tried to scrabble slowly toward her. Blood gushed from its wound.

"Heavens!" Miss Delafield sighed. "That's a moon hare, dear. They're very rare indeed. Very strong. I've never seen one before."

Arianwyn felt Miss Delafield gazing at her oddly.

"They rarely approach humans . . ." And as if to prove her point the moon hare reared up at Miss Delafield, snapping its small jaws. She stumbled back a little and the moon hare continued its purring growl.

"We have to help it, though, don't we?" Arianwyn asked.

"Yes of course, dear." Miss Delafield didn't sound sure. "Well, pick it up and we'd best take it back to the Spellorium and see what we can do there."

Cautiously, Arianwyn reached forward and slowly lifted the moon hare into her arms. It didn't struggle or kick out this time—its growls subsided; it yawned and blinked and then nestled against Arianwyn, closing its gray-blue eyes peacefully.

"How interesting," Miss Delafield said to herself quietly. Arianwyn had noticed the appraising glance her supervisor often gave her, but it was different now, less "never mind!" and more as if Arianwyn was a pair of the most superb driving gloves.

CHAPTER NINETEEN

THE DEMON OF LOW GATE FARM

Arianwyn woke with a start. She had been dreaming about her unknown glyph. She had seen it tangled in the branches of trees in the Great Wood, burned into a stone in a strange place, concealed in the pages of a book in a vast library hidden in shadow and mystery.

She glanced around the room. She'd nodded off by the fire, which still gave off a warm glow. It had been her first day off in weeks and Salle had gone into Flaxsham for another audition at the theater—she'd begged Arianwyn to go with her, but she just wanted a quiet, restful day at home. Her first few weeks in Lull had been frantic and she felt quite worn out.

Outside, the afternoon sky was heavy and gray. Her soup sat cold on the table next to her.

The moon hare lay curled in her lap contentedly, a clean white bandage wrapped over its wounded leg. It had stayed by her side since she had rescued it in the Great Wood over two weeks ago. She had grown quite attached to the little creature, although she knew she would have to return it to the Great Wood once it was healed. It fidgeted in its sleep, making soft grumbling sounds as it dreamed. One of its back legs twitched for a second and then it was still again.

Arianwyn stood slowly, trying to shake the chilly dream she had woken from. She placed the sleeping moon hare back into her seat and crossed to the sink to fetch a glass of water.

Just then, she heard a frantic pounding on the door of the store and a muffled shout.

She hurried downstairs, brushing sleep from her eyes as she went. The moon hare, startled from his own dreams, followed her down the twisting staircase.

Through the door she could see Mayor Belcher, red-faced and panting.

She unlocked the door and the mayor half staggered, half fell inside. He looked to be in a fury and Arianwyn assumed she was about to be scolded for something when he collapsed against the counter and wheezed, "Deee . . . deeeem . . . demon. A DEMON!"

"What? Are you sure?"

The mayor nodded, still trying to catch his breath. Arianwyn had never seen him so flustered.

"I heard people talking about it at the market a while ago." He took a massive gulp of air. "A demon! At Low Gate Farm. Apparently a group of townspeople have gone to look at it!"

Panic fluttered in Arianwyn's chest; she didn't know what to do first. "We have to stop them. They could be in serious danger. Is it the crawler from Clover Hollow?"

The mayor looked terrified. "I have no idea. What should we do?" he asked.

He was asking *her*? *He must* really *be worried*, she thought.

"We need to get there as quickly as possible." She glanced across the room to where her broom stood propped in the corner. She hadn't been flying for weeks, but there was little choice now. "You're going to have to come for a ride on my broom, Mayor Belcher!"

The mayor protested, a lot. He protested as Arianwyn pulled on her coat. He protested as she locked the door of the Spellorium, and he was still protesting as he clambered onto the back of the broom out in Kettle Lane. He gripped her coat tightly. "You will fly carefully, won't you?" he asked, a wobble in his voice.

The broom was much slower with two people on, especially one as rotund as the mayor, and couldn't really gain its usual height, so there was little chance of any danger. Arianwyn moved them quickly through the town. People were pointing and giggling at the mayor, who was trying to remain composed and dignified but not doing a very good job.

They flew out of town, following the mayor's directions.

The first signs of spring shone out on the gray day. Bright daffodils peeked at the side of the road and the trees of the Great Wood were fringed with green.

"Here, it's here!" The mayor waved a hand frantically at the rickety old gate they were just passing.

Arianwyn pulled the broom to a stop, reading the

sign nailed to a post: *F. Caulls—Low Gate Farm—Keep Out!*

Beyond the gate a couple of motorcars, a truck, and several bicycles and carts were parked haphazardly.

They walked quickly down the twisting track alongside a high stone wall. Arianwyn could just make out a cluster of buildings through a small copse of trees. As they drew nearer she could hear raised voices, thick with anger and fear. She glanced at the mayor and they both broke into a run.

The farm had seen better days. The barn seemed to have only half of its door, and that was hanging from a single rusted hinge. Dilapidated, discarded machinery lay everywhere, and the whole place had a feeling of abandonment. A huddle of dirty geese bustled across the farmyard toward a large group of people standing near a small metal shed. The first spots of spring rain started to fall.

A filthy, rangy dog barked a warning at Arianwyn and the mayor as they approached, and the group fell silent and turned toward the new arrivals. "It's just the young witch," she heard someone mumble, and then a stout woman with wispy red hair stepped forward, her meaty arms folded across her chest.

"That's Mrs. Caulls, the farmer's wife," Mayor Belcher whispered quickly.

"Good morning, Mrs. Caulls. I'm Arianwyn Gribble, the new—"

"Yes, I know who you are!"

"I gather you may have a creature causing some trouble around the farm. I've come to help."

Mrs. Caulls eyed Arianwyn suspiciously. "It's a demon we've got and no mistake!" There were calls of agreement from the crowd.

"You're sure?" Arianwyn asked. "Absolutely sure?"

"I'm a simple woman, young witch, but I'm not stupid!"

"No, I, er, didn't mean—"

Mrs. Caulls's face had gone splotchy with large red circles. "I know what I saw," she continued, "and it was a demon if ever there were one! Nasty little thing too, all deformed and bent out of shape. It was trying to get away, but the boys gave it a good scare and it's holed up in the hen shed! We've probably killed it ourselves!" She puffed her already huge chest up even more.

"Wait, did you say it was little?" Arianwyn asked. She was doubtful that a little collection of townsfolk would be able to even tackle even the smallest sort of demon. Such creatures rarely backed away from a fight. It didn't add up: Something odd was going on. "That's very strange," she said, and reached into her satchel, pulling out the handbook. She quickly flipped through the pages until she came to the chapter on demons. She turned the book to show Mrs. Caulls line drawings of the three demon types.

"Which one did it look like?" she asked. Noticing Mayor Belcher's questioning look, she added, "Demons are usually big, never anything smaller than a full-grown man at least. Why would it choose to form into something small?"

"None of them," Mrs. Caulls said dismissively, as though Arianwyn were stupid.

"Well, how big was it?" Arianwyn asked, tucking the book back into her satchel.

"About so high," Mrs. Caulls replied, and she placed her hand as if on the head of an invisible child. Arianwyn thought for a few moments, chewing her lip.

"Well, can you get rid of it?" Mrs. Caulls asked.

"Yes, of course!" Arianwyn said with certainty, and she stepped carefully past Mrs. Caulls and set off toward the hen shed.

The group of townspeople, including Mrs. Caulls and Mayor Belcher, retreated some distance, and Arianwyn summoned a protection spell around them. Although, if it really was a demon, she doubted the spell would hold for long if it chose to attack. She stepped toward the hen shed.

Arianwyn peered into the black oblong of darkness. She saw nothing. Had it hidden anywhere else she would have cast a spell to reveal it, but the spell wouldn't work in the tin shed. This much metal would distort any magic she used. Her best chance was to get a look at the thing and try to lure it back outside. Or drag it out if it really was dead.

She hesitated on the threshold, holding her breath.

"Are you going to wait there all day long? Or are you going to come in?" The voice echoed out of the dark. It was high-pitched and sounded rather annoyed.

CHAPTER TWENTY

ESTAR

A rianwyn turned, wondering if anyone else had heard it. The crowd stood just as it had moments before.

She could hear quiet murmuring and the soothing warble of the hens as she took more steps into the dark shed. The warm smell of feathers and chicken droppings filled her nose. It was so dark that she couldn't see a thing. She breathed Oru, but the metal of the shed meant she only managed to form a weak light globe that flickered before her and followed as she shuffled forward. Arianwyn groped with her hands, worried she might at any moment walk into a wall or some piece of farm equipment with a sharp blade.

The murmuring came to a sudden stop and all was silent except for the occasional sound of Arianwyn's boots scuffing the dirt floor.

She bent forward, the globe light following her movement.

Slumped against the wall of the shed on the straw-strewn floor was a small blue creature. It didn't look like any demon Arianwyn recognized. In fact, it didn't look like anything she had ever seen before.

It had two twisted horns rising from its forehead and sweeping back over its shock of black hair, which was dirty and matted, much like the rest of it.

The creature peered at Arianwyn with luminous yellow eyes and reached out a small blue hand, its fingers long and fine, ending in clawlike black nails. "Have they sent you to dispatch me?" It sounded tired, defeated.

"Not exactly," Arianwyn replied, taken aback by the creature's honest question.

"You're a witch?" The creature gave a loud, sharp cough, a cough that rattled in its chest and made it curl up in pain. Arianwyn winced.

"Yes, I'm the witch from Lull, the town nearby."

"I don't think you are!" the creature replied indignantly. His words crisp and certain.

Arianwyn paused for a second, unsure what to say.

"I know the local witch and you, young lady, are not she!" He sniffed and looked away.

Arianwyn was stunned into silence for a second, until curiosity got the better of her and she asked, "You knew the previous witch?"

"Previous? Whatever do you mean?" He sounded a little bored now.

"I'm the *new* witch, my name is Arianwyn Gribble," she said slowly. "I'm afraid there hasn't been a witch in Lull for nearly forty years . . . until now!"

The creature seemed to be thinking about what she had just said, his face set in deep concentration. "Have I been away for so long?" he mumbled to himself. "Time is so different deep in the wood."

"What . . . what are you?" Arianwyn asked after more silence. "Some sort of gargus or frennark?"

He looked slightly offended at the suggestions. "I am Estar Sha-Vamirian, Alemar of the third Jalloon. I think my mother was a wood sprite, if that helps—a blue one, obviously!" He tried to pull himself up a little more, an action that clearly caused him pain.

Something in his yellow-gold eyes told Arianwyn that there was nothing to fear from him. For a moment her mind cast back to when she had found the moon hare, and even further back to when she had rescued an injured phooka and argued with her grandmother to let her take it back home and care for it till it was well again.

"They are not gentle creatures, Arianwyn," her grand-mother had warned. "It will turn on you as soon as it is well. Leave it here, my love."

"NO!" Arianwyn had said, and scooped the phooka up into her hands defiantly.

She had nursed it back to health, feeding it warm milk sweetened with honey and making it a bed out of a small box. After three weeks when it was well again it had scratched her arm with its sharp little claws and Grand-mother had ordered her to take it to the park or she would have to banish it. She'd watched it scamper off into the park, tears streaming silently down her face. Then it had paused, turned, and raced back to her. It had sung its beautiful song just for Arianwyn until she had forgotten about the angry red scratches on her arm.

She looked at Estar now and wondered if he would hurt her, as the phooka had.

Her heart told her no.

"You're hurt," Arianwyn said.

He smiled weakly. "Times have been tough lately, you might say."

"The crowd out there?" Arianwyn gestured back to the oblong of light and the farmyard beyond.

Estar raised an eyebrow. "They had a good try, but I was in a bit of trouble before that, to be fair." He gazed off, beyond Arianwyn.

"Well, you simply can't go on terrorizing the poor family that lives on the farm!"

"Terrorizing?" he repeated, clearly outraged and clutching his long blue hand to his bony chest. "I did no such thing, I can assure you! *They* set upon *me*!"

It was then that Arianwyn noticed the creature's legs. They were different from each other. The right was scaled and clawed like a bird's or lizard's, with three toes. The left was hairy and ended in a shiny black hoof like a goat's, and around it was twisted a tangle of rusty barbed wire.

The creature noticed her looking and said quietly, "As I said, times have been a little tough."

"Where have you come from?" Arianwyn asked, deciding to start again.

"From Erraldur!" replied the creature, as though she should have known. But when Arianwyn just stared at him blankly he said, "It is the feyling settlement in the Great Wood." As if this would make more sense.

"Feyling." Arianwyn let the word hang in the air briefly. "But that's not possible, that's just old stories."

Estar's eyes widened. "Stories indeed . . . ," he muttered.

Then she remembered the spirit lantern. She fumbled with the strap that held the case closed and then lifted it free. "I just need to take a picture," she said. Estar simply stared back at her.

She lifted the lantern to her eyes and peered through the viewing aperture. The cloud of light that surrounded him was not the pale gold or white of a spirit creature. But nor was it the inky smudge of a dark spirit. The colors that shimmered around him swirled and changed, like an oily rainbow.

He was something different altogether.

Something new.

She sighed heavily. It was forbidden to banish anything other than dark spirits to the void. But she couldn't exactly let him go roaming around the countryside, for his own safety as well as the townspeople's.

Arianwyn sat on the floor, crossed her legs, and stared hard at him.

She looked once more at the scratches and bruises that covered the creature's body; many were fresh but some looked much older. She reached into her bag and found a rather brown banana and a stale cookie. She offered these to Estar, who ate them in just a few bites, including the banana skin, and almost at once his blue skin seemed to have brightened and he sat a little straighter. Next Arianwyn pulled out a clean handkerchief, wetting it in a nearby water dish that looked mostly clean. She reached toward the creature and wiped away at some of the worst-looking cuts. Then she carefully started to untangle the coil of barbed wire. Estar winced and looked away, his small body twitching in pain. As he shifted, Arianwyn noticed a large pattern, elegantly drawn in the compacted earth close to him. There was something so familiar and at the same time quietly disturbing about the shape.

Was it? Could it be? She peered closer still. "What is that?" she asked. Though she was afraid she already knew the answer.

Estar's eyes widened and he was just about to reply when a voice echoed through the shed: "Have you got it?"

Arianwyn turned and saw the faces of Mrs. Caulls and Mayor Belcher silhouetted in the open door. They peered blinking into the dark.

"Yes!" she replied. "I've found . . . it." She glanced apologetically at Estar. "But it's not a demon. Nobody's in any danger."

"Wait here. Please," she whispered, and walked quickly back toward the daylight.

"It's not a demon." Arianwyn repeated as she emerged from the hen shed. "I'm not entirely sure exactly what it is, but I don't think anyone is in any danger from it. He's been rather badly beaten."

"Well, don't look at me!" Mrs. Caulls protested. "How was I supposed to know what it was or wasn't? It didn't have a label around its filthy little neck, did it? I've got children in the house!"

Mayor Belcher stepped in, scowling at Arianwyn. "Dear lady," he began, "I am sure Miss Gribble meant no offense. I am certain she will go and deal with the creature *right now*!" He glared at Arianwyn once more.

"But I can't just banish it . . . ," Arianwyn protested.

Mayor Belcher grabbed her arm and walked her briskly away from Mrs. Caulls. They stopped by the open door of the hen shed. "Get back in there and get rid of that disgusting thing. I don't care what you do or how you do it but I want it gone from the farm. Do I make myself clear?" Mayor Belcher hissed.

Arianwyn nodded mutely. An idea was starting to half form in her head.

"Well, I suggest you get on with it, then!" He gave her a gentle shove toward the shed.

Arianwyn ventured back into the dark, her mind moving quickly.

"It's all right, I will turn myself over to the authorities." She could hear Estar shuffling toward her.

If she handed him over to Mayor Belcher there was no telling what would happen. She might never find out what the strange pattern was, the one that looked so much like her unknown glyph.

"You have to go!" Arianwyn whispered urgently to Estar.

"What?"

"I'm not going to banish you. Can you walk? I can keep them distracted while you escape from the farm."

He looked puzzled.

"Do you remember where the town is?" Arianwyn asked. "Near to the North Gate there's an old mill, it's abandoned. You could hide there for a while . . . until you're fully recovered."

"Why are you helping me?" Estar asked suddenly. He gripped Arianwyn's hand and she was shocked at the warmth of his skin.

"Because it's not fair. You've done nothing wrong. And I'd like to know more about that shape you've drawn in the dirt."

"How is it going, Miss Gribble? Do you need help?" Mayor Belcher called suddenly into the shed.

"Is there another way out?" Arianwyn whispered.

"Possibly—now that I've got a bit more energy!" Estar's eyes sparkled.

He struggled to his feet. Almost at once a strange blue light started to form around him, like an aura. The shed was bathed in its watery glow.

Estar himself shimmered as though he was not really there. Arianwyn panicked. "What's happening?" she asked quickly.

The light increased; Estar was hovering in midair, held in the brilliant blue circle. He reached out a hand toward Arianwyn. "Thank you for helping me, Arianwyn Gribble. I will not forget your kindness," he whispered.

The blue light shone so brightly now that Arianwyn raised her hand to shield her eyes.

It felt as though all the air was being sucked past her, toward Estar. There was a sound like bubbles underwater and the air was suddenly rushing back the other way.

Arianwyn peeked through her fingers and found Estar was gone. So was the symbol that had been drawn in the dirt floor.

"He's gone," Arianwyn said as she emerged from the shed a few moments later.

"You sure?" Mrs. Caulls said, and she poked her head into the shed for a second before disappearing inside entirely. Sounds came from the shed of buckets and things being thrown around. The hens took up a furious clucking.

Mayor Belcher eyed Arianwyn warily. "And where is the creature?" he asked quietly.

"Gone," Arianwyn replied, deciding that it was true—he was gone, even if it was not in the way the mayor expected. She looked out across the farmyard, now wet with fine spring rain.

"But how, what?" Mayor Belcher stuttered.

"I did what you asked," Arianwyn replied firmly. "He . . . I mean, *it* is no longer in the hen shed." She felt she was burning with the lie.

Mrs. Caulls emerged from the shed. "Foul creature," she spat. "Good riddance, I say!" With that she turned and charged back toward the farmhouse, scattering people out of her path.

The rain fell harder. The entertainment over, the watchers made their way out of the farmyard.

"Well, then, Miss Gribble, a job well done!" Mayor Belcher said, a small half smile on his surprised face. "I was worried we might need to reintroduce the curfew."

"Thank you," Arianwyn said, feeling like an utter fraud and wanting to get away as soon as possible. "I think I had best be getting back to the Spellorium. Do you need a lift into town?"

The mayor paled at the suggestion. "Er, no, that's quite all right, thank you. I need a walk and it will be quite pleasant . . . in the rain."

Back at the Spellorium, Arianwyn raided her cupboards for some food and an old blanket. She packed them carefully into a basket and waited until it started to grow dark.

Keeping to the shadows, she made her way quickly to the North Gate and Kurtis Mill. She approached carefully, unsure what to do. She didn't want to leave her parcel by the door, which was locked up tight, for fear that someone would see it and investigate. All the windows looked too high to reach.

She slipped down the side of the mill and pulled a few empty crates to the wall before clambering up to the high window. The small panes of glass were mostly intact, except for a few lower down.

Arianwyn peered into the dark. There was no sign of Estar.

Perhaps he had gotten confused about where to hide. Perhaps he had gone back to the wood. Perhaps he had just run off. She hoped she hadn't made another mistake in letting him go free. She chewed her lip for a moment and watched the dark alleyway.

She tucked the basket carefully on the window ledge and climbed down the crates.

As she made her way back along North Gate Street she stopped and turned, looking over her shoulder.

The basket had vanished from the window ledge.

She pulled her coat tightly around herself and, smiling, headed back home.

On occasion spirits have been known to form
a bond with a witch. In such cases the bond
is usually formed for life. The most famous
instance of this was Gertrude Yates, who
bonded with a stagget spirit that guarded
local moorland. The spirit was known as
Lor'ar and on the death of Ms. Yates appeared
to vanish into thin air.

CHAPTER TWENTY-ONE

THE MAYOR'S NIECE

Arianwyn was hurrying back to the Spellorium, rain pouring down again, overfilling the gutters and streaming down Kettle Lane. She was soaked through and her boots squelched noisily as she ran. She rattled the key in the lock until the door swung open suddenly, causing her to stumble. "Boil it!" she said.

She dropped the spirit lantern in its case with a clatter against the floorboards and a small pool of water immediately gathered around it. Shrugging off her coat, she crossed to the small potbellied stove to stoke the embers, just as Salle burst through the door, skidding on the patches of rainwater.

"We've been invited to the town hall for tea with the mayor," she gasped.

"Tea?" Arianwyn asked, agog. In the two months she had been in Lull the mayor had not invited her over for so much as a glass of water, let alone tea!

"Apparently his niece is coming to visit. Did you know he had a niece? I wonder what she's like?" Salle rambled on.

Arianwyn tried to picture the mayor's niece but she could only imagine the mayor with long hair and wearing a dress. It wasn't a pleasant image.

"So, are you going to go? Shall I meet you at the town hall?" Salle asked.

"Oh, I don't know, Salle. I've been out all day and I'm soaked!" Arianwyn had been looking forward to a nice hot bath and cozying up with the radio, snuggled under her eiderdown comforter.

"Please?" Salle squeaked.

Arianwyn imagined it would not go down well if she refused an invitation from the mayor.

"Yes, all right. I'll see you there!" Arianwyn smiled.

Salle gave an excited cry and skipped out into the rain.

It was still pouring when Arianwyn dashed across the cobbles of the town square, splashing through the odd puddle. The town hall loomed before her, lights shining from the mayor's parlor.

Miss Prynce, the mayor's secretary, greeted her, taking her coat and umbrella, and then led her up to the party. The room was packed to bursting. She saw Salle at once and headed over to the corner where she was standing.

"Where've you been? You're late! Mr. Thorn went to Flaxsham to collect the famous niece and they are due back any second!" Salle said, and glanced quickly out the window, just in case. "The mayor has been groaning on for the last forty minutes about how wonderful she is: top of her class, blah blah blah. Best witch ever blah blah blah . . ."

"What?" Arianwyn said. "His niece is a witch?"

"Apparently so," Salle continued, oblivious to the panic that had gripped Arianwyn. "Oh, come on, Wyn. You're not the only witch in the world, you know!"

Arianwyn scowled at Salle, which only made her burst out laughing.

"And what are you two young ladies up to, giggling in the corner here?" The mayor trotted across the parlor, his arms thrown wide in welcome.

"I was just telling Arianwyn a story about my aunt in Bollington—she . . . fell off her bicycle!" Salle lied.

"Oh, poor lady. That doesn't sound very funny at all. You can be rather peculiar at times, Miss Bowen!" The mayor stared at her suspiciously, clearly not convinced by her story. Arianwyn snorted loudly and tried to cover it with a sudden coughing fit.

"Mayor Belcher, here comes Mr. Thorn now!" Miss Prynce had taken up a position by the window and was pointing excitedly out into the square.

The whole room surged to the long windows, the mayor calling as he ran, "Let me through, please. Let. Me. Through!" He pushed the doors onto the balcony open and a blast of rain and wind gusted into the room. He stepped outside, calling down into the square. Salle and Arianwyn tried to catch a glimpse of the new arrival as she stepped out of the bus, but Mr. Thorn was speedy with an umbrella and all they saw was a pair of shiny black shoes and the swish of a beautiful yellow raincoat.

"Oh, fancy!" Salle cooed.

The room was full of excited chatter as Mayor Belcher dashed back across the parlor from the balcony to the main doors. Everyone followed him, leaving Arianwyn and Salle stranded at the back of the crowd.

"Here!" Salle pointed to two chairs and quickly climbed onto one. "Perfect view!" She smiled.

"Salle, get down! I am not clambering onto a chair—" The doors swung open and, without thinking further, Arianwyn stood on the other seat.

There was the flash of yellow coat once more before the crowd of townspeople pressed in to greet the mayor's niece. Arianwyn's chair wobbled slightly as she craned to see more. There was the mayor, his arm protectively wrapped around his niece, who was still hidden from view as he led her forward.

"So wonderful to see you, my sweet girl!" he was saying as the townspeople broke into rapturous applause.

Salle rolled her eyes. Arianwyn stifled a giggle.

"Ladies and gentlemen, I am thrilled to present to you my dear niece, Miss Gimma Alverston!"

Arianwyn went cold.

She must have heard it wrong. The mayor couldn't possibly have just said Gimma's name. Could he?

Her mind flashed back to Gimma's cruel taunts across the playground and to the last time they had seen each other on the day of the evaluation. Arianwyn's stomach flipped. The crowd parted just at that moment. Arianwyn craned forward and saw clearly that it was indeed Gimma. The mayor held a protective hand on her shoulder as they both smirked at the crowd.

"Gimma!" Arianwyn gasped. She felt her footing go. The chair beneath her veered this way and that as she tried to regain her balance. And then it gave up, tilting too far to the left. It wobbled, it lurched, and Arianwyn crashed to the floor.

She lay there for a second, wishing it was all some nasty dream and that any moment now she would wake up.

Gimma? The mayor's favorite niece? Just as things were sort of smoothing out.

"Are you quite all right, Miss Gribble?"

Arianwyn glanced up and saw the mayor and Gimma standing over her, the townspeople all giggling behind hands and handkerchiefs.

"Arianwyn?" Gimma repeated, her voice full of bright surprise.

Scrambling to her feet, Arianwyn brushed imaginary dust from her skirt, hoping she wasn't blushing.

"What on earth were you doing on the floor?" Gimma asked loudly. More titters from the assembled audience.

Arianwyn glowered at her.

"Heavens, do you two know each other?" Mayor Belcher asked, glancing from Gimma to Arianwyn and back again.

"Yes, Uncle. Arianwyn and I were at school together in Kingsport." Gimma smiled up at the mayor, who continued to gaze at her like a proud mother hen clucking over its chicks.

"Fancy that!" he beamed.

"Yes, and we had our evaluations on the same day. Didn't we, Arianwyn?" Gimma's eyes glittered.

Arianwyn felt everyone's gaze move to the moon badge.

"What are *you* doing here, Gimma?" Arianwyn asked, deciding she'd had enough unwanted attention.

It was Gimma's turn to look a little uncomfortable now. Her cheeks flushed and her eyes darted to her uncle.

"My poor Gimma has overworked herself, Miss Gribble, and has been sent here for a rest. I'm sure she will be eager to be out and about and to come and give you a hand, once she's feeling a little brighter—"

"There's no rush!"

"Maybe next week!"

Arianwyn and Gimma had burbled together at once. The mayor gave a small chuckle. "Now, I do hope you girls are going to get along together," he said, his eyes narrowed at Arianwyn.

Arianwyn smiled at Gimma. They stared at each other for a long moment; the air in the room seemed to crackle.

"Of course, Uncle!" Gimma said in her singsong voice. "We're going to be the very best of friends, aren't we, Arianwyn?"

Arianwyn shivered as though a cold draft had tickled her skin. She could feel everyone watching her.

"Of course," she said, a little hoarsely.

There was a long silence. Gimma pulled out a small

mirror from her little beaded purse and gazed at herself until Salle stepped forward. "Hello there, I'm Salle Bowen." She extended her hand.

"Miss Bowen's aunt and uncle run the Blue Ox," Mayor Belcher offered.

"Oh! How charming!" Gimma sniffed and put the mirror away and took the tiniest step back from Salle, who immediately turned slightly pink. "Well, perhaps you wouldn't mind fetching me a cup of tea?"

Gimma pointed to the table nearby, which was laden with buns, cakes, and a huge steaming tea urn. Salle, unsure what to do, hovered between staying and going, hopping from one foot to the other.

"Salle!" Arianwyn hissed, pulling on her arm to hold her still. "She's not a waitress!" Arianwyn said to Gimma, not caring how angry she sounded.

"Oh?" was all Gimma could muster as a response, thoroughly bored. She stared at the wall, the floor, and then at her own nails.

"It's fine!" Salle said in a small voice, and headed off to the table.

Mayor Belcher was called away and for a few seconds Gimma and Arianwyn stood staring at each other in tortured silence. Eventually Gimma caved in, saying, "I don't know how you can stand it here, Arianwyn. It's a rather ghastly little place, isn't it?"

A well-dressed couple standing just behind Gimma overheard and glared at Arianwyn as if it were her fault. "Well, I quite like it!" Arianwyn said brightly.

"I suppose it suits *you*. But I think when you're used to a certain class of things, not to mention a certain class of people . . . well, it's . . ." She pulled a sour face and the couple walked off, casting filthy looks over their shoulders.

"But I suppose you won't be here all that long, anyway," Arianwyn said hopefully.

"Hmmm?" Gimma pretended she hadn't heard her. "Where has that waitress girl gotten to, do you suppose?"

"She's not a waitress, Gimma!"

Just at that moment Salle returned, carrying a cup and saucer. Tea sloshed over the sides of the cup as she thrust it into Gimma's hands. "Oh, thank you!" Gimma smiled.

"Don't mention it!" Salle said, rolling her eyes at Arianwyn. "And how long are you staying in Lull for? A week? Two?"

Gimma paled and started to stammer a response when Mayor Belcher returned from the other side of the room. "Now then, ladies, I trust you've all been getting along nicely. My niece is going to be with us for the foreseeable future and she'll be needing some companions her own age! Can't spend all her time with her old uncle!"

Arianwyn was sure she had heard wrong. He couldn't have just said that, could he? She looked at Salle, who pulled a face and sighed heavily.

"Isn't it marvelous?" Gimma squealed. "I just know us three will be great pals! And I can't wait to get to work!"

"*Work?*" Arianwyn spluttered.

"Yes, I was saying earlier." Mayor Belcher beamed. "I spoke to Miss Delafield yesterday and she is going to see about Gimma providing you some assistance with your duties. Isn't that nice? And won't you benefit from having a fully qualified witch to assist you and show you the ropes?"

"Wonderful!" Arianwyn said eventually, though her voice croaked a little, dry with shock. It was a million things other than nice or wonderful. She was going to have to speak to Miss Delafield about this situation as soon as possible.

CHAPTER TWENTY-TWO

RETURN TO THE GREAT WOOD

It was nearly a week later before Arianwyn had a chance to speak to Miss Delafield. The moon hare had made a full recovery from its injuries and she and Miss Delafield had decided to return it to the Great Wood.

It was early afternoon, and Arianwyn heard the now-familiar sound of Miss Delafield's silver-green motorcar pulling up in Kettle Lane. A few seconds later she charged through the door, twirling her driving goggles around her fingers and whistling a bright tune. "Afternoon, Arianwyn!" She grinned. "Everything okay? All ready for a trip back into the Great Wood?" She cast her usual cautious glance around the Spellorium.

"Yes," Arianwyn muttered. The encounter with Gimma was still playing on her mind, even though she hadn't seen her since that first night, thankfully. Presumably she was still "resting."

The thought of returning the moon hare to the wild was not filling her with enthusiasm, either. She'd become used to having the spirit creature around. It stared at her now, bright blue eyes expectant. Arianwyn felt a twist of guilt inside her. She bent to lift it up and it purred loudly as she stroked its long silvery ears. "Come on, then, little one," she said, heading out into Kettle Lane. She clambered into the car beside Miss Delafield, making sure to fasten her seat belt tightly.

The drive to the Great Wood was mostly silent. It was hard to have a conversation over the engine's roar and Arianwyn wasn't feeling talkative. She held tightly to the moon hare as the line of trees grew larger, Miss Delafield occasionally glancing in her direction.

They didn't drive in as far as they had before. Miss Delafield stopped in a small clearing full of yellow-green dappled light. "This should do, I think. Let the little thing find its own way back. Probably doesn't want to go back to that clearing, anyway . . . I say, is everything quite all right, dear?"

"Not really," Arianwyn said as she clambered down from the car. She placed the moon hare into the soft grass and watched it scamper happily around for a few moments. "It's about Gimma Alverston."

"Ah. I thought as much." Miss Delafield sighed. "Well, dear, what's the bother?"

"I can't work with her, it's not possible. I'm sorry, but I just can't!"

Miss Delafield didn't look surprised but still she asked, "Why?"

What could Arianwyn say? *She hates me? She's a bully? I don't like her?* It all sounded childish and silly in Arianwyn's head. "We don't . . . get along!" she eventually muttered to the trees and the grass.

"Speak up, dear. You know I can't abide mumblers!" Miss Delafield said. Then she suddenly wandered off to study a nearby tree.

"We don't get along very well!" Arianwyn said loudly and all at once as she followed Miss Delafield across the clearing.

The moon hare had hopped off to the edge of the trees and was scraping in the earth, chewing on long blades of grass. It seemed entirely relaxed and at home.

"Oh, of course you'll get along," Miss Delafield said distractedly as she bent close to the tree. "And it's not forever . . . just a few weeks, a month at most."

"A *month*?" Arianwyn couldn't contemplate having Gimma around for a month. "Can't she go and work in Flaxsham?" she asked desperately.

"I'm sorry, Arianwyn," Miss Delafield said, turning to look at her. "My hands are well and truly tied on this— not a thing I can do about it, dear. But don't you worry: If she gives *me* any trouble she'll be off faster than you can say broomstick! Now, this looks a bit nasty to me, what do you think?"

Miss Delafield's gloved hand rested just below a loose curl of tree bark. As Arianwyn peered closer she could see that beneath the bark was a large patch of hex. Miss Delafield pulled on the loose bark and revealed thick black ridges that enfolded the trunk.

"Is this how it was on the Myddletons' house, dear?"

Arianwyn shook her head. She had never seen hex so dark or thick or spread over an area so big.

It was smothering the tree from within!

"Oh dear, oh dear." Miss Delafield sucked in air through her teeth and tutted. "Not good, my dear! I need to report this ASAP. Have a quick look and see if there are any other trees affected—but don't touch any of it!"

Arianwyn ran from tree to tree, checking for any more signs of hex, but they all looked clear.

Miss Delafield was busy tying a strip of bright-colored cloth around the trunk. "That should keep people from coming too close," she said, but Arianwyn wasn't listening.

She glanced through the trees, looking for the moon hare, but it had vanished from sight. Off gamboling through the dappled shade of the Great Wood, no doubt, or busy finding itself a new den.

She felt more than a little sad at having to say good-bye, though she didn't know why. It had been a comfort to have it in the store in the dead of night or when she felt lonely. She had chatted away happily to the little creature and it always seemed to have been listening to her. She sighed.

"Chin up, old girl, you did a wonderful job getting the little tyke back on its feet, you know! Better off for it to be out here in the wild, where it belongs!" They both looked out across the clearing once more.

"Will you drop by and make sure the hex at the Myddletons' hasn't returned?" Miss Delafield asked.

Arianwyn nodded, although she didn't relish the prospect of a return visit to Mrs. Myddleton's house. She watched carefully as Miss Delafield pulled a glass tube from her bag. Next she took out a small pocketknife and scraped some of the hex and tree bark away. There was a foul smell and Arianwyn felt the rough feeling of dark magic. "It's best not to use any magic near this type of hex," Miss Delafield warned. "You know it can distort spells horribly—you can't burn it away as you did at the Myddletons'."

Arianwyn nodded and looked out across the clearing once more. But there was still no sign of the moon hare.

"Right, let's get you back to town. I need to report this to the CWA and prepare for a parade meeting in Flaxsham—ghastly business," Miss Delafield said, heading back to the motorcar.

Just as Arianwyn pulled her door shut she saw a silver-white streak dart across the clearing, like a bolt of silvery sparkling moonlight. The next second the moon hare was sitting alert by the side of the car, looking up expectantly at Arianwyn.

"How curious!" Miss Delafield said. She started the engine.

"Go on!" Arianwyn said to the moon hare. "Off into the wood now. It's where you belong." The moon hare hopped a few yards away from the car but turned again to stare at Arianwyn. Miss Delafield moved the car in a slow circle and the moon hare hopped alongside it, sparkling eyes fixed on Arianwyn.

"It's not going," she hissed.

"It will!" Miss Delafield said, shifting the car into another gear. It roared and jolted forward over the rough ground of the Great Wood, back toward Lull. But the moon hare kept pace with the car.

It followed them through the wood.

It kept up with them across the meadow.

And as Miss Delafield's car rattled over the bridge and through the South Gate the moon hare was leading the way. It darted ahead of the car, like a blur of brilliant light. Back through town and along Kettle Lane it weaved in and out of shoppers. And as Miss Delafield brought the car to a halt outside the store, the moon hare was waiting patiently on the steps. It looked at them both and its long ears twitched playfully.

As Arianwyn climbed out of the car it bounded toward her, leaping up and into her arms. Purring with happiness.

"Well I never." Miss Delafield sighed. "You are a very odd witch, Miss Gribble. This creature seems to have taken more than a shine to you. Doesn't look like it will be going anywhere soon." She seemed to be considering something for a moment. "Look—how's about I assign Miss Alverston some work to do, keep you two separate for a bit? Think it would make things easier?"

Arianwyn felt a surge of relief wash over her. She smiled. "Thank you," she said and, with the moon hare in her arms, she unlocked the door and went back inside the Spellorium.

CHAPTER TWENTY-THREE

THE UNEXPECTED BOGGLIN

Arianwyn's return trip to Mrs. Myddleton's was not the most pleasant experience in her life. The woman, as harassed as before, had only grunted in response to Arianwyn's request to look at where the patch of hex had been. There was now just a dirty smoky smudge against the wall. The hex hadn't shown any signs of reforming, thankfully.

"Thank you, Mrs. Myddleton!" Arianwyn had said brightly as she left the woman's cottage. She sighed deeply in relief as the door swung shut behind her and as quickly as possible she headed back to the Spellorium.

Something made her walk back a different way. Perhaps it was the bright sunny day, the blue sky high above, and the way the light flooded into the streets of Lull. She passed the tearooms on Blossom Terrace and decided to stop for some lunch. Mr. Bandoli showed her to a seat outside and Arianwyn sat down and sipped her tea quietly for a few moments, thinking about nothing in particular except for the lovely feeling of warm spring sun on her face.

Her peace and quiet was suddenly broken by a loud scream from the doorway of a small cottage opposite the tearooms. The door stood wide open and various boxes, crates, and pieces of furniture were stacked on the sidewalk. Arianwyn noticed that the *For Sale* sign attached to the side of the house had a *Sold* label plastered diagonally across it.

Something small and fast darted out of the open doorway, followed by another scream from inside. Arianwyn, thinking it was a pet, stood up to try and stop it running away, but something about the creature's movement told her it was neither a dog nor a cat. Then she noticed the gray skin, matted hair, and the bulging yellow eyes.

It was a bogglin, she was sure of it. It gave a loud screech and scuttled a little farther down the street.

Arianwyn was stunned. She'd never seen a bogglin out in the open like this, and it was rare to see them in broad daylight. A young woman and man emerged from the house and watched in shock and relief as the creature scampered down the street, growling and lashing out at passersby as it went.

Without thinking too much about it, Arianwyn summoned a stunning spell and sent it hurtling straight at the bogglin. There was a bright flash, followed by gasps from the watching bystanders, and then the sound of the bogglin sliding across the cobbles and coming to a crashing halt against some trash cans at the top of a narrow passageway.

"Oh, thank heavens, Miss Gribble," the young woman sighed. "We didn't know what to do. We found that thing in the basement and the other witch didn't seem to be getting along very well at all, you see. We've only just moved in today . . ."

"Other witch?" Arianwyn asked the young woman. "Is Miss Delafield here?" She peered into the darkness of the cottage doorway.

"No, it was the new young lady."

"Oh, Gimma," Arianwyn said. She had almost forgotten about Gimma, *almost*!

Gimma appeared in the shadows of the empty hallway. Her hair, usually so perfect, was wild and tangled. Her face was flushed and her clothes rumpled and dusty. She carried a broom, just an ordinary and rather cobwebby broom, which she clutched like a weapon. Her eyes swam with tears. She reached out, and her hands were shaking. "Oh, Arianwyn! I'm so pleased you're here." She fell against Arianwyn and sobbed, very loudly.

"What on earth happened?" Arianwyn stood rigid for a few moments before patting Gimma tentatively on the shoulder.

"The bogglin . . . ," Gimma began, then stepped away a little, cheeks red with embarrassment. "I couldn't, um, get my spell to work properly. Think I might be a bit rusty." She looked quickly at the cottage owners and then back at Arianwyn.

"It's okay," Arianwyn said, unsure exactly what to do

or say. She reached out a gentle hand again and rested it on Gimma's back. "I'm sure it was fine . . . really." She glanced at the young couple. The woman looked bemused.

"I don't think she knew what she was doing." Arianwyn heard the young man grunt.

"Ssshh!" the young woman replied, bundling him back inside the house.

"What happened?" Arianwyn asked once the fuss had died down.

Gimma looked at Arianwyn. Her mouth opened slightly as though she was about to speak but at the last second she looked away and burst into tears again. Arianwyn watched in puzzled silence, patting Gimma's shoulder again once, twice, and saying, "It's all right!" as Gimma howled louder and louder. Arianwyn recalled her own fiasco with the crawler in Clover Hollow. She couldn't quite believe she actually felt sorry—for Gimma Alverston! She rubbed her shoulder more gently and made soothing noises.

"It's really not going according to plan!" Gimma said through hiccups and slowly subsiding sobs. "You won't . . . tell . . . Uncle, will you?"

"Um—"

"Please, Arianwyn? He won't understand." She reached into her little beaded bag and pulled out a clean handkerchief and dabbed at her eyes very delicately.

Arianwyn couldn't imagine Mayor Belcher ever being angry with Gimma. But she thought back to the mayor's little notebook and found herself agreeing. "Okay. You know, I didn't get off to the best start either when I arrived," she admitted.

Gimma peeked from behind her curtain of tangled hair. "Really?" she croaked.

Arianwyn nodded and sat on the curb; Gimma sat beside her and Arianwyn found herself telling Gimma all about the snotling incident. Gimma listened, her mouth open wide; she even gave a small laugh as Arianwyn reached the part where the snotling exploded. After she finished her own catalog of disasters they sat silently for a few minutes, thoughts churning through Arianwyn's mind. Then out of nowhere she found herself saying, "Look, perhaps it's best if you come to the Spellorium and we work together, while you're here."

Gimma stared at her in wonder, her eyes red and watery. Arianwyn thought she looked quite unlike her normal self: She looked a little bit fragile, more real and human. Perhaps she had been wrong about Gimma; perhaps she wasn't so bad anymore.

"If you're sure I won't be in the way? It was Uncle who insisted on me helping. I didn't want to bother you, honestly, Arianwyn. I know . . . I know I've not always been the nicest person." She sniffed again.

Unsure she wanted a teary apology from Gimma in the middle of the street, Arianwyn stood. "Well, just come to the store—"

"In a few days? When I've recovered," Gimma added theatrically, more like her old self at last.

Arianwyn smiled. "Yes, of course. I'll see you in a few days, Gimma." And she wandered down the street to deal with the stunned bogglin. She'd only gone a few steps when she heard Gimma call, "Wait. I'll give you a hand . . ."

CHAPTER TWENTY-FOUR

THE WATER SPIRIT

It was nearly a week later when Gimma appeared at the door of the Spellorium for the first time. Her uniform was pristine; her star badge glinted in the morning light. She stifled a yawn as Arianwyn opened the door and let her in. They watched each other carefully and quietly for a few moments. Arianwyn felt a knot of anxiety in her stomach; she hoped this was going to be okay. She had never imagined—not in a million years—that she and Gimma would be spending a day working together.

Gimma flashed one of her familiar smiles, charming and winning. Then she turned slowly, taking in the Spellorium. "I suppose it might not be *too bad* a place . . . once you've given it a good clean!" She ran her gloved fingers over one of the shelves and examined its tip carefully. Her nose wrinkled.

Arianwyn turned back to the desk, determined not to let Gimma annoy her. She pulled open the ledger of outstanding appointments and idly scanned across the list of jobs that required her attention.

Suspected bogglin at Belldon's Warehouses, Percy Lane.

Probably not a good idea! She wasn't sure Gimma would want to be faced with another bogglin just yet!

Pisky nest in chimney, 12 Drury Street. Boring!

Three charms for Farmer Devott (new tractor). Arianwyn couldn't imagine Gimma wanting to stay in the store all day making charms.

And then, scrawled in Jucasta's bold handwriting and underlined was:

Calvaria (water spirit) spawning, Torr River—ASAP! Surely that was just asking for trouble!

"So!" Gimma said, leaning across the desk and peering at the ledger. "What have we got to keep us busy, then?"

Arianwyn sighed a little and turned the ledger around so that Gimma could see it. She carefully kept her hand over the entry about the water spirit, though.

Gimma looked up slowly and considered what she saw in front of her.

"Oh, that all looks rather dull, don't you think? Isn't there something more interesting to be doing?" Gimma peered closer at the ledger. "Oh, look, what about this?" she pointed at the entry half hidden under Arianwyn's hand.

"No, I really think we should go and deal with—" Arianwyn began, but Gimma started to talk over her at once.

"Well, you know best, I'm sure. But I think it might be fun if we go together . . . and just think how pleased my uncle and Miss Delafield would be if we got that sorted before she comes back on her next visit . . ."

Arianwyn stared hard at Gimma, searching for a twinkle of familiar malice or scorn in her face. But there was nothing at all. Perhaps she was starting to mellow at long last. Maybe without the audience she wasn't going to be the way she had been back in Kingsport: sneaky and cruel, calling Arianwyn names as she walked along the street or putting thumb tacks on her chair. Arianwyn shook her thoughts away and remembered her grandmother's words: "Cruelty is a sign of weakness, Arianwyn. And you are neither weak nor cruel!" Perhaps it was time to put all of that firmly behind them, once and for all.

"Well, I suppose it would be easier to sort it out with two of us—" she started.

"Oh, it really will, I promise! But what exactly do we have to do?"

How did she not remember about calvaria? They'd spent nearly a month learning about them last year! "Calvaria only spawn once every few hundred years, and there's no record of the spirit in the Torr River having spawned ever before. We need to see if it really has spawned this time, check the eggs are safe, and make sure there are no other spirits nearby that might interfere when the eggs hatch. We should probably try and get it captured with the spirit lantern as well."

"Well, that doesn't sound too hard, does it?" Gimma clapped her hands together and jumped up and down on the spot.

"Okay, okay. Let's go, then," Arianwyn replied slowly. Still, something niggled at the back of her mind. "But don't start whining if you get wet or muddy. Have you got some Wellington boots?"

Gimma smiled broadly at Arianwyn, clapped her hands together, and gave a high-pitched shriek of delight.

The Torr River twisted sleepily along the edge of the Great Wood, twinkling and shimmering in the light. The trees reflected in the wavering water. Spring flowers lined the bank with patches of bright blue or buttery yellow.

Gimma was trailing along behind, taking in the sights. Her Wellingtons were bright red and looked as though they had never been worn. "They're from Leighton & Dennison's, on Queen's Parade in Kingsport—have you been?" Gimma had asked when Arianwyn mentioned them. Arianwyn had quietly shaken her head and looked down at her own Wellies: old, slightly too large, and covered in mud. She wasn't even sure they were a matching pair.

"So it says in your book that the water spirits spawn in the shallows of the river, most likely in a patch of water grass or river weed . . ." Gimma was reading from *The Apprentice Witch's Handbook*. "Oh, look—there!" she cried excitedly, pointing just ahead of them.

A little farther along, the river broadened to twice its width and the grassy bank gave way to a deep shoreline of pebbles, stones, and small round rocks. A thick patch of river weed grew at the water's edge. The perfect spot for calvaria spawning, Arianwyn thought.

"Shall I have a look?" Gimma asked, unable to hide the excitement in her voice.

"Be my guest!" Arianwyn placed the spirit lantern case on the bank and stretched her aching shoulders. She took a deep breath, stared up at the pale blue sky, and thought about the warmer days ahead.

"Oh my goodness! Arianwyn, look! Come here, quickly!" Gimma was jumping up and down on the bank and pointing at the patch of river weed.

Curious, Arianwyn clambered onto the pebbles and moved quickly toward the water's edge.

"Look, look!" squealed Gimma, pointing down into the swirling mass of hairlike weed.

Arianwyn leaned out over the water and peered down. Tiny fish and insects darted about. Light flashed against the surface. There was no sign of the calvaria spawn.

But then, in the very center of the patch of weed, Arianwyn saw a shimmer of gold. It was just for a second and then it was gone again.

"Did you see it?" Gimma squeaked.

"Sssh!" Arianwyn said, and she glanced out across the river. The water ran deep and fast at the center and something was moving against the flow. She caught a glimpse of a long sinuous tail, which quickly disappeared.

Arianwyn crouched down to see better through the fluttering strands of weed.

Unmistakably, now, she saw them. Hundreds of them, perfect but very, very tiny calvaria eggs nestled down safely among the river weed. They glistened and shone, golden like tiny suns beneath the water. Arianwyn had never seen anything so beautiful in her life.

There was another large splashing eruption from the river and both girls turned to watch as the calvaria launched clean out of the water. It was twice as long as a bus and covered in fine black scales that glistened with water. Along its back were spines and rainbow-colored fins that fluttered in the air as it arced gracefully above the river. It gave a loud trumpeting call and a spout of water rose from the top of its head, high into the air. It twisted itself, the sun catching its silky scales, flashing brilliantly in the sun. Then it dived back below.

"The calvaria!" Gimma called in excitement.

"I'll get the lantern!" Arianwyn said, and dashed across the bank. She wrestled the spirit lantern free of its case and turned back to the water's edge. Her heart froze.

Gimma was now standing knee-deep in the river weed, peering down into the water.

"Gimma, get out of the river. The calvaria! What are you doing?"

There was a sudden movement, closer to the river weed this time. The water bulged as the spirit moved toward the bank and its nest, spines breaking the calm waters.

"I just wanted to get a better look. Honestly, you are such a worrywart, Arianwyn. You always were, but I think you've actually gotten worse." Gimma waved a hand lazily at Arianwyn.

Arianwyn took a deep breath and, for a moment, she considered walking away. But just then the calvaria reared up out of the water. Its long serpentine body swayed hypnotically, icy droplets falling through the air. Its dark scales flashed in the sun as it towered over Gimma, its red mouth open wide, its brilliant rainbow crests fanned out.

CHAPTER TWENTY-FIVE

THE RIFT

The calvaria's cry screamed out across the river and into the wood. Gimma stumbled in her haste to move away and fell backward, splashing into the cold water and swirl of river weed.

Arianwyn quickly set the spirit lantern down and then she was running, stumbling across the stones and pebbles toward her.

The calvaria reared back again, trumpeting a cry of anger across the river and into the trees beyond. Then it threw its long sinuous body forward. Gimma screamed and Arianwyn skidded to a halt on the pebbles. The calvaria crashed past Gimma and into the shallow water close to its nest. Then there was a rushing sound and, before she could think, Arianwyn felt the icy embrace of the river as the massive tidal wave engulfed her. She stumbled back under the weight of water, felt stones at her back as she fumbled in the dark to right herself. She had no idea which way was up or down and the water roared in her ears.

Just as she thought she was going to run out of breath the water seemed to be rushing back past her and she felt cold air on her damp face. She opened her eyes and wiped away a straggle of weed, checking carefully for signs of calvaria spawn.

Arianwyn peered through her wet curtain of hair. The wave had thrown her back up onto the stony beach, clear of the river and the angry calvaria that still thrashed and churned just a few yards away. In its rage it had beached itself. Gimma was nowhere to be seen.

"Gimma!" Arianwyn called, gripped with fear. She forced herself up and ran, her Wellingtons sloshing full of water. Shivering with cold and fear, Arianwyn waded into the river. Drowning the mayor's favorite niece was not something she wanted to explain to anyone. She plunged her arms into the water, searching for an arm, leg, or hair—she didn't mind which.

Suddenly, a desperate hand wrapped tightly around her wrist and Arianwyn pulled hard, the calvaria still struggling wildly close by. Gimma broke the water, gasping for air. Weed and a few stray calvaria eggs wrapped through her hair and stuck to her coat. "Come on!" Arianwyn called. "We need to get the calvaria back into the deeper water quickly."

"What?" Gimma gasped, half laughing. "I'm not going near that thing again. No way!" She tried to pull away.

"Yes, you are! Come on!" She dragged Gimma closer to the spirit. It tumbled and turned in the shallow water. Stones rattled beneath it and it snapped its wide mouth at the two witches.

"It's okay," Arianwyn cooed soothingly. "We're not going to hurt you."

She turned to Gimma. "On three we're going to push it back into the deeper water. Ready? Watch out for the spines, okay? One, two . . . THREE!"

Together the girls pushed hard against the side of the twisting calvaria and it tumbled over. Despite the cold water, the beast was incredibly warm and the scales, though smooth and wet, were not slimy. They pushed again and it tumbled some more, moving slowly toward the deeper water of the river.

"Nearly there!" Arianwyn shouted as she felt the water spill over her boots again. The calvaria seemed to calm itself, as though it knew what was happening, and then, with one last shove, it splashed into deeper water and snaked sharply away and out into the center of the river, slipping below the water, disappearing in seconds.

"Well, I'm glad that's over . . ." Gimma sighed. But just as they started to turn back to the bank the spirit reared up high above them. Its mouth was bared wide once more and its rainbow fins stood on end, rattling noisily.

"Oh, what now?" Gimma wailed, flicking her wet hair back over her shoulder.

"Oh, boil it, the eggs!" Arianwyn cried. She quickly started to pick the tiny sunlike eggs from Gimma's straggly hair and her coat. "Stand still!" she said angrily, as Gimma fidgeted.

"But I'm cold!" Gimma moaned. Arianwyn glared at her through her own tangled wet curls and carried on extracting weed and eggs.

The calvaria watched carefully; its fins continued to

rattle a warning. Once or twice it bellowed its displeasure and snapped forward with its large head, causing Gimma to jump back.

Eventually the last egg was plucked from Gimma's coat. The girls moved swiftly to the patch of river weed and gently placed the eggs back with the others. Gimma was about to turn back to the shore when Arianwyn hissed, "Bow to the water spirit!" *How had she forgotten that?* Arianwyn wondered.

Slowly the two witches knelt in the water, lowering their heads in honor of the great water spirit. There was a long moment of silence, followed by a gentle splash as the calvaria sank below the surface once more.

Arianwyn lowered herself down against a large rock and sighed deeply. The river was calm once more, the eggs were safe, and the calvaria seemed perfectly able to defend its territory. She glanced at Gimma, who was shivering and looked slightly blue.

"I'm freezing. Can we light a fire or something?" Gimma whined.

"Not here." Arianwyn glanced at the water. "It's not a good idea; let's walk on a bit first." She wrapped a reassuring arm around Gimma's shaking shoulders.

A few minutes later they were standing in a small clearing on the edge of the Great Wood. Gimma hadn't spoken once since they left the river. She had let Arianwyn lead her without complaint and now she waited by a tall fir and stared into the distance.

"I'll get a fire lit, okay? It'll just take a second." Arianwyn hurriedly cleared a small patch of ground and sketched Årdra, the fire glyph, into the earth. But she was so cold she couldn't concentrate on the flow of magic nearby and her hands shook as she traced the glyph for a second time.

"I don't remember being so cold since we went on that school visit to the pier in Horton, and it was snowing . . . do you remember?" Arianwyn kept her voice bright and cheerful, glancing over at Gimma, who was still motionless by the tree. Was she in shock?

With the third attempt of the fire glyph the ground slowly started to glow with magical warmth. Arianwyn scooped a handful of dry leaves and small twigs onto the glyph and it brightened some more but mostly billowed smoke.

"Come and sit by the fire," Arianwyn called, and she watched as Gimma moved slowly across the clearing as if in a dream. Gimma hunched by the tiny fire, rubbing her hands, then she shrugged off her coat, which fell damply to the ground, wafting up a small cloud of leaves and dusty earth.

"I didn't go on that trip," Gimma said quietly. "But my aunt and uncle have a house there and we used to visit in the summer. This could do with some more wood to really get it going, don't you think?" she said, rubbing her arms and inching closer to the magical glow.

Arianwyn stared at her for a moment. "I'll go, shall I?"

"Oh, you are a love, thanks!" Gimma half smiled and then gave a loud, theatrical sneeze.

***

Arianwyn's boots squelched as she walked slowly from the clearing and along a broad avenue of tall trees. The echoing sound of bird calls rang overhead and pale spring light filtered in through the new leaves. She kept glancing back over her shoulder, down the avenue, to where Gimma sat warming herself by the fire.

"Keep calm, she can't help it. She was trying to be helpful," Arianwyn muttered to herself quietly. "It'll only be for a few more weeks and then she'll be off to some other swanky assignment and you won't have to deal with her again. Except for when she comes to visit for a vacation! Oh, jinxing-jiggery!"

Arianwyn stomped her way farther along the avenue of trees.

She spotted a collection of twigs and fallen branches at the foot of a grand oak. She checked first for any spirits that might have decided to nest there or close by, but there was no pull of magic. With the branches and twigs cradled in her arms, she walked back the way she had come, seeing occasional drifts of smoke wafting toward her as she drew closer to the clearing. And then she heard an earsplitting scream that was without a doubt Gimma's.

"I suppose she's found a worm or a woodlouse or

something," Arianwyn grumbled to herself, and continued her slow walk back to the clearing.

But then there came a second scream, louder and more frantic, followed by a shrill blast of Gimma's witch whistle and two bright flashes. The unmistakable whiff of magic reached Arianwyn.

The branches tumbled to the ground and she broke into as fast a run as her damp heavy clothes would let her.

"Gimma?" she called frantically, but the only answer was another anguished scream. She shouldn't have left her on her own. She burst into the clearing, now filled with thick gray smoke and the very definite tingle of magic.

"GIMMA!"

"Here! Arianwyn! I'm here!" Gimma's voice trembled. Arianwyn could just see her through the smoke. She was backed up against a tree, a tiny pale spell orb cupped in her shaking hand. Her face was ghoulishly white in the light of the spell. "There's something here!" she said, her eyes scanning the clouds of billowing smoke.

"What is it?" Arianwyn whispered quickly, summoning her own crackling spell. It hovered above her palm, tumbling and turning in the air. It was much larger than Gimma's and brilliant green.

"I have no idea, but it was small and vicious. It came right for me! I'm not going to let it get away—I've made too many mistakes already!" Gimma pulled her gaze away from Arianwyn, a blush now spreading across her pale skin.

There was a sudden darting movement through the smoke. Gimma gave a small mewl of fear mixed with anger and shoved herself in front of Arianwyn.

"Get back!" she roared into the fog, just as Estar stepped forward.

He wafted smoke from his face, coughing gently into a handkerchief. He looked thoroughly bemused. Arianwyn's heart stopped. Her breath caught in her throat and for a split second, time seemed to be held in place, suspended on a thread.

Gimma's spell orb was held high, ready to be thrown.

"No, Gimma, stop! It's all right, he's not dangerous!" Arianwyn grabbed Gimma's wrist, shaking it until her weak spell fizzed to nothing.

"What are you doing?" Gimma asked in amazement.

"You can't . . . you don't understand. He's . . ." Arianwyn was breathless with fear. She glanced at Estar.

"He's my friend!" she said finally.

Gimma edged back and stared in horror at Arianwyn. The wood was suddenly silent but for the crackle of the little fire buried beneath the expanse of foglike smoke.

Estar watched them both carefully.

"But it's a demon or some other dark spirit creature!" Gimma said slowly, as though she were telling this to a child or someone simple.

"He's not," Arianwyn began. "Well, not entirely. He's some sort of hybrid. A . . ."

"Ahem! A feyling, if you don't mind!" came Estar's polite and polished reply. He bowed slowly.

"Yes, sorry. A feyling."

Gimma stared at Estar and then looked back at Arianwyn; her mouth hung open slightly.

"Oh my god!" she suddenly cried. "He's got you under some sort of spell, hasn't he? Don't worry, Arianwyn. I'm going to banish him. Right now! Back to the void with you, you—you . . . fey-*thing*!"

Estar rolled his eyes.

As fast as lightning, Gimma had wrenched her arm free of Arianwyn's grip and shoved her backward into a tangle of bush. Without saying anything else, she reached forward and in the smoky air sketched the banishing glyph, L'ier. It slid through the smoke, splitting the very fabric of the air in two. Out of the space spooled the darkness and icy cold of the void.

But something was wrong. Almost at once the rift grew to twice the size it should have been. It twisted and turned, straining as it grew larger still.

"Oh, boil it, what have you done?" Arianwyn cried, grabbing Gimma again and pulling her away from the rift.

"I was just trying to help you—what's wrong with the spell?" Gimma shrieked, and already tears were coursing down her face.

"I suspect it was the hex over there." Estar was now beside them. He glanced at Arianwyn and pointed behind them.

"No wonder the fire spell wouldn't take properly," she said.

As Gimma saw him, she gave another earsplitting scream.

"I think you'd better just go," Arianwyn hissed at Estar.

"But I—"

"Estar, please!" Arianwyn moaned. He arched an eyebrow and suddenly the smoke enveloped him like a cloak and he vanished from view.

Now, even through the swirling smoke from the feeble fire, Arianwyn could see the patches of thick hex growing all across the trunks of the trees in the clearing.

How had they not seen it before?

The rift pulsed, expanding and contracting again, and Arianwyn felt its icy pull on her damp clothes, the tingling chill on her hands and face. "Close the rift, quickly," she said to Gimma, who simply stared in horror as the rift contracted again and again.

"Gimma?" Arianwyn prodded.

"I can't!" she whimpered.

Arianwyn wanted to help, but it wasn't easy to undo another witch's spell—it was almost impossible. "You opened it, you have to close it!" she said, pointing at the rift.

Eventually, Gimma stepped forward, tracing the glyph backward in the air, canceling the spell. But the rift did not vanish as it should. Instead it shuddered briefly and throbbed. Gimma fell to her knees, her voice swallowed in uncontrollable sobbing.

The rift pulsed once more and this time Arianwyn thought she could see a shape moving in the darkness, large and swift. Something lurked beyond.

Arianwyn knew they had to close it now before anything crossed through. "Throw as many spells at the rift as you can, straight at it and don't hit the hex, whatever you do—that'll just make things worse!"

"I'm sorry!" Gimma sniffed and wiped her nose across her sleeve.

"Let's just get this fixed, shall we?" Arianwyn replied, and the next moment the air was lit up as Gimma and Arianwyn hurled their spells across the clearing and at the dark twisting tear.

Bright explosions, smoke, and vapor drifted across the clearing, making it even harder to see. There was a shower of smoking, charred wood as a stray spell exploded against a tree.

"I think we need to get out of here now!" Arianwyn shouted.

"But what about the . . . fey-thing?" Gimma sniffed.

"Don't worry, Estar can look after himself quite well!"

They ran for the cover of the trees, Arianwyn glanced back and peered through the smoke. She searched for the rift, but couldn't get a clear view. She had to hope that the spells they had bombarded it with had done their work.

Her heart stopped. Between the clouds of smoke and magic she thought she saw a large, dark, twisted shape moving quickly, like dark water. It danced through the mist of smoke and magic, a trick of the light, perhaps? Or something else—something worse?

"Wait, Gimma!" Arianwyn called.

"What's wrong?"

She turned back and, squinting, peered once more through the smoke, her eyes stinging, her vision blurred.

But whatever it was it had disappeared. Arianwyn couldn't be sure anything had ever been there at all.

She looked at Gimma, who was still in tears.

"Promise me you won't tell anyone about this," Gimma wailed.

THE APPRENTICE WITCH'S HANDBOOK

✦ ✦ ✦

All things have their opposite, and dark magic can be found in different forms in our world. Hex, usually produced by dark spirits or stagnant or degraded spells, can be lethal to humans and spirits. Several "hex plagues" are recorded throughout history.

CHAPTER TWENTY-SIX

THE EXPLODING KITCHEN

Arianwyn jerked awake. She was tangled in her bedsheet and blanket. Scrabbling to sit up, she saw bright daylight flooding in through the windows that looked out over Kettle Lane.

She shivered, damp with sweat and fear.

The small clock declared it to be after nine and the sounds from outside confirmed that she had overslept quite spectacularly. Taking a deep, shuddering breath, she slumped back against her pillows and closed her eyes just for a second.

FLASH!

The unknown glyph burned in her memory—reaching out from her dream.

"No!" she cried, tumbling from her bed and scrabbling away from it as though it were on fire. The moon hare approached cautiously from its spot by the stove. It sniffed at her bare ankles and sneezed, casting her a cautious glance before scuttling under the bed.

"What's wrong with you?" Arianwyn asked. She reached out to reassure it but it gave a low growl and backed away, its claws scratching against the floor. Arianwyn shrugged. As she stood back up again the room spun and her head throbbed.

She'd gotten up too quickly, that was all. She just needed a glass of water.

She padded across the cool floorboards, yawning and stretching as she went. She picked up a glass from the drying board and reached out to turn the tap.

CRACKLE!

Sparks flew from her fingertips as she touched the metal. She leapt back from the sink, the glass slipping from her hand and shattering on the floor.

"Boil it!" Arianwyn shouted. Her head throbbed again and her vision grew dark at the edges. She reached out to steady herself against the cupboard and it started shaking and rocking violently. Was it an earthquake?

She glanced around the room. Everything else was still. But the cupboard still danced furiously, the plates and cups inside rattling noisily.

All at once it stopped, as suddenly as it had begun. The doors flew open and crockery spewed across the floor, crashing and breaking.

That was when Arianwyn noticed dark smoke curling from her outstretched hand.

She had done this.

She closed her eyes again but there was the glyph shape once more. Fainter, but still in her mind, drifting slowly away. But still there.

She wanted to go back to bed, but she was scared to close her eyes. She was scared to move. She glanced around her. The moon hare still growled beneath the bed.

Terrified, she sank to the floor and hugged her knees to her chest, hoping it would pass quickly. She felt sick, cold and alone. She stared straight ahead at the opposite wall, at a patch of peeling wallpaper.

She wasn't sure how long she had been sitting there when she heard the door charm jangle in the Spellorium below.

"Wyn?"

It was Salle.

"Wyn? Are you here?" she called a little louder, then there were quick footsteps downstairs as she crossed the Spellorium.

Was it safe for Salle? Arianwyn glanced at the wreckage of her kitchen. She didn't want to risk hurting her friend! Perhaps if she just sat still, Salle would go away again . . . but then she heard footsteps on the stairs.

"Wyn? Are you okay?"

The moon hare scampered from under the bed to greet Salle.

Arianwyn thought about trying to get into the bathroom to hide. She started to stand just as Salle's head appeared from the stairs. Salle had already seen her, still in her nightdress, crouched amid fragments of broken glass and china, her eyes red and dry from trying not to blink.

"What on earth?" Salle gasped. She dashed across to Arianwyn, reaching toward her.

"NO!" Arianwyn said, scrabbling back. "Don't come too close. I'm not very well. I'm sick."

Salle stopped dead. She folded her hands and stood still, the toes of her shoes crunching in the glass. "Flu?" she asked, but her eyes swept around the room: the glass scattered on the floor, the cupboard with its contents spewed out.

Arianwyn nodded, but she could see Salle was not convinced by her feeble little lie.

"Let me help you get back into bed, then . . ." Salle reached out again but Arianwyn moved to bat her away. As their hands touched Salle jumped a little. Arianwyn felt the charge of magic pass between them. Jolting, sharp, painful. Sparks flashed in the air.

"Ouch!" Salle snatched her hand away. "That was some electric shock!" She smiled, laughing a little. But her eyes stayed focused on Arianwyn. She reached out again, slower this time, and wrapped a comforting arm around Arianwyn's shoulders.

"Let's get you tucked in, shall we?" she soothed.

Arianwyn nodded and allowed herself to be led back to bed.

As Salle straightened the blanket around her the moon hare jumped up and cautiously approached Arianwyn. Ears high and alert, its nose twitched. It sniffed at her hand, sat back on its hind legs for a second, as if considering something. Then it yawned wide, scratched its ear, and curled up against Arianwyn's side.

"I'll get you some water," Salle said calmly.

As Salle busied herself filling an unbroken cup from the tap, Arianwyn took a deep breath and quickly scrunched her eyes closed.

There was only darkness now and the murky blobs of color you see when you squeeze your eyes closed. She felt a moment of brief relief.

"Okay?" Salle asked, putting the cup on the bedside table next to Arianwyn.

Arianwyn nodded. "Just tired."

Salle went back to the kitchen and started to tidy the mess, humming to herself as she worked. It was soothing, relaxing.

For a while the fear went away.

CHAPTER TWENTY-SEVEN

EUPHEMIA

It was late afternoon and Arianwyn had sat wrapped in a blanket all day. After Salle had left she'd curled up into a tight ball, still too afraid to close her eyes.

The moon hare nestled beside her. She glanced at the clock. It would be night soon and she would have to sleep. But sleep meant dreams and dreams meant the glyph. She was scared, and the one person she thought might be able to help her was Estar.

She waited until dusk, until the town had grown quiet and the shops along Kettle Lane were closed. Pulling on a cardigan against the cool evening, she slipped out of the Spellorium and headed through town.

All day the half-sketched symbol Estar had drawn into the earth of the hen shed had plagued her memory. She was sure now that it *was* a glyph: the very same one she had seen so many times. Estar was the only one that might be able to tell her more.

Slipping quietly along Kettle Lane and out across the town square, Arianwyn was greeted by a few people out for evening strolls but she moved on quickly, businesslike, and nobody wanted to interrupt the witch when she was busy.

A few people were wandering past Kurtis Mill as Arianwyn arrived: families taking a walk through the meadow in the spring sunshine. She slipped quickly down the side of the ramshackle building. At the side door, which now stood partly ajar, a slice of darkness welcomed her. "Estar . . . ," she whispered as she pushed on the door. "Estar? Are you here?"

Her only answer was the low moan of air moving through the empty building. She stepped forward, her eyes adjusting slowly to the darkness. Perhaps he really had left this time.

Strange shapes loomed out of the shadows, solidifying as her eyes adjusted, large wooden crates stood haphazardly about the room. "Estar!" she hissed, slightly louder this time, and peered farther into the gloom of the mill.

"Yes?"

She jumped.

He was suddenly there, standing beside Arianwyn and staring up at her, his yellow eyes luminous in the gloom.

"Oh, Estar. I was getting worried. I thought something terrible had happened to you . . ."

"Something did, remember? Who was that rather stupid girl with you the other day?"

Arianwyn sighed. "That's Gimma . . . you shouldn't have frightened her, you know!"

"Frighten her indeed! Well, I think it was all the other

way! She's made a real muddle in the wood, you know, with that rift."

"I thought we closed it—did something come through?"

"Perhaps . . . but what's one more creature in the wood, eh?" Estar smiled.

Arianwyn suddenly felt scared again and didn't want to tell Estar what she had seen in the rift. Whatever would he think of her? Besides, she really didn't know this creature at all. Her hands felt hot and sweaty; she could feel her breathing quicken.

"Bad dreams?" he asked, his eyes sparkling now as well as glowing, half a smile on his sharp little face.

"How . . . how did you know?" Arianwyn asked, flooded with relief and shock all at once.

"I can hear them buzzing around you still. Dreams can haunt us, you know." He shuffled away from Arianwyn in his slow hop-along walk, moving farther back through the mill. He stopped by a small pile of boxes and clambered onto one. He sat up regally, as if the stack of crates were a throne. "So, is there something you would like to ask me, young witch?" He peered down his long blue nose at Arianwyn.

They stared at each other for a long moment.

"That shape, in the hen shed, it was drawn in the dirt—it's magical, isn't it? Powerful?

"Perhaps . . ." Estar shook his head. "But I don't really want anything to do with it. I promised to keep it a secret."

Sudden tears brimmed in her eyes. Estar was her only hope of understanding the strange glyph—what would she do if he wouldn't help her? Her hands curled into fists and she chewed on her lip in frustration.

"I need your help . . . please!" Arianwyn said eventually, staring levelly at Estar. "I'm frightened. There is something about that shape. It's tempting and terrifying all at the same time. I've seen it all my life and each time I see it something bad has happened. My mother died, I failed my evaluation, and this morning—"

"You nearly blew up your kitchen?" Estar bent closer.

She nodded her head, warm tears on her face and a lump in her throat that stopped her words.

Estar stroked his narrow chin, his lips pursed in concentration. "Hmmm." He sighed, considering. "The other witch—the one I knew before. Euphemia. She was interested in those strange shapes you witches use to control the magic."

"The glyphs?" Arianwyn asked.

"Yes . . . glyphs!" Estar said the word slowly, as though he were letting it roll around on his tongue. "A very clunky way to control magic, in my opinion," he added quietly. "She asked me to find a book of glyphs from the demon library in Erraldur."

"What did she want to know?"

"Oh, this and that. It wasn't easy—cost me a lot of trouble, you know. I didn't manage to retrieve the whole book, but I got her a page—and the page showed that glyph."

"Where's the book now?" asked Arianwyn. If she could

read it, perhaps she could find out what all this was about!

But Estar shook his head. "Lost. I went back to Erraldur to try and find it again, but it must've hidden itself from us. I didn't realize I had been gone from the human world for so long; time works in strange ways when you're that deep in the Great Wood. Where is Euphemia now?" There was a glimmer of hope in his voice.

"I don't know," Arianwyn replied sadly. "Nobody seems to know."

"Poor Euphemia. She was kind, funny, and brave. Rather like you, Arianwyn Gribble. She told me that anyone who could recognize the glyph would help us, could be trusted." His yellow eyes flicked to Arianwyn's. "That's why I drew it in the hen shed . . . for help."

"I don't understand." Arianwyn paced back and forth, staring into the shadows. "That symbol is dark and dangerous; it can't be a help to anyone, surely?"

Estar reached out and took Arianwyn's hand in his own. "I don't know about that." He added, "The spell might well be dark, but *you* most certainly are not, Arianwyn Gribble."

Arianwyn felt her cheeks flush for a moment.

"If only we knew what had become of the page . . . ," Estar mused.

They were silent for several long minutes. Outside the window the sky was a deep purple color, the evening drawing in.

In a sudden moment of clarity, Arianwyn saw the small case that Salle had tucked away at the back of her wardrobe in the apartment. She had packed all of the previous witch's things away in it. All those dresses that had hung in the wardrobe and the photograph and old papers! Had the answer been in the Spellorium all this time?

CHAPTER TWENTY-EIGHT

THE UNKNOWN GLYPH

Arianwyn flipped the *Closed* sign around on the door and pulled down the long blinds to hide Kettle Lane from view. She flicked off the lights so only the twilight glow illuminated the store. The moon hare skittered excitedly at her feet, darting this way and that, sensing her excitement and trepidation.

She let Estar in through the long windows that opened onto the small yard at the back of the Spellorium. The moon hare rushed toward him at once and rolled over and over in ecstatic glee by the feyling's feet.

"Wait here!" Arianwyn said, and she bounded up the curling staircase into the apartment. She threw open the wardrobe doors and shoved her own clothes and spare uniforms to one side. There, at the back of the wardrobe, sat the case. She pulled it forward and snapped the catch at the front. Carelessly she rifled through the contents until she had the collection of papers in her hands. She also took the photograph. Then she returned downstairs to the dark Spellorium.

On the polished wooden counter she fanned out everything. She saw Estar reach a small blue hand out to touch the photograph gently, but when he realized she was watching he moved the photograph to one side and pretended to be helping to sort the papers.

"Aha!" he said. "I think this is it!"

He pulled free a curled piece of ancient-looking parchment, dusty and faded brown. It was roughly the size of Arianwyn's palm. He held it up for her, expectantly.

"It's blank!" she said.

"What?" Estar stared at the paper. "But Euphemia saw something there . . ."

He dropped the page, which fluttered to Arianwyn's feet. The moon hare sniffed at it and growled, a low rumbling sound that filled the store. Its long ears flattened against its body and its fur rose in a sharp spine along its back.

"Whatever's wrong with you?" Arianwyn asked, shooing it away from the page.

She bent to pick it up and gave a small gasp. As her fingertips brushed the parchment, a symbol started to form at its center.

"Oh!" Arianwyn gasped. "Estar, look!"

The shape seemed to be bleeding through the paper, dark and bold. "I think it's a glyph. I think it's *the* glyph!"

Estar didn't move. He was watching Arianwyn very carefully now.

Arianwyn couldn't pull her eyes away from the piece of paper. It was real. She hadn't muddled things or imagined them. The glyph was truly real! She clutched the curl of paper tightly in her hands. Proof at last!

"Do you know anything more about it?" Arianwyn asked.

There was a long pause and then Estar said, "I cannot read it; none of my kind would be able to read it. And you witches seem to have long forgotten it—well, most of you." He winked.

"Euphemia . . . she could see it too?"

"Perhaps not so clearly as you do."

Arianwyn studied the piece of paper again for a few minutes, an idea forming in her mind. There was really no need, though—she knew the glyph so well from memory.

The moon hare worried at her feet, snapping and jumping up, growling and mewling for her attention. She scooped it into her arms and carried it to the small storeroom at the back. She didn't want to be distracted now. She shut the door quickly and crossed back to the counter. She could do this, she had the page, and there was nothing to worry about . . . probably.

Her hands were shaking as she prepared to sketch the glyph, not too large, into the air in front of her.

"What are you doing?" Estar asked, backing away to the window.

"I have to know. I have to know what this glyph is, what it does. I'm going to summon it."

"Is that wise? It could be dangerous. You said yourself it had heralded dark things in your life. What makes you think it won't be some sort of dark magic?" His voice was uncertain.

She hesitated for a moment but the glyph had always appeared unbidden before. This time, she would call it and control its power. "Only one way to find out." Her confident words did not match how she felt, but excitement and curiosity won out over her fear.

They looked at each other for a few moments and then Arianwyn said, "You will stay with me, won't you?"

Estar sighed and sat down on the floor. "Of course."

Arianwyn took another deep breath and started to sketch the glyph into the dark air of the Spellorium. The glyph hung in the air for a few seconds.

It was dark.

Black.

Unlike the cardinal glyphs, it gave off no feeling of heat. It was as cold as stone and ice.

But nothing happened.

Instinctively, Arianwyn reached for the glyph, which shimmered briefly before drifting away like smoke from a candle.

The store was as quiet as before, late evening shadows reaching across the floor, the far-off sounds of Kettle Lane just as they had been. Estar sat still on the floor, his long shadow splayed out across the boards.

Arianwyn turned around. Everything was as it had been a moment before. Nothing had happened. "I think it must be dormant or dead." She sighed. "It has no power!" She reached for the page that still lay on the counter. As her hand stretched out, her fingers fanned, the shadows spread across the floorboards of the store moved in a sudden jerking motion toward her, like daggers of darkness.

Arianwyn pulled her hand back and stood still. She stared at the floor. The shadows were just shadows. They hadn't really moved at all . . . had they? "Did you see that?" she asked Estar.

He shook his head. "Are you all right?"

"I think I just need a good night's sleep!" Arianwyn scolded herself and reached for the page again.

There was no mistaking this time. None!

The shadows shifted. Leapt. Convulsed. Just for a second.

"Oh my goodness!" Estar jumped to his feet and scuttled behind the counter. "I saw *that!*"

Arianwyn turned her hand, curling her fingers into her palm. Testing. The shadows inched closer toward her, darker and darker as they approached. And they were changing. They moved like a mist now, black phantoms shifting across the floor. The room was suddenly cold. Arianwyn could see her breath in the air. Her hands ached with ice.

There was a frantic scratching from the storeroom door as the moon hare tried to free itself.

Arianwyn heard a small voice, twisting and cruel. "Useless!" it said snidely. "You are useless!" She spun around, half thinking it was Estar, but she knew deep down it wasn't.

It was the shadows that spoke to her.

Whatever had she done?

She reached forward—pushing away with her hand, hoping it would make the dark twisting shapes move back. Return to just being shadows once more.

The gloom simply swirled more vigorously at her feet. Panic rose in her chest. Darkness was thickening now, growing deeper and deeper. It churned like black water. "Stop!" Arianwyn called, as though she were shouting over a raging ocean, but there was only the dreadful silence and the scratching sounds from the moon hare in the storeroom.

"Make it stop, Arianwyn. Please make it stop!"

She looked at Estar, who had backed up against the wall, as far from the darkness as he could, but it drew closer.

"Idiot!" came the voice again. And it was louder, right next to her ear.

She *was* an idiot: How stupid to have summoned this glyph without knowing what it was! But she had felt so certain that there were answers waiting for her.

A sly cackling laugh filled her ears and she shivered from head to toe. She could feel the darkness creeping over her; her feet and legs were buried beneath the rolling shadows.

The darkness was consuming her.

She felt a terrible sadness and loneliness. Thoughts of her mother washed over her. She remembered her grandmother's cries as she raced across the road and her mother's too-still body. The look on her father's face and all their tears—so many tears.

The power of the glyph pulled her like a strong tide, but Arianwyn knew she had to fight against it. She had been so foolish. This was very dark magic indeed.

But the sadness was heavy, like a great weight pressing against her, making it hard to breathe or move.

What was she doing? This was madness, so dangerous. She was stupid to have thought she might be able to control the power of this glyph.

Estar had probably tricked her into summoning something terrible and dark. Why had she thought she could trust him? She remembered the horrid shape in the wood, and the shadows grew darker still. How was this happening to her? Had she really allowed herself to be such a fool *again*? The darkness, ice, and loneliness swirled around her, obscuring all the familiar sights of the Spellorium.

She could hear the frantic scrabbling of the moon hare and its anxious call. She knew she should release it . . .

The shadows surged and she staggered back from them, wanting to run and hide. Where had the light gone?

Suddenly determined, Arianwyn pushed herself forward, batting away at the air. Instantly the shadows retreated, twisting and tumbling away.

The room returned to normal, the Spellorium once more. The last rays of light flooded Kettle Lane.

Arianwyn felt a surge of hope and then heard the door rattle. She turned just in time to see Miss Delafield staring in through the window, her face twisted in shock. And beside her was Gimma.

"Hide!" Arianwyn hissed at Estar.

CHAPTER TWENTY-NINE

SISTERS

I t's not what you think!" Arianwyn protested as Miss Delafield marched through the door, her driving coat flapping angrily in her wake. Gimma trailed in behind, silent and careful.

The older woman pulled her goggles from on top of her head and threw them down onto the counter along with her long driving gloves. They landed next to the piles of papers and the photograph of the other witch. Miss Delafield's eyes widened briefly and she glanced away. Arianwyn noticed the page with the glyph—now invisible—waft away and tumble to the floor behind the counter.

"What on earth were you doing?" Miss Delafield roared, her cheeks blazing red, her eyes wide.

Arianwyn, unsure what to say, looked down at the floor.

"Look at me, young lady!" Miss Delafield boomed, and the glass jars on the shelves jingled.

Arianwyn's head snapped up and she looked into Miss Delafield's eyes. She could try to lie but what could she say? How could she explain away what had just taken place—what Miss Delafield had obviously seen through the window?

"Well?" Miss Delafield asked. "I am waiting for an explanation, Miss Gribble."

Arianwyn sighed again. She reached for a piece of loose paper and a pencil and quickly sketched the unknown glyph onto it.

"Do you know this glyph?" She held the paper out.

Miss Delafield snatched it from Arianwyn's hand and studied it carefully. It seemed hours before she folded the paper and slowly but definitely tore it in half. She handed the scraps of paper to Gimma. "Put them in the fire, please, dear," she said firmly.

Gimma crossed to the little potbellied stove.

"Where did you see that glyph, dear?" Miss Delafield asked. Her voice was softer now, quiet, but in place of the anger was concern.

"I've seen it for years and years," Arianwyn replied. "Ever since . . ." But the memory of her mother made her stop. She heard the door of the stove swing shut. Gimma looked on silently.

Miss Delafield stood still. Her eyes flashed back and forth, her face twisted in concentration.

"Are there more glyphs than the ones we know and use?" Arianwyn asked. She could feel herself shaking with anticipation.

Miss Delafield pulled away and marched to the opposite side of the room. She gripped the edge of the shelves and bowed her head.

"Miss Delafield . . ." Arianwyn made to move forward but Miss Delafield spun around and grabbed Arianwyn by the shoulders and shook her, once, twice, three times.

"Promise me, you will never, *never* summon a glyph like that again. *Promise!*" Her face was wet with tears. She was crying!

"What is it?" Arianwyn asked gently, placing one hand on her supervisor's shoulder.

"They're dangerous, dear—full of dark, terrible magic, beyond our understanding and ability."

"They? So there *are* more of them . . . ," Arianwyn said quickly. She looked across at Gimma but the other girl was hanging back in the shadows by the stove, watching everything unfold.

Miss Delafield nodded, dabbing her eyes. "There are rumors that there were once more glyphs than we know today and that the witches of the Four Kingdoms stopped using them for some reason. But we don't know anything about them, what they do, or if they are connected to dark spirits. So please promise me you won't try to summon one ever again." Miss Delafield continued, "I couldn't bear for you to go through—" Her voice broke as more tears coursed down her face. She suddenly reached out and snatched up the old photograph from the counter.

Arianwyn gently led her to the chair by the stove. She fetched some teacups, setting the old copper kettle on top of the stove. Gimma watched, frozen by Miss Delafield's outburst. Suddenly remembering the moon hare still trapped in the storeroom, Arianwyn dashed to let it out. It sat tense under a tumble of boxes. It growled lightly as Arianwyn entered the room before bounding past her to nuzzle against Miss Delafield's leg.

"Hello, little one!" Miss Delafield sniffed, petting the moon hare's ears gently.

Arianwyn set about making the tea. She handed Gimma and Miss Delafield a cup each and suddenly Miss Delafield started to speak, quietly and distractedly, as though recalling something from another lifetime. She cradled the photograph in her hands.

"I lied to you, Arianwyn. I'm sorry. You asked me if I knew the previous inhabitant and I lied. I did know her. I knew her very well indeed."

Something twigged in Arianwyn's mind. The photograph. The beautiful witch with the golden curls that tumbled over her shoulders and the gangly younger girl with the thick braids who stood awkwardly at her side. Arianwyn went cold.

"She was my . . . sister . . ." Miss Delafield's voice wobbled and cracked as she spoke.

"Her name was Euphemia, but we all called her Effie." Miss Delafield slurped from her teacup and eyed Arianwyn cautiously. "She was like you, Arianwyn. She had visions of glyphs that only seem to exist in the oldest of legends, myths and half stories long forgotten. And when she tried to summon them as a young witch . . . well . . . it drove her quite insane. And eventually the power consumed her . . . and she died."

Arianwyn glanced across at Gimma, who had tears in her eyes that she quickly wiped away.

Miss Delafield sniffed once more and extracted from her pocket a huge handkerchief that was embroidered with flowers and birds. She blew her nose noisily into it.

Arianwyn rested against the bookcase nearby and considered what Miss Delafield had just said.

"So if your sister and I have both seen different glyphs, there might be others out there—"

"This is not the sort of thing you would want to go about telling people, dear. Trust me. They'd lock you up as quick as a flash. In truth it's why I never told anyone poor Effie was my sister. I was ashamed and worried they might think I was similarly affected . . ."

For a moment, Arianwyn wondered if she should mention Estar, hiding nearby. But she decided now was not the time for that particular revelation.

Miss Delafield gulped the rest of her tea and wiped the tears from her cheeks. "Say nothing about this to anyone, *either* of you!" She scowled at Gimma. "And under no circumstance attempt to summon that thing ever again. You could kill yourself and those around you. Do I make myself quite clear, dear?"

Arianwyn, slightly frustrated at not being able to ask more questions, nodded mutely. Gimma nodded as well.

Miss Delafield rose silently from her chair and handed Arianwyn the teacup, the discussion over.

"We had come to practice for the parade, but I suggest we put that on hold for another evening."

"Of course, Miss Delafield," Arianwyn replied. It seemed the evening's dark events had swiftly been forgotten.

Or perhaps not. For, just as Gimma had gone back out into Kettle Lane, Miss Delafield gripped Arianwyn's arm tightly and pulled her into a sort of haphazard hug on the doorstep of the store. "You really mustn't. For your own good, dear. Promise me?" Her voice was soft and pleading.

Arianwyn nodded.

There was a long moment of silence at the door. Miss Delafield's eyes searched Arianwyn's face. It was a similar look to the one Estar had given her earlier, the cat and the mouse, as if she was suddenly scared of Arianwyn.

Arianwyn looked away at last.

"Well, see you in a few days, then, dear. Good night!"

Arianwyn waited on the doorstep until the sound of the engine had died away into the night, until the first stars blinked high in the clear sky and the distant sounds of wood owls sang out from the Great Wood.

CHAPTER THIRTY

THERE ARE SHADOWS SINGING

Don't you think you ought to give that moon hare a name?" Gimma asked. She sat between Arianwyn and Salle. The two young witches were taking a break from Miss Delafield's parade training session in the Spellorium. "What about Lancelot or Umberto?"

Salle snorted loudly and looked at Gimma. "You can't call it that. It's a girl!"

"Is it?" Arianwyn asked.

"Surely it's a boy," Gimma said, studying the moon hare carefully.

"Neither!" Miss Delafield said brightly.

"What?" Salle asked, unable to hide the shock in her voice. All three girls turned quickly to look at the moon hare, who was busy washing its feet rhythmically.

"You know, like a snail or a worm!" Miss Delafield said. "Oh!"

"Hmmm," Salle said. "Well, I agree with Gimma, we really ought to give it a name if it's staying here with you."

"But what?" Arianwyn said. "I don't know any popular snail or worm names!"

"Why don't you just call it . . . Bob, then?" Salle suggested, and as she did, the moon hare sat up on its hind legs and twitched its nose at her. "Oh, I think Bob likes it!" She smiled. "Don't you, Bob?"

"We can't call it *Bob*!" Arianwyn said, a chuckle rising in her voice.

"Well, it'll be Bob until you come up with a better alternative," Salle said.

"Right, if you ladies have had enough of a rest, shall we continue?" Miss Delafield said, getting to her feet. Arianwyn and Gimma followed, while Salle sat stroking "Bob's" ears and watching. But after only a few moments chaos had descended as Gimma spun too sharply and at the wrong point and crashed headlong into Arianwyn for the twentieth time that evening. Salle collapsed in helpless giggles.

"Oh, for heaven's sake, Miss Alverston, you have all the coordination of an octopus on roller skates!" Miss Delafield growled. "I thought you'd be perfect at this!"

Arianwyn cast a quick look at Gimma. She was just as surprised that Gimma hadn't gotten this perfect straight off. Whatever was wrong with her? Gimma seemed to have no coordination at all and Miss Delafield had run out of patience quite quickly.

"Sorry. Sorry, Arianwyn," Gimma mumbled.

"It's really not that taxing, I'm sure. Left right, left right. Turn! Left right, left right. Pause and salute!" Miss Delafield chanted, wafting her glass to and fro as she called out her commands.

"As the new recruits, you'll be head of the procession next week and I can't have you turning the wrong way and messing up the whole line, dear!" She sighed and glared at Gimma. "Shall we try once more? And one, two, three . . ."

Arianwyn and Gimma set off in perfect unison. But after only three or four steps, just as they should have been turning, Gimma collided with Arianwyn again. This time they both collapsed into a pile of giggles on the floor of the Spellorium. Bob, intrigued by all the noise, hopped over and peered at them both. Then it gave Arianwyn a quick wash with its rough pink tongue and scampered off to rest in the corner again.

"Oh, for pity's sake!" Miss Delafield groaned and buried her head in her hands. "What am I going to do with you?" Then she gave in and joined the chorus of giggles.

There was a frantic tapping on the door. "Hello . . . hello? Miss Gribble, are you there?"

It was late; nobody generally came to the Spellorium after dark. Arianwyn immediately felt a knot of panic in her stomach. Brushing herself off, she dashed to the door and pulled open the locks and bolts. On the doorstep stood Mr. Turvy and the mayor. The mayor appeared to be dressed in his pajamas and dressing gown with a large coat thrown over them. He had taken time, however, to tie his purple sash over the top of it all.

"Ah, Miss Gribble, is my Gimma still here with you? It's awfully late, you know. Ah, good evening, Miss Delafield."

The mayor and Mr. Turvy wandered into the store. Mr. Turvy was pale and he fiddled anxiously with the repaired charm that hung around his neck, the golden locket catching the light.

"Well, then, Turvy," Mayor Belcher grumbled, "tell Miss Gribble what you wanted to say. Some of us were just about to go to bed."

"Hmmm, yes," Mr. Turvy muttered quietly. He took a few careful steps closer to Arianwyn and whispered loudly, "There is something in the wood!"

Arianwyn, puzzled, looked at the mayor, then at Miss Delafield and back to Mr. Turvy. Was it some sort of test or joke?

"There are lots of spirit creatures in the wood, Mr. Turvy. Have you seen one?"

Mr. Turvy sighed and jangled the charm more furiously. "No, no, no . . . something else. Something *different*."

"Yes, of course," the mayor replied, patting Mr. Turvy reassuringly on the shoulder. Then in hushed whispers he said, "I think he's gotten himself confused. Probably just saw a badger or some such thing and gave himself a fright. But he insisted on coming along to see you." Mayor Belcher placed a comforting arm around Mr. Turvy and tried to lead him away.

"I think he may be a little . . ." Mayor Belcher pointed at his own head and rolled his eyes slightly. "All alone and no one to keep you company, Mr. Turvy. You should come into town more often and join one of the clubs or societies."

But Mr. Turvy, with unexpected strength and speed, shrugged off the mayor's arm and dashed back to Arianwyn, gathering her hands in his own. "There is something terrible and dark in the wood!" he whispered, his eyes darting to and fro. "Something angry and dangerous—there are shadows singing!"

"What do you mean?" Arianwyn asked. "There have always been spirits in the Great Wood." But something worried at the back of her mind and fear tickled at the back of her neck.

"Not like this." His voice wobbled; he was truly terrified. "Something huge and dark. Twisted, it was, and moved fast. Like water!"

Arianwyn felt a surge of cold; the knot of anxiety tightened. She resisted the urge to glance at Gimma and looked to Miss Delafield instead. "Should we go and look?" she asked, hoping beyond all hope that Miss Delafield would say no.

"I don't think there is any need for that at this point, certainly not this late." She stood up, hands planted firm on her hips. "It might be best to let everyone know not to go too deep into the Great Wood for now, until we have had a chance to investigate further. Can you arrange that, Mayor Belcher?"

"I'll ensure notices go up tomorrow." He busied himself scribbling frantically into his little black notebook.

"We'll carry out some further investigations after the Flaxsham Parade. Speaking of which, we need to get back to our preparations, if you don't mind?"

"Oh, of course not. I'll let you ladies get back to your work. See you later, Gimma, sweetie!" Mayor Belcher waved as he left the store, Mr. Turvy following closely behind. He cast several anxious glances back at Arianwyn.

"Girls, I'm just going to get something from the car!" Miss Delafield called, and disappeared out into Kettle Lane behind the mayor and Mr. Turvy.

Arianwyn quickly took hold of Gimma's arm and pulled her close. "Do you think that's from the rift?" Her heart raced suddenly.

"What?" Gimma shrugged her away. "Don't be silly, Wyn. It was nothing."

"What?" Arianwyn gasped.

"It was a tiny little rift, barely anything there at all."

"But—"

"But what?" Gimma hissed. She glanced over her shoulder to check Miss Delafield was still distracted outside.

"I think something came through, Gimma. Through the rift, from the void."

"Like what?" Gimma sounded genuinely shocked at the suggestion.

Arianwyn couldn't quite believe her ears—was Gimma so blind or dumb? "Like a dark spirit! I thought I saw something. Something just like Mr. Turvy described."

Gimma grabbed Arianwyn's arm a little too roughly. "You didn't see anything, okay? I think you're just confused, that's all." Her fingers squeezed a little tighter.

Arianwyn winced. She stared at Gimma; her eyes were steely and shone brilliantly.

"Everything all right in here, girls?" Miss Delafield called as she came back through the door.

"Fine!" Gimma called, her voice all light and cheerfulness again.

Arianwyn glanced down at the angry red mark on her arm, already blossoming into a yellow bruise.

Arianwyn couldn't sleep that night. Mr. Turvy's words rang in her ears and Gimma's suddenly odd behavior worried at her as she turned this way and that. The knot in her stomach grew tighter and tighter. When she did doze she dreamed of dark shapes stirring in the trees, tall and monstrous, faceless creatures that watched and waited. And always there was her glyph, terrifying and cold.

As soon as it grew light she left the store and ran to the Blue Ox. She was grateful to see Aunt Grace by the front door as she arrived, taking a basket of bread from the baker's boy. "Arianwyn!" she called brightly. "Everything okay?"

"Could I use the phone, please?" Arianwyn said.

"Of course, love. Help yourself."

She hopped across the freshly mopped floors, glistening and slick, to the little corridor between the bar and the kitchen. She picked up the receiver and dialed the number of the bookstore.

"Hello!" Her grandmother's voice was expectant, urgent.

"Grandmother!" Arianwyn said, and suddenly she was crying, the sound of her grandmother's voice making her feel homesick and lonely, which she hadn't felt in months and months.

"Arianwyn?"

"Yes!" Her voice cracked.

"What's the matter?" Grandmother said. "It's so early!"

"I . . ." Could she tell her grandmother about the rift and Gimma? She couldn't be sure that whatever Mr. Turvy had seen was truly anything to do with Gimma's rift. She was suddenly uncertain.

"I was just missing you, that's all."

"Really?" Grandmother asked. She was clearly not convinced. "What is it?"

"Nothing, just a local saw something odd in the wood and I think I scared myself. I'm fine. Really fine." She swallowed, her voice catching again.

"What sort of thing?" Grandmother's voice was urgent, alert.

"Honestly, it's nothing. Just some crazy old chap from town."

The line went suddenly quiet. Arianwyn could only hear her grandmother's breathing. Then Grandmother was talking hurriedly, urgently: "Stay away from the wood, Arianwyn. Promise me. Until it's checked out."

"Of course," Arianwyn answered.

There was a long moment's silence. The telephone line crackled. "Grandmother?" Arianwyn asked. "Are you still there?"

"Yes, yes, I am. Do you want me to come? You only have to say . . ." Her voice sounded distracted and far away, as though she wasn't fully paying attention.

"You sound busy. I'd better let you go," Arianwyn said. She could feel her throat tighten and tears threaten. Her vision blurred for a second.

"I love you!" Grandmother's voice was bright and cheery but it masked something else, something worrying, threatening.

"I love you too. Bye!" Arianwyn said quickly, and before she put the receiver down she heard the click as Grandmother hung up at the other end.

"Everything all right, Wyn?" It was Salle, standing at the end of the corridor by the kitchen door.

"Yes, fine!" Arianwyn lied.

Salle stared at her. "Are you going to go and look for the creature Mr. Turvy saw in the wood? Can I come?"

Arianwyn, in no mood to start a conversation about it and feeling bruised and muddled from the conversation with Grandmother, snapped before she had time to think. "Oh, just leave it alone, Salle, will you. It's nothing. Just some confused old man!"

Salle took a step forward, she opened her mouth to say something, but Arianwyn didn't want to draw her into this mess. "I have to go," Arianwyn mumbled, and turned and marched as quickly as she could from the Blue Ox. She ignored Aunt Grace on her way through the bar, and Uncle Mat, who was busy washing the windows. She walked as quickly as she could across the square, down Kettle Lane and back to the store.

She felt quite alone.

THE APPRENTICE WITCH'S HANDBOOK

✦ ✦ ✦

As with all magic, charms will degenerate over time; in most cases this can simply be a weakening of the magic and the potency of the charm. In rare cases, though, the charm can start to reverse its magic, turning dark and causing all manner of related problems. Charms should be checked regularly to ensure this does not occur.

CHAPTER THIRTY-ONE

A PARADE OF WITCHES

A s Arianwyn, Gimma, and Salle emerged onto Flaxsham market square on the day of the parade, they were nearly swallowed up by the huge crowd of people.

"Where is it you need to meet Miss Delafield?" Salle called over the noise.

Gimma ignored her. "Where are we meeting Miss Delafield, Wyn?" she asked, as though Salle hadn't just spoken. Salle pulled a face behind Gimma's back.

Arianwyn was a little frustrated. Gimma seemed unable—or unwilling—to get along with Salle.

"Near the courthouse. Do you know where that is, Salle?" Arianwyn asked.

Salle glared at Gimma and then said, "Yes, it's just over there!" She pointed to a grand-looking building, all warm golden-colored stone with high windows. Its balcony was draped in swags of cloth in the colors of the flags of Hylund and the Four Kingdoms.

They were shoved and jostled as witches, cadets, police officers, and row upon row of schoolchildren filed past. There seemed to be no order to anything at all.

Gimma squealed at the spectacle. "Amazing!"

"GIRLS!" A loud voice boomed above the bustling noise of the market square.

Spinning around, Arianwyn scanned the nearby faces.

"Girls! Over here!"

A flash of bright red hair caught Arianwyn's eye. Miss Delafield towered over everyone around her; she was waving frantically at them. "Come on, come on!"

Squeezing and weaving in and out of the mass of people, Arianwyn, Gimma, and Salle made their way toward Miss Delafield. They emerged into a space that had been partly roped off and was full of witches of all ages, shapes, and sizes—all navy and bright silver stars. Arianwyn glanced forlornly at her bronze moon brooch. There must have been about fifty witches altogether, with more arriving each second.

"Ah, there you are. Morning, Salle! Now, we're at the head of the procession today!" Miss Delafield puffed up with pride. "And there is a film crew here from Kingsport, apparently, for the Central News Program!" Her cheeks flushed a color almost as fiery as her hair.

"Oh my goodness!" Gimma shrieked again and jumped on the spot, clapping her hands together. A few older witches nearby cast her sideways glances.

"I need to go and check my hair!" Gimma said urgently. "Do you know if there's a bathroom somewhere nearby?" She rifled through her little beaded purse, pulling out a small comb and mirror. Arianwyn was amazed she managed to cram so much unessential stuff in there.

"What?" Arianwyn asked. "Are you crazy? The parade is about to start any second. You can't just go off now."

Gimma was paying no attention at all. "Come with me, come on!"

"Five minutes, everybody!" Miss Delafield boomed through her megaphone.

"I'll be right back!" And just like that Gimma was swallowed up into the crowd of witches.

"Oh, boil it!" Arianwyn hissed.

"I have to go," Salle said reluctantly. "I'll be late for my audition and it was good of the director to see me again." She looked pale and kept checking her coat buttons every few seconds.

"You'll be great, I'm sure!" Arianwyn replied. She was so excited for Salle. She pulled her into a tight hug. "Good luck!" she said.

Salle gulped and smiled. "Thanks, Wyn! I'll meet you back here at one!" She turned to go.

"Salle. Wait!" Arianwyn shouted, suddenly remembering the object in the bottom of her pocket.

"Here, take this, for luck!" She pressed a small charm into Salle's cool, shaking hand.

"Oh, Wyn! For me?" Salle stared down at the small glass orb that held tiny pale green thyme leaves, a dark pala seed, and a small polished lump of bloodred veren stone.

"It's a really old charm for luck; I found it in the handbook."

"Oh, thank you!" Salle gave her a quick hug and disappeared into the crowd.

Arianwyn sighed contentedly and turned back to the crowd of waiting witches. Miss Delafield was entirely distracted organizing everyone. "No, no, NO!" Miss Delafield wailed, "I've already told you, Mrs. Barnaby—stand to the left of Elder Moorcroft, please!" Two witches shuffled places.

"Excuse me, aren't you Arianwyn Gribble?" a quiet voice asked.

Arianwyn turned. A girl about her age was smiling at her. She was neat and well turned out in her uniform. Her star was bright against the dark material of her coat. She seemed very familiar.

"Do I know you?" Arianwyn asked

The girl blushed a little. "I'm Polly Walden; we had the same evaluation date, back in Kingsport." The girl tossed her long dark hair across her shoulder and gave a small smile. "And I'm a friend . . . *was* a friend . . . of Gimma Alverston."

The penny dropped, with a bang!

She was one of Gimma's little gang. Arianwyn recoiled slightly, folding her arms across her chest. She stared at the girl.

"I saw you with Gimma just now. I didn't know you two were—"

"Friends?" Arianwyn asked, her voice sharp. Was it such a surprise that the two of them could have become friends?

The girl nodded and blushed again. "Sorry, I thought Gimma had been stationed in Kingsport. She was always going on about how she had a post to go to and blah blah blah." She waved her hands theatrically above her head.

"No," Arianwyn said simply. "She's visiting Lull, which is where I'm stationed."

"Well, good luck with that." The girl grinned. "Just a word to the wise: Don't let her do any magic if you know what's good for you. She's hopeless."

"What?" Arianwyn asked, stepping closer, assuming she had misunderstood.

Polly grabbed her hand and hissed loudly into Arianwyn's ear, "Gimma is utterly useless when it comes to spells."

"But—" Arianwyn tried to respond.

"She only passed her evaluation because of who her parents are and because we all helped her through instruction and tests. She can barely summon a basic spell orb!"

Arianwyn suddenly pictured Gimma running from the house after the bogglin, brandishing the broom. The day in the wood with the banishing glyph and her tiny spell orbs with their weak light.

"I'd better go," Polly said, drawing away from Arianwyn and glancing over her shoulder. "But I thought you should know."

Twisting, Arianwyn could see Gimma weaving in and out of the waiting witches. She turned back to Polly, to ask more, but the girl had already gone.

"Everything okay, Wyn?" Gimma asked as she reached her. She beamed as usual.

Arianwyn stared into her face. She didn't know what she felt. Anger? Hurt? Had it all been another of Gimma's cruel tricks, one in the long line of many? Had she been using Arianwyn? Masking her own failings behind somebody a little more competent and hoping nobody would notice? How had she been so shortsighted?

"What's the matter?" Gimma asked. "Who was it you were talking to?"

Arianwyn looked her squarely in the eyes. "It was Polly Walden." She let the words hang in the air for a few seconds and watched as Gimma's perfect smile slipped slowly from her face.

"What did she have to say?" Gimma's voice was bright but forced. "I haven't seen Polly in months."

"I think you already know," Arianwyn said sadly.

The small battalion of witches shifted, anxious to move out across the market square. The band struck up a cheerful tune. Gimma stared at Arianwyn and her mouth opened as if she was about to respond, but just at that moment Miss Delafield's voice echoed out across the square. "Right, ladies, let's not make a colossal hash of this, shall we? On my mark, please, Miss Gribble, Miss Alverston. One. Two. And go!"

The long line of witches started to move slowly out across the market square. All around the edge people watched, cheered, and waved small bright flags this way and that. For a few moments they marched on in silence. Arianwyn stared straight ahead, watching the smiling faces of the crowd and the bright bunting fluttering in the breeze.

"Arianwyn," Gimma hissed loudly, trying to get her attention. Arianwyn ignored her and picked up the pace.

"Why are you being like this?" Gimma demanded. She stumbled, missing a turn and colliding with one of the witches behind her. She scrambled to catch up with Arianwyn again.

Arianwyn kept her eyes focused on Miss Delafield and kept marching. "You tricked me! You never said anything about not being able to use magic properly. Polly told me," she whispered angrily at Gimma.

"And you believed her?" Gimma spat. "Thanks a lot!"

"Is it a lie?" Arianwyn paused for just a second, causing the entire line to shudder to a halt. Elder Moorcroft, who was right behind her, stood on her heel. "Oh, sorry!" she muttered.

Miss Delafield cast a stern glance over her shoulder. Arianwyn lurched forward quickly, dragging Gimma along with her.

"I *can* cast spells. I'm not stupid, Arianwyn!" Gimma blurted suddenly in a nervous hurry.

"You need to tell someone. You ought to tell Miss Delafield."

"Why? So they can chalk this up as another failure? I don't think so!" Gimma looked away into the crowd of happy people. They all called and cheered as the witches marched past. The band played on, one tune sliding into the next.

"Gimma, I want to help. I do understand what it's like," Arianwyn said after a while.

"You have no idea!" Gimma hissed. "Not one! Perfect Arianwyn, who can never do anything wrong!"

Arianwyn laughed out loud. "Don't be ridiculous; I'm always getting things wrong, Gimma. You know I do!" She prodded at her coat and the moon brooch.

"But it's different for you because it always seems to work out in the end, doesn't it?" That was when Gimma's voice broke and Arianwyn saw fat tears welling around her eyes. Gimma brushed at them angrily.

They had turned again and were heading now for the far corner of the market square.

"Not always, no," Arianwyn replied. She reached out to take Gimma's hand again. "I do understand. But if this is why you lost your post in Kingsport—"

"Girls! What on earth is going on back there?" Miss Delafield suddenly snapped her head around and glared at them both. Even so, she kept in step with the band as they marched past the courthouse. There was a loud cheer from a group of schoolchildren. "Pay attention, for pity's sake!"

They marched on for a few more yards without speaking. Until Gimma paused and turned to Arianwyn. "I did *not* lose my post in Kingsport!" Gimma said through gritted teeth. "I'm taking a break. That's all!" Tears started to trickle down her cheeks. She pulled out a handkerchief and turned away.

The line collapsed around them once more. Miss Delafield turned and gave a loud moan and threw her hands up in despair.

Arianwyn reached out to Gimma, but she turned on her heel and ran off, sobbing.

Arianwyn hesitated for a moment. Should she just let her go? She watched as Gimma crashed headlong into another witch.

"Watch where you're going!"

Arianwyn sighed. She couldn't let her go off on her own, upset. "Gimma!" she called, and started to follow her. But a few more steps and Gimma quickly disappeared in the confusion of parading witches.

She searched down alleyways and in courtyards, but it was as though Gimma had never existed. There was no sign of her anywhere.

Glancing at her watch, Arianwyn saw it was nearly one o'clock. She'd been searching for more than an hour already.

She retraced her steps, peering down more narrow streets and into shop doorways. There were so many uniformed witches—how would she ever spot Gimma?

When she heard the clock over the courthouse sound out two o'clock Arianwyn realized she had forgotten all about Salle. Her heart sank. She was an hour late! She dashed back to the market square, running through her excuses as she went, and just at the corner near Hetherington's department store she saw a flash of red coat as Salle disappeared inside.

Arianwyn followed, calling as she slipped in through the revolving doors.

"Salle, wait! Salle, I'm sorry I forgot to meet you. I was looking for Gimma!"

Arianwyn reached out and caught Salle's arm. Her friend spun around, her eyes blazing, her face red.

"What's the matter? What's happened?" Arianwyn asked.

"What do you care?" Salle spat, turning down an aisle beside a display of bright scarves.

Arianwyn paused, as though she'd been struck. "Salle, please. I'm sorry, Gimma ran off—"

"Oh, and of course *Gimma* is your new best friend, isn't she? So you just forgot all about me!"

This time Salle's blow landed heavily. It seemed to knock all the wind out of Arianwyn. All she could do was reach out a tentative hand to her friend, but Salle turned sharply and disappeared down another aisle. It was busier and she weaved quickly in and out of the shoppers.

"Salle!" Arianwyn called, bumping and pushing to reach her friend.

She found Salle sitting on a small stool, dabbing her face with a handkerchief.

"I really am sorry. Look, tell me what happened, please?" Arianwyn asked.

Salle glared at her. "The audition went terribly. And all I wanted was to see you so we could talk about it and you'd make me feel all right. But you weren't there."

"Gimma—" Arianwyn tried to explain.

"Oh, don't bother!" Salle said, getting to her feet. "We need to be back at the bus or Mr. Thorn will go crazy."

"Let's go, then," Arianwyn said, reaching for her hand.

"I'll go on my own, thanks. Don't bother trying to walk with me, Wyn. I'd rather be on my own!"

The words stung.

Salle stomped away. Arianwyn watched her move through the shoppers and then after a few moments she made her own way out of Hetherington's and back to the street where Mr. Thorn had dropped them off that morning.

As she turned the corner she saw Salle waiting next to the bus, her arms folded tightly across her chest. She was relieved to see that Gimma was already on the bus, stony-faced and staring into space as Mr. Thorn tried fruitlessly to talk to her.

Salle and Arianwyn climbed onto the bus and each took a seat on opposite sides in total silence.

CHAPTER THIRTY-TWO

UNEXPECTED ARRIVALS

Arianwyn stood in a small line outside the post office a few days later, waiting for it to open. The first gentle days of summer had arrived. The sky above was bright blue, there was a warm breeze, and everyone seemed to be in a happy mood.

Except for Arianwyn.

She flicked through the letters in her hand: an order to the Civil Witchcraft Authority, a letter to her father, and one for her grandmother, telling her about the parade. She thought Grandmother might find it amusing. She hadn't mentioned the falling-out with Salle. They had not seen each other since the bus ride home and Arianwyn missed her friend.

The doors to the post office were pulled open and Mrs. Attinger, the postmistress, called an enthusiastic "Good morning!"

Arianwyn reached into her bag for her wallet, ready to pay for her stamps. But her wallet wasn't there. "Oh, jinxing-jiggery!" she muttered, and turned quickly, planning to dash back to the Spellorium. As Arianwyn turned, still rootling through her bag, she walked straight into Salle.

"Ouch, look where you're—Oh, it's you!" Salle said icily.

They stood facing each other in silence for a few moments, both blushing. Then Salle looked away. Arianwyn felt hot and suddenly awkward, as though everyone passing in the street was watching them.

"I'm . . . sorry about the other day, Salle. Gimma was so upset and I felt bad. I had to go and look for her."

"I really don't care, *actually*!" Salle said, and then she turned on her heel and headed away from the post office.

"Salle, wait!" Arianwyn scurried after her, calling as she went. "Salle, please let me explain." Arianwyn's fingers grasped the edge of Salle's cardigan.

"Let go!"

"Not until you listen! You have to let me explain."

"So you can feel better about forgetting to meet me?" Salle folded her arms across her chest. "I thought you were my friend, Wyn. But as soon as Gimma clicks her fingers you come running."

"No I don't!" Arianwyn replied, but she worried for a second that maybe she had just lately, ever since the rift . . . "Oh, all right, Salle. Maybe I did. But you see, I bumped into someone Gimma and I both knew from Kingsport and she told me something about Gimma." Arianwyn lowered her voice. "Something that worried me . . ."

Salle stepped closer. "What?" she asked, curiosity getting the better of her.

Salle and Arianwyn moved farther away from the bustle of the post office and shops. In a hushed voice Arianwyn told Salle what Polly Walden had said and her own worries about Gimma's abilities.

"I haven't seen Gimma since," Arianwyn said as she finished the story.

"Oh my goodness. You have to tell somebody," Salle said quickly. "You have to tell Miss Delafield!"

Arianwyn shook her head. "I don't know. Miss Delafield's been so busy checking for whatever it was Mr. Turvy thought he saw in the wood."

"Did she find anything?"

"Just a few more patches of hex, but no dark spirits, thankfully." The thought of the rift spell made her feel suddenly cold and agitated.

"Well, you could always just tell . . . the mayor!" Salle said mischievously.

"I don't think I would feel comfortable doing that, Salle." Arianwyn laughed, then added with more seriousness, "Gimma trusts me."

"Well, I think she'd turn you in if *you* were keeping a secret," Salle huffed.

"What does that mean? What secret?" Arianwyn felt her cheeks burn. "I don't have a secret!" she said quickly.

"I know!" Salle said, laughing a little. "And I'm sorry about the other day as well. I was upset about the audition, that's all. I didn't mean to take it out on you, Wyn!"

They hugged briefly, the horribleness thankfully behind them at last.

There was a loud roar of an automobile engine and the shrill call of a horn as Beryl, the town bus, surged around the bend in the road. Arianwyn and Salle stepped quickly out of her path and waved to Mr. Thorn, who peered over the top of the steering wheel. He raised a hand in brief greeting and tooted the horn again.

The bus looked busy: probably tourists from Flaxsham come for a glimpse of the Great Wood, Arianwyn thought. A familiar-looking young man waved enthusiastically at her and was trying to complete some sort of complicated sign language through the glass.

It looked decidedly like . . . but surely couldn't possible be . . . Colin!

"Colin!" Arianwyn said excitedly, and waved. He beamed from inside the bus and gave her a thumbs-up.

"Who's that?" Salle asked. Arianwyn grabbed her arm and set off down the street after the bus, which was heading for the town square.

"Come on, Salle!" Arianwyn dragged her friend along the sidewalk. They dodged shoppers and emerged into the town square as Beryl was unloading her passengers. People milled about, collecting luggage and meeting friends and families in the bright sunlight. There was a small crowd of people clustered around the bus.

Colin was surrounded by bags, cases, and trunks. He twisted and stretched, obviously grateful not to be experiencing Beryl's unique bouncing anymore.

"Colin!" Arianwyn called, darting across the town square.

"Miss Gribble!" The boy waved and broke into a broad grin.

Arianwyn sidestepped a few other passengers, and their luggage, and Colin reached out for her hand and shook it warmly. Salle followed, staying back just a little.

"Such a pleasure to see you again." He smiled.

"And you too." Arianwyn grinned. "But what on earth are you doing here?"

"Oh, um." His face clouded a little. "Didn't you get the telegram?"

Arianwyn shook her head.

"Well, you see, I'm here for your reevaluation!"

Arianwyn felt as though she had been submerged in ice water. She'd sort of forgotten about the reevaluation, hoping perhaps she could just carry on like this forever and not have to do the test ever again.

"Miss Delafield sent a special request through a few months ago, but we've been so busy this was the first chance we had to send anyone."

"Not Miss Newam?" Arianwyn asked, scrunching her face up.

Colin laughed and then stood a little straighter, adjusting his jacket. "No, it's me. I'll be doing the evaluation. I've qualified now!" he said delightedly.

"Oh, that's wonderful, Colin!" Arianwyn said, and without thinking she leaned forward and hugged him.

This nearly made up for the prospect of the evaluation, although she was still far from thrilled.

"Ahem." Salle coughed rather loudly and theatrically behind them.

They pulled apart quickly, both blushing.

Colin glanced at Salle, who had a gigantic grin on her face.

"Oh, I'm sorry," Arianwyn said. "This is my friend Salle Bowen. Her aunt and uncle run the Blue Ox. You must be staying there." Arianwyn gestured toward the inn.

Salle shook Colin's hand and winked at Arianwyn. "You don't travel light, do you? Would you like a hand with all your things, Colin?"

"Oh, this isn't all mine. There's the equipment for the evaluation." He indicated a large shiny wooden case with bright brass handles. "But most of the luggage is your grandmother's!"

"What?" Arianwyn gasped.

As if by some strange magic, just at that moment the crowd around Beryl parted and Arianwyn could see across to the doorway of the Blue Ox. There, chatting happily to Aunt Grace and Mayor Belcher, was her grandmother.

"Your grandmother requested to be escorted to Lull on official business for the Council of Elders, so I was given the task," Colin burbled on.

Tall, with silver hair flowing over one shoulder, Grandmother broke into a wide beaming grin as she saw Arianwyn.

"Oh wow, Wyn. Your grandmother's beautiful!" Salle whispered.

Arianwyn dashed across the square and straight into her grandmother's arms. "I can't believe it. What are you doing here?"

"Well, I thought it was about time I visited my granddaughter. Let me get a look at you." They stepped away from each other briefly, still holding hands tightly. Grandmother's appraising gaze swept up and down. "I knew the CWA was sending someone for . . ." She paused, and the silence that rushed in was awkward.

"The reevaluation?" Arianwyn offered quietly.

"Yes," Grandmother replied carefully. "But I'll keep out of the way of all that, don't you worry. I was only tagging along." Her face broke into another smile, her eyes twinkling in the sunlight.

Arianwyn stared hard at her grandmother. Hadn't Colin just said she was here on official business for the CWA? Perhaps he had just misunderstood.

"How long will you be staying?" Salle asked brightly, breaking the silence.

"Well, the evaluation will be next Thursday morning, if that's okay," Colin said.

Today was Friday. Arianwyn spun quickly to stare at him. "So soon?" she asked, her voice breaking a little.

Colin nodded. "And then we have to be off to Kingsport again, is that right, Madam Stronelli?"

There were sounds of disappointment. "But you'll be staying for a few days more, surely?" Aunt Grace asked.

"Yes, I insist you stay on as my special guests!" Mayor Belcher interjected.

Grandmother seemed to consider for a moment. She looked at Arianwyn, her lips pursed in thought. "Yes, of course, we can stay until next weekend, perhaps. Don't worry, Colin: I'll deal with Miss Newam for you!"

"And let's arrange for the evaluation to take place in the town hall," Mayor Belcher added. "We can invite people along. It would be just like it is in Kingsport, all wonderfully grand and what have you!"

Arianwyn felt fear grasp her guts and twist. She couldn't face her reevaluation in front of Colin and Grandmother, let alone in front of the whole town! She felt certain something would go wrong again, that she'd fail, just like last time. She looked pleadingly at Grandmother.

"We had best check with Miss Delafield first, but that's a very kind offer, Mayor Belcher. Very kind indeed." Grandmother smiled warmly and the mayor dashed off, full of excitement.

"Please, Grandma. I'd really rather not . . ."

"Don't be silly, everything will be fine. I'm sure!"

Arianwyn fell silent, but her nervousness remained. She looked at Salle and then at Colin.

"Well, I'd better get all this luggage into the hotel." Colin smiled. "I hope I'll get a chance to see you again before the evaluation."

"Oh, Wyn practically lives in the Blue Ox. She's here all the time, aren't you, Wyn?" Salle winked theatrically at Arianwyn. "Here, let me give you a hand with those,

Colin." And they disappeared inside the inn, chatting away as they went.

"Can we go for a walk?" Grandmother asked. "I'd like to hear how you've been getting along."

Arianwyn gestured to the town square and they walked a little way from the Blue Ox and the curious stares of passersby.

"You look well!" Grandmother smiled. "Very well indeed. And I hear from Miss Delafield that you have been doing excellent work for her—"

Arianwyn couldn't hold it in a second longer. "Where have you been?" she said, her voice louder than she had expected.

"What?" Grandmother looked genuinely shocked.

"When I've called the store you've been either off on some trip or another or sounding distracted. I've had three postcards from you and that's it. No letters, no phone calls, no visits."

"Well, I'm here now . . ." She trailed off.

How could Arianwyn tell her it was all too late now? She'd already messed up everything!

"Look, I decided to take the chance to go on some trips and to do a little bit of research work for the CWA, that's all." Grandmother gazed out across the town square. "It really is lovely here."

"Grandma!" Arianwyn said desperately, anxious for answers.

"Come on now, let's not argue. You're still my Arianwyn, aren't you?"

Arianwyn wasn't sure. She looked at Grandmother carefully. So much had changed in the last few months—had Arianwyn changed most of all?

"I'm not the same as I was back in the winter, you know," she said softly, little more than a whisper.

"I think I can see that," Grandmother replied, "and I am so anxious to see how you get on with your evaluation test—not that it matters to me, of course—you know that. But I know Miss Delafield was quite insistent on getting your retest brought forward. Something to do with a moon hare?" Grandmother chuckled. "My little girl!"

Arianwyn stopped walking. She *wasn't* a little girl anymore. She was a witch. She had taken care of herself and of Lull for six months now—without any help from Grandmother—and things were different. She might've made mistakes, but she'd helped people too. Did her grandmother think she was just going to find the same little girl who left Kingsport? She felt her cheeks grow hot.

"I should be getting back to work," she said, rather formally, hoping it masked her anger.

Grandmother was obviously taken aback but she simply replied, "Of course, please don't let me keep you."

Arianwyn nodded.

"I hope I'll see you later? I can't wait to see the Spellorium," Grandmother added.

"Please come and inspect it whenever you wish," Arianwyn said, though she hadn't meant it to come out quite as shortly as it did.

"Well, yes. All in good time," Grandmother replied quietly.

Arianwyn turned and walked across the town square. She didn't glance back.

She had to get ready for her reevaluation.

At the end of her apprenticeship a witch will serve her community for approximately twenty years before being declared an elder witch. It is at this point that a witch is encouraged to take on the training of apprentices, therefore ensuring the continuation of skills. A quorum of fifteen elder witches serve as the Council of Elders, the governing body of the witches of Hylund. They are led by the high elder.

CHAPTER THIRTY-THREE

THE REEVALUATION

The week passed slowly and quietly. There seemed to be only a handful of jobs that took Arianwyn out of the Spellorium and she had lots of time to worry about her coming reevaluation. The mayor had become rather obsessed about it and was telling everyone—he was obviously delighted at the prospect of having a "proper" witch in Lull at last. Each time Arianwyn thought about it she felt hot and sick.

Grandmother had not spent as much time with her as she had thought: lunch one day and a couple of dinners at the Blue Ox. But she seemed to be either visiting Flaxsham with Miss Delafield or keeping to her room. "I've got lots of papers to read through," she explained when Arianwyn asked her.

There was so much Arianwyn wanted to tell her and so much she didn't feel she could.

Late one evening, two days before the reevaluation was due to take place, Arianwyn was startled when a small shower of stones rattled against the window of the apartment. Peering out over Kettle Lane, she saw two dark figures in the lane below. "Who is it?" she called.

"Ssssh!" Salle hissed back. "It's me and Colin, let us in quickly!"

"I was just about to go to bed!" Arianwyn complained.

"Just let us in, Wyn. Hurry up!" Salle replied.

She raced downstairs. Bob the moon hare was close behind her, alert, magic crackling around it. She pulled open the door.

Wrapped in black velvet cloaks with hoods pulled over their faces, Salle and Colin bundled into the store. Salle immediately—and a little theatrically, Arianwyn thought—pulled down the blinds on the window and flicked off all but one of the lights, leaving them in some sort of mysterious gloom.

"What on earth are you doing?" Arianwyn laughed, assuming it was some sort of game. But then she noticed that Colin was carrying the polished wooden case of the evaluation gauge. Bob, fascinated by a new person, raced around Colin's feet, making excited noises.

"Hello there!" Colin said, gazing at the creature.

"We've been plotting!" Salle exclaimed. "You don't want to face everyone for your evaluation so we're going to do it right now instead." She pulled the hood back away from her face and grinned.

"Won't we get in trouble, though? Does it count?" Arianwyn asked.

"Yes, now I'm qualified. They can't ignore the results, even if it's not done with an audience!" Colin said, placing the case on the counter and pulling off his cloak. "This wretched thing is strangling me!"

"Why *are* you wearing cloaks, anyway?" Arianwyn asked.

"So nobody would see us coming here, of course. We're incognito!" Salle spun, swishing her cloak dramatically. Colin rolled his eyes and laughed.

There was an urgent tap at the door and Gimma's voice called, "Arianwyn. Are you there?"

Everyone froze; Salle in mid-swirl looked as if she was about to fall over.

"I saw Colin and Salle coming in," Gimma said. "Let me in, come on!"

"What's she doing here?" Salle hissed, glaring at Colin.

"I guess your cloaks didn't quite work as well as you thought!" Arianwyn replied. There was no point trying to keep Gimma out now; if she'd seen the cloaked Salle and Colin, she wasn't going to let it rest.

Arianwyn pulled open the door. Gimma walked in and stared at them all, smiling. "What's going on?" she asked. Then her eyes fell on the evaluation gauge box and they sparkled.

"Ooooh," she cooed. "You're not actually going to do Wyn's evaluation in secret? Won't you get in trouble?"

"Don't you tell anyone about this!" Salle's voice was quiet but menacing. She stepped in front of Arianwyn.

"Oh, relax, Salle," Gimma replied. "Wyn and I keep each other's secrets *all* the time, don't we, Wyn?"

Arianwyn felt her cheeks burn. She glanced away.

"So, shall we give it a try?" Colin said in a singsong

voice. He glanced at the evaluation gauge and back at Arianwyn.

She thought of crowds of people watching her fail for the second time. She looked quickly at Gimma, then at Salle. She shuddered. "Okay. Let's do it!"

Colin carefully lifted the gauge onto the counter and removed the cover. He uncoiled the power cable and plugged it into the nearest wall socket.

Arianwyn could feel herself start to shake. She sank down in a chair and watched Colin unravel the other cream-colored wire that attached to the probe, with its familiar shiny sphere at the end. He carefully checked the length of the wire for signs of damage. Then he unfolded the poster that displayed the cardinal glyphs:

BRIÅ

ALUNA

ERTE

ÅRDRA

"All ready?" Colin asked haltingly. His shaking fingers hovered over the tiny metal switch.

Arianwyn nodded.

Colin stretched his arms toward Arianwyn, the probe trembling slightly.

"Remember, focus!" he said gently.

She closed her eyes briefly. There was a large seam of magic running right past the window. Her skin prickled.

"Please let this be all right," she whispered to herself.

Her heart quickened and she felt a twinge of panic as the cold metal sphere connected with her skin.

This is a bad idea; it's not going to work. Her mind raced. Her eyes flew open in fear.

"Focus!" Colin whispered. "Stay calm, everything's all right."

She took several steadying breaths. The room felt suddenly too small and airless. She wanted to run away.

There was the first flicker of power, passing quickly through her.

She focused on the poster. The glyphs seemed to swim and merge, as she had almost expected them to. She closed her eyes and immediately she saw the unknown glyph. Her mind began to reach toward it and she felt the flow of energy change. She heard the fizz of the single light and knew that it was flickering just as they had at the Civil Witchcraft Authority offices.

"Arianwyn!" Salle's voice was cautious, warning.

The unknown glyph hung there, bright and real and tempting.

She felt Bob nudge against her leg, a low threatening growl rumbling in its throat.

No, don't reach for the glyph, she told herself.

She stared hard at the poster again, but she could still feel the icy grip of the unknown glyph, as though it lurked just behind her eyes.

Eventually, after what felt like forever, Colin shifted in his seat. "I've got a reading!" he said quietly.

Arianwyn's eyes flashed open.

She looked at the gauge right away. There was no smoke rising from it this time. Colin sat studying the thin strip of paper churning from it, his brows knitted in concentration. Salle hovered close by, fidgety and distracted. The moon hare was curled at Arianwyn's feet. Gimma watched coolly from a distance.

The only sound was the ticking of the clock and the whir of the gauge.

"Well?" Salle and Gimma asked simultaneously.

"Just give me a minute." Colin waved his hand, dismissing them. He scanned the strip of paper again.

Arianwyn took a deep steadying breath. She was thirsty, her head foggy as if she had a cold, and her vision swam a little. She shouldn't have reached for that glyph.

Colin got to his feet very slowly. He gazed at Arianwyn, his face white.

"What? What is it?" Arianwyn muttered.

"The reading is . . . strange. I've never seen one like this."

"I've failed again?" Arianwyn said, sinking a little in her seat.

"No, no, it's not that. But I can't figure this out. I need to go and look at some notes. I might have to check with someone at the CWA in the morning."

Arianwyn still couldn't quite understand it all. Everything was blurry and it sounded as though everyone was underwater.

"Are you sure you're okay?" Colin asked. "You look a bit pale—perhaps you should go and lie down?" The air crackled around Arianwyn's fingers. She saw tiny sparks.

Not again, she thought.

"Want me to help you up?" Salle asked. She reached out to help Arianwyn from her seat. "Ouch! You gave me an electric shock!" The girls stared at each other for a long moment, the memory of the last time flooding them both.

"Sorry!" Arianwyn said. "I'm pretty tired . . . I think I'd just like to go to bed . . ."

"Yes, come on, we'd better get away before anyone notices we've gone out." Colin smiled at Arianwyn, but she didn't have the energy now to smile back. She could still feel the magic fizzing around her. She was thankful nothing worse had happened than the electric shock she had given Salle. Gimma hadn't moved from where she had stood and watched everything happen, as though she was watching a play. Was she worried or scared by what she had seen? Arianwyn had no idea. Then she casually tossed her golden hair over her shoulder and looked away, heading for the door.

When Colin, Salle, and Gimma had left, Arianwyn locked the door and climbed back upstairs. She sat on the edge of the bed and stared at the wall.

It felt as if everything had come to a head at last. She felt lost, more lost than ever.

She was lying to herself if she thought she knew what was going on. She had made a colossal mistake—or several!—and she had no idea how she could unravel it all. The unknown glyph, the rift in the wood, and the strange creature . . . even if Miss Delafield hadn't found anything, Arianwyn was certain something was out there.

It was all her fault. And now she'd probably failed another evaluation! She was sure of it, no matter what Colin had said. She had no hope of being able to sort everything out, however hard she tried.

CHAPTER THIRTY-FOUR

CONFESSION

Arianwyn looked into the mirror. There were dark shadows beneath her eyes—she had barely slept all night, her mind whirring over and over. The reevaluation had been the final straw.

She splashed cold water on her face and peered into the mirror again. She knew what she was going to do. She had to go and see Mayor Belcher and tell him everything. About the rift that she and Gimma had failed to close and the creature that was probably roaming the Great Wood somewhere. About the illegal evaluation she had willingly taken part in last night. And about the unknown glyph she kept seeing and the trouble it had brought her, time and time again.

And then she would resign.

The usual people waved and called greetings as Arianwyn walked along Kettle Lane and across the town square, which was being dressed in festival bunting and flags. Arianwyn ignored it all as she passed by.

"Morning, Miss Gribble!"

"Hello, miss!"

"Hi, Arianwyn."

She smiled faintly at them all but kept on her course toward the town hall. Miss Prynce was at her desk, the large black receiver of the telephone wedged against her neck.

"Oh, I know! And did you notice that hat she was wearing? What a sight! Oh, Miss Gribble, you're early. The mayor is busy right now. Miss Gribble? Did you hear me?"

Ignoring Miss Prynce's calls, Arianwyn climbed the stairs up to the mayor's parlor two at a time. She could hear Miss Prynce's shoes click-clacking down the hall, hot on her trail.

The mayor's parlor door stood ajar and, without knocking, Arianwyn pushed the door wide and strode in.

"Miss Gribble, what on earth?" Mayor Belcher jumped from his seat, shuffling a pile of papers across his desk, unsuccessfully hiding a plate of cakes. He blushed and wiped stray crumbs from his little beard.

At that moment Miss Prynce trotted through the door, theatrically out of breath, a hand held to her chest. "Mayor Belcher," she puffed. "I am so, *so* sorry. I informed Miss Gribble you were not to be disturbed but she just barged right past me. I couldn't stop her!"

Mayor Belcher studied Arianwyn carefully and a flicker of concern flashed across his eyes. "It's quite all right, Miss Prynce. I am sure Miss Gribble would not have dreamed of rudely bursting into my parlor, uninvited, without good and proper reason!" His stare was questioning.

"But Mayor Belcher, this is quite against protocol!" Miss Prynce's usually serene and organized manner was giving way and her face glowed with two large angry red splotches.

The mayor raised a hand. "Yes, that will be all Miss Prynce, thank you!"

"But—"

"*Thank you*, Miss Prynce!"

Arianwyn heard the door click shut and the secretary's slow retreating click-clack footsteps.

"Now then, Miss Gribble, how might I be of service?"

The calm and certainty that Arianwyn had been feeling up till now was suddenly gone. Her legs trembled and her throat was dry; her tongue felt twice its usual size.

The mayor waited. Still standing, he folded his hands across his velvet-clad belly. "Well?"

"Mayor Belcher, I've come to ask you. No, to tell you, actually . . ."

"Yes?" Mayor Belcher peered at Arianwyn.

"You see, the thing is, I've been doing an awful lot of thinking and I think—no, I *know* it would be best if I—"

"MAYOR BELCHER! WHERE IS THE MAYOR?"

The scream startled Arianwyn so much that she lurched forward in fright and grasped the mayor's desk.

Out in the town square came the sounds of a commotion. Voices full of fear and anger filled Arianwyn's ears. And beneath these angry shouts was the gentler sound of a woman sobbing.

"Good heavens, whatever can be happening now?" The

mayor moved quickly to the long glass doors that opened onto the small balcony that overlooked the town square.

"There he is!" somebody called as the mayor came into view.

Something made Arianwyn edge a little nearer to the doors so she could hear, though she couldn't see past the mayor into the square below.

"What seems to be the matter?" the mayor called.

"It's my boy, Your Worship. He's been hurt!" The woman's voice was strained and terrified and fractured with sobs.

"Hurt how?" The mayor leaned farther over the edge of the balcony.

"He was attacked!" came another voice, louder, angrier.

"Attacked by whom?" the mayor called.

"Not a 'whom,' Worship. A what!"

Arianwyn felt a nervous chill fall upon her and she stepped through the doors onto the balcony to stand beside the mayor. Below stood a small crowd of children and adults. Two women carried a still and pale figure in their midst. The boy's shirt was in tatters and across his chest was a huge black mark. The bitter tang of dark magic wafted on the air. There was something familiar about the boy. Arianwyn peered closer.

"He was attacked near the Great Wood, by one of them demon creatures—a terrible, black thing it were, like a shadow come to life." The woman who spoke knotted her grubby apron between her fists. Arianwyn locked eyes

with her and realized with a sickening lurch of her heart
that it was Mrs. Myddleton and the boy was her son, Cyril.

Arianwyn went cold. She thought back to Mr. Turvy's
warning in the store: "There are shadows singing." Her
blood turned to ice. She gripped the edge of the balcony
and stared out across the rooftops of Lull, unable to look
down into the square again.

CHAPTER THIRTY-FIVE

BLACK AS A HOLE AT MIDNIGHT

What had she done? What had *Gimma* done? *Why* hadn't they stayed and closed the rift for certain?

Arianwyn staggered back, away from the balcony, her heart pounding deep in her chest. She felt sick.

She should tell the mayor right now about the rift. But, just as she was about to, the sounds of the crowd echoed up the staircase, punctuated with gasps and cries from Miss Prynce. Mayor Belcher followed Arianwyn back into the parlor and they stood staring at each other, Arianwyn biting her lip and the mayor fiddling with his tie. He had gone pale as well.

Suddenly the study was full of people, shouting, crying. Arianwyn kept well back until she saw Cyril being laid slowly onto the small couch by the fireplace.

There was a loud gasp from Miss Prynce.

The group of women and children spread away from the couch where Cyril now lay, his skin sickly gray and shiny with sweat.

"Miss Gribble?" The mayor's voice wavered although it was deep and grave. He gestured to the couch. Arianwyn took two halting steps forward and crouched down. She took Cyril's small hand in her own. He was so very cold and still—but alive. The pungent stench of dark magic filled her nose, so strong she thought she might gag.

"The wood . . . monster!" Cyril's voice came between huge ragged breaths.

Arianwyn could feel everyone's eyes on her. All thoughts of her planned conversation with the mayor had now fled: This was more important. "It's all right, Cyril. Just stay calm now." She placed a soothing hand on his forehead. "Can you tell me what the creature looked like?"

The boy's eyes widened in sudden fear and he started to struggle, as if trying to escape the memory.

"Sshh, stay still or you'll hurt yourself." Arianwyn put a hand on Cyril's arm, holding him down. He was too weak to resist.

"I think you'd better send for my grandmother and Miss Delafield at once." Arianwyn looked at Miss Prynce, who nodded mutely and ran from the room.

"And the doctor as well!" Arianwyn squeaked, unable to hide the panic in her own voice.

"Found 'im near the orchards," Mrs. Myddleton said. "He was playing with his ball and then . . . we heard him screamin'."

Hot angry tears blurred Arianwyn's vision. This had happened because of what she and Gimma had failed to do.

"It hurts, Miss Witch . . ." Tears trickled down Cyril's face.

"You're brave, young Cyril. Very brave indeed." Mayor Belcher came to stand beside Arianwyn.

Cyril was suddenly racked with a coughing fit that shook his whole body; the spittle and phlegm were blackened and a foul smell of dark magic was on his breath as well.

"Did you see the creature, Mrs. Myddleton?" Arianwyn asked.

"It were enormous, miss," she said. She was nearly as pale as her son. "Bigger than any of 'em spirits I ever saw before. Black as a hole at midnight and with long tentacles, not arms! It didn't have no face either, just blank except for its huge gaping mouth. Was like looking at terror itself."

Just then, Cyril moved to touch the wound on his chest but winced and cried out in pain.

"Miss Gribble, you have to do something for the boy's pain at least," Mayor Belcher hissed into Arianwyn's ear.

"But there's nothing I can do," she replied quietly. She so wanted to help him, to not have another person be in pain or frightened because of her mistakes. She looked at Mrs. Myddleton, still furiously wringing her apron between her hands. She knew she had to try.

Arianwyn rifled through her bag and pulled a charm free. "Without knowing more about the creature that attacked him, it's too dangerous to use a spell, but a charm might . . . help a little." She could hear the desperation in her own voice.

"Anything you can do, miss." Mrs. Myddleton smiled

weakly and came to stand by her son. She placed a trembling hand on the back of the couch and gazed at Cyril.

Arianwyn tied the charm carefully around the boy's neck. "There."

"Uncle? Uncle?" Gimma's voice echoed out in the hallway, startling Arianwyn from her moment of concentration. Seconds later she burst into the parlor. "Uncle, what's happened? Mrs. Oliva was just . . ." She stopped, taking in the horror of the scene.

The mayor moved to her side quickly. "Gimma, dear one, there has been the most awful attack near the Great Wood. Mrs. Myddleton's son has been wounded!"

Gimma's eyes flicked to Arianwyn and then away at once.

"Mr. Turvy was correct, it seems, and some terrible dark creature appears to be on the loose." The mayor swallowed hard. "It must have eluded Miss Delafield's search."

Silently, Gimma stepped slowly and carefully around the couch. She gasped as she took in the full view of Cyril's small frame and his dark festering wound. Her hands covered her mouth and she looked away.

"Miss Gribble has placed a charm—she says there is nothing more to be done. What do you think?"

Clouds of fear rushed across Gimma's face. She appeared to struggle to find an answer for her uncle. "I'm sure Arianwyn has done what's best, Uncle. But perhaps Arianwyn and I should have a quick chat. Out. In. The. Hallway!"

Without waiting for a response, Gimma swept past Mrs. Myddleton and out of the door. Arianwyn followed, uncertainly.

"Oh my word, Wyn! This is because of the rift, isn't it? Something got through." Gimma's voice shook.

Arianwyn nodded mutely.

"What are we going to do? I'll be in so much trouble! Have you said anything?"

"No!" Arianwyn gasped. She grabbed Gimma's arm and dragged her farther away from the door. "Of course I haven't said anything. It's not really up to me to say anything, is it? I didn't summon the rift in the first place!"

Twisting her arm free, Gimma looked down at the floor, knotting her fingers together and chewing on her lip. "Perhaps you could just—"

Arianwyn didn't wait to hear more. "No!" she hissed. "Poor Cyril's been hurt, Gimma. He might die! You have to tell them what happened. Now!"

Silence filled the hallway.

"You're right," Gimma said, her voice small. "It's time to face up to things at last. Thank you, Arianwyn." She reached out and took Arianwyn's hand. "I couldn't do it without you by my side. You've been such a good friend to me, I really don't deserve it."

Arianwyn felt her cheeks warm and then in silence she followed Gimma back into the mayor's parlor.

"Well, then, ladies. What's the plan?" Mayor Belcher asked, his voice laced with false cheer.

Gimma smiled weakly at Arianwyn and went to stand beside her uncle.

"I have something important to say about the creature in the Great Wood. I should have told you a long time ago. It's not fair to keep a secret from you any longer, despite how personally difficult it might be for me." A huge tear rolled down her pale cheek. Arianwyn felt sick with worry.

"Heavens, sweetheart. Please don't upset yourself."

"Thank you, Uncle. But I can't keep lying about this." Gimma took a deep breath and looked pleadingly at Arianwyn.

"It's okay. You can do this!" Arianwyn mouthed to her.

Gimma nodded.

There was the sound of more hurried footsteps. Grandmother, Miss Delafield, Colin, and Miss Prynce entered the room and stared at the sick boy on the couch, before glancing up at the mayor and the two young witches. Quickly, Gimma carried on.

"Arianwyn opened a rift in the Great Wood and let that creature through."

CHAPTER THIRTY-SIX

A FINE OLD MESS

I t didn't quite sink in at first. Arianwyn heard exactly what Gimma had said, but she didn't seem to understand the words. Then she realized everyone was looking right at her.

Miss Delafield's hand hovered near her mouth. Grandmother's eyes were wide.

"Is this correct, Miss Gribble?" Miss Delafield choked out the words.

"What?" Arianwyn mumbled, still not quite understanding.

"Did you open a rift that caused all of this?" Miss Delafield stepped forward and gestured to the couch and Cyril Myddleton.

"NO!" Arianwyn finally said. She looked at Miss Delafield pleadingly. "I didn't. Gimma, that's not what happened."

"Then pray tell us, Miss Gribble, exactly how did all this occur?" Mayor Belcher positioned himself in front of Gimma and glared at Arianwyn.

Arianwyn allowed the memory to unfurl in her mind, the calvaria, the smoky fire spell, Gimma encountering

Estar and the rift. "It was Gimma who opened the rift. Something went wrong with the spell and we couldn't close it again." Arianwyn's voice shook a little. She felt as if she was on fire and her head throbbed.

All eyes in the room flicked to Gimma. "How can you tell such lies, Arianwyn?" Gimma gasped. "It was you. And when *I* tried to close the rift it was already too late." Her perfect face was pulled into a mask of concern and angelic confusion. A performance Salle would have been proud of.

The room erupted into a volley of voices as everyone tried to speak and ask questions all at the same time.

"THAT'S ENOUGH!" Miss Delafield's voice boomed across the parlor, silencing everyone at once. "Miss Gribble, please explain what you think caused the rift to open."

Arianwyn took a deep breath. "We were in the Great Wood after we had been to check on the calvaria spawning. We'd gotten wet by the river and decided to light a small fire to dry off. I went to fetch more wood and while I was away . . ." She paused, thinking how best to avoid mentioning Estar. ". . . Gimma must have been frightened by something in the wood and summoned a rift." Arianwyn couldn't meet Gimma's eyes. Her cheeks burned. She glanced up and saw a slow, sly smile spread across Gimma's face.

"Miss Alverston, would you like to say something?" Miss Delafield asked.

The sly grin vanished as everyone turned to look at Gimma once more. "Arianwyn was showing off in the wood and opened the rift. And she was helped by some strange little blue creature . . . with funny legs!"

"That DEMON!" shrieked Mayor Belcher. "I knew you'd lied to me about banishing that beastly creature!"

"And last night Colin carried out an evaluation test on her, which I don't suppose she's mentioned," Gimma added gleefully.

Arianwyn closed her eyes for a second and hoped she would just vanish.

There were more gasps of shock from around the room. Gimma seemed to be working them like an audience. "And if she lied about *that*," she added, her eyes flashing, "why wouldn't she lie about *this*?"

Throughout all of this, Arianwyn hadn't known how to look at Grandmother. It was like the evaluation day all over again. Waves of disbelief crashed against her, mingling with a crushing sense of shame and humiliation.

"Okay, yes, I lied about Estar," Arianwyn blurted. "But that's because you wouldn't listen to me: I *knew* he wasn't dangerous. He's not even a demon, he's a feyling. Even the spirit lantern could see that. And I didn't tell you about the evaluation, which I think I failed again, anyway. But I swear I didn't open the rift!"

From the corner of her eye, Arianwyn watched as her grandmother slumped into a chair and gazed out the windows across the town square and far away.

"Miss Delafield?" Arianwyn pleaded. "You believe me, don't you?"

The mayor snorted. Gimma folded her arms across her chest and leaned back against the desk, satisfied at a job well done.

Miss Delafield crossed to Arianwyn quickly and said, so only she could hear, "You lied about banishing a suspected demon. You took part in an illegal evaluation. Did you use *that* glyph? Is that what caused all of this?" She shook her head sadly.

There was nothing Arianwyn could say. They all believed Gimma. "I'm sorry." Arianwyn's voice was swallowed up in the silence of the room.

"Not as sorry as I am, dear." Miss Delafield carried on past Arianwyn and stood next to the mayor and Gimma.

Arianwyn felt her last sliver of hope wither away.

"Well, Miss Delafield? What do we do now?" Mayor Belcher inclined his head toward Arianwyn.

"Our first priority will be to deal with whatever creature is in the Great Wood. It must be something clever if it managed to evade my searches. And we have to close the rift," Miss Delafield said sharply. "We'll deal with Miss Gribble later."

Standing between the mayor and Miss Delafield, Gimma's face was lit up with a broad smile. Fighting back the urge to throw herself across the room, Arianwyn turned away.

Mrs. Myddleton stepped forward and smiled at her. "Thank you for all you've done, Miss Gribble," she said quietly. It was a small chink of comfort, but it didn't make Arianwyn feel any better.

"Right, then, off to the wood!" Miss Delafield rolled her shoulders and pulled her bag strap tight across her chest. The mayor beamed and returned to his papers and Gimma flopped into a chair and swiped up a magazine. Miss Delafield glared at them both.

"What?" Gimma asked.

"Well, obviously, you'll be coming along to assist me!" Miss Delafield said.

"Oh yes, of course!" Gimma blushed, looked at her uncle, and reluctantly tossed the magazine aside.

"And you as well, Mayor Belcher!"

"But hadn't I better . . . stay here to keep an eye on Miss Gribble?"

"She's not dangerous! Perhaps a little foolish. Besides, I'm sure her grandmother will make sure she doesn't disappear."

The mayor muttered and stood up again.

"Where was the glyph summoned?" Miss Delafield asked Gimma as they peered at the huge map of Lull and a tiny portion of the Great Wood.

"I don't know where we were." She stared intently at the map. "It was near the river, I think."

"Arianwyn?" Miss Delafield gestured to the map.

Arianwyn let her eyes rove over the map for a second, snaking along the twists of the Torr River. There was the clearing: not far from the old woodsmiths' cottages. Her finger hovered there for a second.

"Well?" Mayor Belcher huffed.

"There," Arianwyn said pointing to the clearing just along from the bend in the river, where the calvaria had spawned.

"Let's go, then!" Miss Delafield marched toward the parlor door, Gimma skittering along behind her, trying to keep up with her long strides. As she reached the door, Miss Delafield turned. "Wait here," she said to Arianwyn. "I'll deal with you when I get back!"

CHAPTER THIRTY-SEVEN

SOMETHING GREAT INSIDE

Grandmother got to her feet and walked slowly around the mayor's office, chewing her lip and humming quietly, thoughtfully. Arianwyn watched. She could feel herself glowering, hurt that Grandmother had not tried to defend her.

All of a sudden Grandmother stopped, planted her hands on her hips, and stared at Arianwyn. She looked as though she was just about to speak when there were hurried footsteps from the hallway and then Salle, Colin, and Bob the moon hare burst through the door.

They skidded to a halt, picking up on the evident tension in the room. But Bob skipped across the dark floorboards and silky rugs to greet Arianwyn, all the same. She gathered the creature up into her arms, burying her face against its brilliant white fur. At last she let a small sob escape.

"What's going on?" Salle asked. "We just saw Miss Delafield and Gimma and the mayor heading off to the wood."

Arianwyn turned away, quickly wiping hot tears from her face. She heard Grandmother explain it all in a hushed and broken voice.

As Grandmother's tale ended, Arianwyn burst out: "I swear I didn't open that rift! But nobody believes me!"

Grandmother spoke, her words firm. "I know you would never lie, except to protect someone or something. Never to protect yourself. You're always looking out for others. But even a blind man could see that that girl doesn't need protecting—"

"She needs to be locked up!" Salle added quietly.

"So what's the plan?" Colin asked, glancing from Arianwyn to Grandmother cautiously.

Arianwyn looked away. "No plan. I'm done now." She placed the moon hare on the floor and it ran around her feet.

"What? You can't mean that," Colin said.

"Well, I do. Leave it to Miss Delafield to sort out. She'll be fine. I was going to resign anyway."

"Resign?" Salle and Grandmother gasped together.

"I've done everything wrong and I'm frightened, Salle. The power of that glyph! This creature! I don't want anyone else to get hurt."

Salle's face became stormy. "You can't just run away," she declared, her hand slapping down hard on the mayor's desk. Her eyes sparkled with tears. Everyone turned to look at her. Bob jumped and ran for cover under the sofa.

"You don't understand, Salle. I've put a whole town in danger!"

"You're right, I don't understand. *My friend* Arianwyn Gribble would never back down from anything. She's amazing, she's not scared of anything, and she *always* helps and she *always* does the right thing."

"But I don't, Salle. I've made so many mistakes!"

"Everyone makes mistakes, Wyn! But you will put things right, won't you?" She looked at Arianwyn; her eyes were willing her, pleading for her, to do the right thing.

"I . . . I can't, Salle; I don't know what to do."

Salle looked at Arianwyn, Colin, and Grandmother, and she fidgeted, anxious and angry. "Well, I'm not going to stand by and do nothing!" Quick as a flash she turned and ran out of the parlor.

"Salle, wait!" Arianwyn called, but only her own voice echoed back to her.

The room was silent for a long time.

Colin stood like a statue by the door. He was watching Arianwyn and Grandmother carefully. Grandmother paced the floor like a caged beast ready to pounce. Arianwyn sat in the mayor's seat, staring at the piles of paper and half-eaten pastries on his desk.

She felt sick and foolish and helpless.

After a time, Grandmother came to Arianwyn's side. She reached for her hand and said softly, "You know that undoing another witch's spell is the most difficult kind of magic. You had no chance of closing that rift."

The words hung in the air for a minute.

"Then why didn't you say anything before?" Arianwyn asked, pulling her hand slowly away.

Grandmother gazed levelly at Arianwyn. "Because I feel partly responsible. I thought I was doing the right thing by sending you here. I thought things would be easy and you could build your skills slowly, until you were ready for your reevaluation—"

"Oh, don't even mention that!" Arianwyn groaned. "Another disaster!" She hid her face behind her hands.

"Oh! The evaluation!" Colin said, the words a burst of excitement. He darted forward and fumbled in his pockets for a second.

He pulled out the thin strip of paper from the evaluation gauge and held it out to Grandmother.

She studied it for a second. Then glanced up at Arianwyn, her eyes wider still. "Is this reading—?"

"Yes!" Colin said quickly, proudly. "It's Arianwyn's!"

Grandmother slowly straightened from where she had been crouched beside the mayor's seat. The reading quivered in her hands.

"You're sure this is accurate?" she asked.

Colin nodded. "And I've verified it with the CWA this morning. They weren't happy about the unscheduled evaluation, but . . ." He smiled broadly.

Arianwyn felt as though there was a secret that they were not sharing with her. She looked from Colin to Grandmother and back again.

"But this means . . ." Grandmother paused, a smile blooming across her face. "There's no way you could have failed the evaluation before—"

Colin explained quickly, "You *broke* the machine because your reading was *so high* and we didn't adjust the settings accordingly!"

Arianwyn listened but she didn't seem to understand what Colin was saying.

"I knew you were going to be an amazing witch, Arianwyn Gribble. I knew you had something great inside you!" He smiled and his cheeks flushed.

"With a reading this high I think you could do just about anything!" Grandmother laughed and she did a little dance right there on the rug in the middle of the mayor's parlor.

But their joy was to last only a few seconds more.

Outside came a screeching, wailing noise, like a siren or the howl of some wild animal or perhaps a mixture of the two.

Arianwyn turned toward the tall balcony doors, which still stood wide open. She could see out across the town square and the roofs of Lull, over the walls that circled the town and toward the Great Wood. Rising high up above the trees was something bright. Like a flare, or firework. But it was brighter than either, brighter almost than the sun, and a deep, fiery, bloody red. As it curved up into the cloudy summer sky, the wailing intensified, until Arianwyn felt the need to cover her ears.

"Someone's in trouble! That's an old spell flare!" Grandmother said quickly.

"Miss Delafield and the others!" Colin said, looking at Arianwyn.

Arianwyn stopped dead, fear clamped around her heart.

"Salle!" she said quietly, and then she turned and raced for the stairs.

CHAPTER THIRTY-EIGHT

THE NIGHT GHAST

The spell flare had attracted a lot of attention.

As Arianwyn emerged from the town hall she saw people peering up at the sky, their faces marked with worry. They wandered around, swapping ideas about what was occurring. Arianwyn had to push past a few clots of people as she headed toward Wood Lane. She glanced back and was relieved to see Grandmother a little way behind her. She didn't know what she was going to do, but she felt better knowing she was with her. Colin had stayed behind to contact the CWA and send for help from Flaxsham.

The crowd grew thicker as she drew closer to the town wall and the East Gate, some pointing up at the fading spell flare. People were slow to move aside, even though she called ahead, "Can you make way, please? Coming through!" She tried not to think too much about what she might be about to find. She felt breathless with worry and her legs seemed to be turning into lumps of stone.

Arianwyn pushed forward, toward the East Gate. The high stone arch framed a glimpse of green meadow and woodland that pulled her onward.

"Out of the way!" she shouted, unable to keep her voice sounding polite any longer. The last few townspeople in the lane pulled to one side and Arianwyn got her first clear sight of the meadow and the Great Wood beyond.

Blasts of magical energy flashed somewhere just inside the line of trees and, even from this distance, the rancid stench of dark magic caught in her nose and throat.

Grandmother stood at her side and lifted a handkerchief over her mouth.

"This is not good," she whispered quietly to Arianwyn.

"We need to keep everyone safe. Can we cast a protection spell over the East Gate, at least?" Arianwyn asked.

"Yes, but one of us will have to stay here to maintain a spell of that size," Grandmother said.

"I'll go and help the others, you stay here. It's more important to keep the town safe," Arianwyn said quickly, though she didn't know if she could go on without Grandmother at her side.

"You'll be fine!" Grandmother said, as if she had read her thoughts. She lifted her hand to Arianwyn's cheek and smiled. "You'll be amazing!" She then raised her hands high and turned toward the people gathering around the gate.

"Everyone needs to stay within the town until we've figured out what is going on." Grandmother's voice was full and commanding. "We're concerned that there is a very real danger to Lull and all of you from a dark spirit creature that is at large in the Great Wood. Nobody must pass beyond the gate!"

She turned to her granddaughter. "Will you help me with the spell, Arianwyn?" Grandmother asked.

Arianwyn glanced toward the wood, the bursts of magic growing in intensity.

"We'll be quick!" Grandmother reassured her. "Just a moment or two!"

Grandmother pulled off her jacket and folded it on the ground. She paused for a moment, considering, and then she raised her hands and started quickly to sketch glyphs in the air in front of her. Arianwyn saw the flash of magic as each one formed and she slowly began to copy her grandmother's spell.

The watching townspeople fell quiet. Arianwyn caught sight of faces she knew among the crowd. They looked frightened, but each smiled warmly at her and she felt a small surge of confidence. All was silent but for the breeze through the grass and the sound of Grandmother humming softly to herself.

"Why do you hum like that when you're casting spells or concentrating?" Arianwyn asked. Grandmother glanced at her and for a second she was worried she had offended her. But then she chuckled, a light joyful sound that was swallowed up by the unnerving silence as quickly as water down a drain.

"Old habits die hard. When I was an apprentice, I used to get so nervous casting certain spells. I would get sick with worry and fright each time and so I used to hum this little tune to myself." She sang a few lines of the song:

Don't be scared, my little one,
the clouds roll in and hide the sun
but deep within our true light shines
and keeps us safe in darker times.

"*You* were scared?" Arianwyn asked, unable to hide the shock from her voice. She looked harder at her grandmother, glimpsing the girl she had once been all those years before.

Grandmother nodded. "And I still am sometimes. Fear is with us all at some time or other. It's nothing to be ashamed of, Arianwyn." She carried on singing and humming as she worked.

The soft rose-colored light of the spell flowed toward the gateway. Grandmother twisted her hands, helping the flow of magic to tumble this way and that to the opening. The magic fizzed and crackled as it sealed the gates with magic.

"There! Not bad for an old witch, eh?" Grandmother grinned. "You go on; I'll stay here to maintain the spell and make sure everyone stays safe."

Arianwyn beamed; she had never felt more proud of her grandmother.

She turned back to face the Great Wood. Dread crept around her again.

"You can do it!" Grandmother said reassuringly. Arianwyn smiled, but she could already feel tears forming as she pushed the gate open, the spell tingling under her fingers. She felt all the watching eyes on her as she turned back toward the wood and started to walk quickly across the meadow without looking back.

The long grass swayed in the breeze; it was dotted here and there with bloodred poppies and brilliant white daises, but it all seemed a blur to Arianwyn. As another screaming spell flare rose into the sky high above the tops of the trees, she broke into a run, summoning her own spell orb as she did. It crackled and fizzed ready in her palm.

She had only gone a few yards into the wood when the trees directly in front of her started to tremble and shake as if whipped up by a storm, even though the breeze itself was only just strong enough to stir the meadow grass.

Shapes shifted and lurched between the trunks and behind the branches. Arianwyn ducked this way and that, trying to see clearly. And then she heard a cry: "Help, please! Someone help!"

It was Salle!

Without thinking a second longer, Arianwyn charged through the trees.

The scene that awaited her was nothing short of bizarre and terrifying.

Slumped against a tree was Miss Delafield, her left leg twisted at a very strange angle. It was clearly broken. Salle sat beside her, partly shielded by the older witch, who hurled spell orb after spell orb through the trees.

And growing on every tree trunk and across large patches of the ground was a black carpet of hex, like thick hairy cobwebs, smothering everything it touched!

"Oh, rune rot!" Arianwyn breathed. Her own spell orb extinguished in fear. How had the hex spread so far, and so fast? A shower of leaves drifted through the air, falling far too soon because of the hex that now riddled the trees.

Arianwyn dashed toward Miss Delafield and Salle. Twin looks of relief passed across their grubby, scratched faces. Miss Delafield took a deep breath and leaned on Salle.

"Are you okay, Salle?" Arianwyn asked quickly, glancing at her friend, who was muddy and covered in scratches but didn't seem to be in any more trouble than that.

Salle nodded. "I'm fine but Miss Delafield's leg is broken," she said quickly. "We need to get her back to town."

"Oh, Arianwyn, dear," Miss Delafield said. "Thank heavens you're here. I'm afraid I've bitten off more than I can chew! The creature . . . it's a night ghast!"

"A what?" Arianwyn asked, and looked through the trees, but all she saw were dark moving shapes, like shadows. She had never heard of such a creature.

"A night ghast. It's a very ancient dark spirit, dear. They haven't been seen for hundreds of years," Miss Delafield said, her teeth gritted in pain. "They're vicious, though, and rather tougher to get rid of than I imagined. Nothing seems to be working, dear."

"Where's Gimma and Mayor Belcher?" Arianwyn asked, panic crashing against her like a wave.

Salle nodded to a large rock just to her left and a little farther back. She rolled her eyes.

Arianwyn could just see Gimma and the mayor huddled together, crouching behind the rock. They were both covered in bits of tree and mud and looked beyond terrified. Arianwyn dashed to them as Miss Delafield sent another volley of spell orbs into the distant trees.

"Mayor Belcher, are you all right?"

The mayor looked up. His regal purple sash was rumpled and torn and twisted around his neck. His golden medal was nowhere to be seen.

He was out of breath, his face purple. "You have to get us back to town, Miss Gribble," he pleaded. "I don't think Miss Delafield knew what she was doing when she brought us out here, it's really not safe!"

Arianwyn looked at Gimma. "We need you to help keep this night ghast thing at bay, so we can get back to town."

Gimma said nothing and avoided Arianwyn's gaze.

"It seems my niece's abilities are . . . very much affected by the dark magic and the hex, Miss Gribble. She's struggling with her spells at the moment." Even the mayor didn't sound convinced.

Gimma's eyes flicked to Arianwyn, and then away again.

Arianwyn sighed and hurried back to Salle and Miss Delafield.

"We really need to get out of here," she said, looking back over at Gimma and the mayor. "The hex is affecting Gimma!"

"Oh, that's nonsense, Wyn, and you know it!" Salle said suddenly.

"All right, Salle, dear!" Miss Delafield said, patting her hand and looking carefully at Arianwyn as she lobbed another spell orb. It arced high, its bright yellow trail lighting up the trees briefly before it disappeared among the branches and trunks. "I think we all know it's not the hex that is Miss Alverston's problem, don't we, Arianwyn?"

Arianwyn glanced from Salle to Miss Delafield and then across to Gimma. Salle had apparently told Miss Delafield everything.

"She'd have figured it out sooner or later," Salle said, lifting her chin and glaring at Arianwyn.

"Now then, girls, let's not argue at this precise moment in time!"

From within the thicket came a rasping, clicking, insectile sound.

"Cuk cuk cuk!"

Arianwyn looked at Miss Delafield and Salle.

"It's coming again!" Salle said, pointing deeper into the wood.

"Well, let's get out of here, then. Grandmother's put a protection spell up around the East Gate. If we get back there perhaps we can hold it off until help arrives."

"A very brave plan!" Miss Delafield said, but something in her eyes made Arianwyn feel suddenly much more afraid than she had before.

"Gimma, Mayor Belcher, get ready to run!" Arianwyn called back to the rock.

Then she nodded at Miss Delafield and they sent a massive volley of spell orbs flying into the trees. The clicking sound retreated and then stopped briefly.

"RUN!" Arianwyn shouted.

Salle and Arianwyn helped get Miss Delafield to her feet. She cried out in pain as they pulled her along, her broken leg limp and useless, dragging behind.

Gimma and the mayor were already running ahead. They didn't glance back to check if Arianwyn and the others were following.

They shuffled clear of the trees, emerging at last into the meadow. The sky was dark, steely gray clouds filling the sky, a few light spots of rain falling against Arianwyn's face. The honey-colored stone walls of Lull looked a million miles away. Arianwyn could see crowds of people watching and waiting behind the gates. A soft rose-colored light surrounded them; Grandmother's spell was still in place.

Arianwyn and Salle pulled Miss Delafield along but had only gone a few yards when the "cuk cuk cuk" sound filled Arianwyn's ears again. She glanced over her shoulder just as the creature finally emerged from the trees and she saw the night ghast for the first time.

The twisted shape looked like a stunted tree, blackened, menacing, and moving slowly toward them. It twisted its long branchlike tentacles, swinging them wide. It was a vortex, a black whirlwind. "Cuk cuk cuk" came the sound again, dry and echoing through the trees.

As it drew closer, Arianwyn could make out its smooth featureless face—featureless but for the angry jagged shape that was its mouth. Its tentacle arms snapped and writhed around it. It felt for the patches of hex, its limbs snaking across the ground, feeling and searching this way and that. Arianwyn was sure it was drawing power from the dark magic.

"Arrrgh!" Miss Delafield cried out in pain and frustration. She turned with Salle's help and, with another scream of fury, she fired another round of spell orbs. But this time she was aiming for the trees and the ground beneath the creature.

It seemed as though a small portion of the wood exploded. Trees were torn from their roots, the earth opened up, and massive trees came toppling down onto the night ghast.

CHAPTER THIRTY-NINE

DON'T DO IT

Arianwyn and Salle held tight to Miss Delafield as she hobbled across the meadow. The supervisor was pale and her eyes fluttered with exhaustion.

The thunderous cracking and creaking noise of trees toppling seemed to engulf them.

Just ahead, Mayor Belcher was hunched in the grass, his face purple. He panted and clung tight to Gimma's arm.

"Did . . . you . . . stop it?" he wheezed, looking back at the wood.

"Unlikely!" Miss Delafield said grimly. "I think it would be a good idea to put up some spell barriers now. To keep it back for as long as possible."

Arianwyn nodded and started to create a barrier spell that would form close to the pile of charred trees. It wouldn't hold the night ghast for long but it should slow its progress.

"Why isn't anyone coming to help?" Gimma moaned, looking back at Lull.

"Madam Stronelli has sealed the East Gate with a spell," Miss Delafield said, "to keep everyone safe."

"Colin was going to call the CWA for help," Arianwyn offered, as the first barrier formed.

"Good." Miss Delafield nodded. "They'll coordinate help from other local witches." But something in her voice told Arianwyn that this would still not be enough.

They all looked back at the night ghast.

"But we're not going to be able to stop it, are we, Miss Delafield?" Salle's voice was grave but clear.

Miss Delafield shook her head.

An idea was forming in Arianwyn's mind. She slipped her trembling hand into her pocket and her fingers brushed the page that held the unknown glyph. Perhaps Miss Delafield could control it. Perhaps she was a skillful enough witch to wield its dark magic?

Arianwyn's fingers tightened now around the page. She lifted it from her pocket and offered it to Miss Delafield.

"I think we should try this—"

"No!" Miss Delafield cut her off, her voice full of anger and fear. She turned away and busied herself with another barrier spell. Her shoulders tensed as she drew more glyphs into the air in front of her. "I thought we'd gotten rid of that!"

The air was suddenly filled with a loud cracking noise. Like thunder but much louder, as though the earth itself was being ripped apart.

Arianwyn turned just as the tumble of trees was thrown high into the air in an explosion of earth, tree, and rock. The night ghast crawled slowly from the blackened, charred mess.

"Cuk cuk cuk!"

It surged forward but came to a halt at the first barrier spell. Magic flared and sparks illuminated the meadow as the night ghast threw itself against the barrier, its tentacles flailing against the spell again and again.

"It's not going to hold for long," Arianwyn shouted back to Miss Delafield. She could already see fractures forming. The thought that had been blooming in her mind was now fully formed and demanded her attention.

The unknown glyph.

It was the only way.

"I'm going to summon the glyph!" Arianwyn called. "It's the *only* chance we have."

"No! Completely out of the question," Miss Delafield shouted back. "Don't even think about it, dear! I can't ask you to risk yourself like that."

"What's going on?" Mayor Belcher called. He was less wheezy but still rather purple.

"Miss Gribble wishes to use an unknown spell to stop the night ghast," Miss Delafield explained loudly. "One I have forbidden her from using! It's not safe!"

"Heavens, let her do it, Jucasta!" Mayor Belcher's voice rose in pitch and volume. "She might be the only one who can save us all. Gimma's clearly no use!"

Arianwyn glanced over her shoulder at the mayor. Gimma, who had been at his side, took several deliberate steps away. She looked hurt, as though the mayor had given her a good slap.

The mayor, noticing his error, reached out quickly, "Oh, Gimma, precious. I am sorry—"

She wasn't listening; she batted his hand away. "Well, I'll show you!" she said, her voice flat and quiet, but everyone heard her. She undid the ridiculous little bag that she always carried, and from it she pulled a small slip of paper. It was crossed with a line of tape. As she unfolded it a sickening knot of dread tightened around Arianwyn's heart.

It was the piece of paper Arianwyn had drawn the unknown glyph onto for Miss Delafield. Gimma had never thrown it into the stove. She had kept it all this time.

"You can't use that glyph, Gimma!" Arianwyn shouted, fear shaking her voice. "Its power is as dark as the night ghast, darker perhaps. It's too dangerous for you!"

"Too dangerous for *me*, is it?" Gimma asked. "But not too dangerous for *you*, I suppose." Gimma spat the words. "You always thought you were better than me, didn't you, Arianwyn *Dribble*?"

"NO!" Arianwyn said, her voice shaking but loud. "It's the truth, Gimma. Please!"

There was a rush of air and a flash of blinding blue light.

"Miss Gribble is correct. It is an incredibly dangerous glyph." A small voice filled the moment. "It's proper name is Skygε, the shadow glyph. One of the ancient *quiet* glyphs."

Everyone turned to see Estar. He stood only yards away, surrounded by a halo of fading blue light. He smiled at Arianwyn and then bowed to the others.

"You!" shrieked the mayor. He surged toward Estar, jabbing a finger and roaring, "You're making all of this up. This is the creature Miss Gribble has been in league with all this time!" He shook, and little specks of spittle flew from his mouth. "We will not listen to any more lies! You'll be banished along with the night ghast; back to the void with the lot of you!"

Estar blinked calmly and stared up at the mayor.

Arianwyn froze for a moment, aware everyone was looking at her.

"That's enough!" Miss Delafield shouted. "Arianwyn and this . . . creature, are telling the truth. That glyph is far too dangerous for Gimma to use."

"If you attempt to use it you will fail, young lady," Estar continued. "Of that there is little doubt. Miss Gribble, it would seem, is unusual in being able to see and summon the quiet glyphs. As was Miss Delafield's sister, my dear friend Euphemia." Estar glanced at Miss Delafield and smiled warmly.

"Well, this is most irregular!" Mayor Belcher huffed, and turned to Gimma. "Give Miss Delafield the piece of paper and come away," he said quietly.

"NO," Gimma said, her eyes flashing, her cheeks flushed.

"Pity's sake, child, do as you're told for once!" the mayor roared.

"I will not! I can do it. I'll show you, I'll show all of you!" Without another word, Gimma turned and ran through the long grass toward the night ghast. It had just broken through Arianwyn's first barrier spell and was heading for the second one.

"Stop her, oh please, Miss Gribble!" the mayor called.

Arianwyn ran after Gimma. Behind her, Miss Delafield threw more spell orbs, as fast as she could create them. Again and again, spell orbs, binding spells, blasts of fire and ice. But the night ghast seemed to cut through each spell like a blade.

A fleeting thought brushed Arianwyn's mind as her feet pounded across the meadow. She could let Gimma try and use the glyph. It wouldn't work, she knew that much. And she would be on hand to pick up the pieces as Gimma finally made the most colossal mess of the whole thing. And with an audience watching from across the meadow.

She let the thought play across her imagination for just a few seconds and then shook it away. What was she thinking? Gimma could be killed by the night ghast or this quiet glyph.

Whatever she'd done, she didn't deserve that.

She was just a few paces away, and without thinking she threw herself forward. Her arms wrapped tightly around Gimma and they both tumbled to the ground.

"Boggin' well get off me!" Gimma spat, lashing out with her hands. She scratched at Arianwyn, screaming like a cat. She pulled on Arianwyn's hair and tried desperately to break free from her grasp. But Arianwyn held on tighter and tighter in fear. "You don't know what you're doing, Gimma, please!"

"Cuk cuk cuk."

There was a flash of light and a shower of sparks as the second barrier failed.

As they fell over again in the grass Arianwyn noticed the dark shape drawing ever closer, only a few yards away now. She released her grip and scrabbled to stand again, pulling Gimma with her. The night ghast towered over the two young witches, dark and twisted, its tentacles swirling around their boots.

A dry scream escaped Gimma's mouth and she tried to back away. The night ghast shifted. It had detected her movement.

Arianwyn tried to shove Gimma to one side, but the night ghast was too fast. It swung one of its long sinewy scaled arms, sending Gimma soaring up and over its head. For a second it looked as though she was flying. But then her body twisted and plummeted down to the ground. She fell into a tumble of shattered tree stumps amid a thick patch of hex, where she lay worryingly still.

"Gimma!" Arianwyn screamed, terror ripping through her body in waves. She had to move fast before the ghast reached for her. She dodged past it and ran toward Gimma, skidding to a halt before she reached the hex. Gimma was out cold, but appeared to be breathing.

Arianwyn shook with fear, tears blurring her eyes.

The night ghast grew closer and closer.

The storm broke above the wood and meadow, rain pouring down through the branches, soaking everything around her, the ground beneath her feet quickly becoming slick and muddy. She turned, facing the night ghast.

She was ready to summon the shadow glyph and bring everything to an end, one way or another. She could see the glyph even through her tears. She could feel its power already. Maybe it would be different this time. She couldn't let it overwhelm her: She had to control it somehow.

She shuddered, her heart raced in her chest. She thought it must be drowning out the noise of the storm, it was so loud. She took a quick breath, knelt on the damp ground, and reached forward.

Her arms outstretched and hands shifting in the dying light, she formed huge, wide, sweeping shapes in the air, drawing the shadow glyph before her as large and quickly as she could.

The glyph hung in the air for a moment, its snakelike curving shape bold and dark. Magic thrummed all around, pulsing and moving through earth and rock and air.

The spell formed so easily.

And as the glyph faded she could sense the cold creep of the shadows all around her, stretching, folding, and tumbling from every direction.

The edge of her vision was a dark inky blur and as she got to her feet she felt the chilly press of all the darkness in the wood. All foreboding and dread, heavy as stone and cold as ice, it draped itself around her like a thick blanket. She shuddered and slumped a little under the weight of magic. *Mustn't give in*, she thought as her feet slipped in the wet grass.

The night ghast stopped and watched her. She sensed that it could feel the strength of magic just as she could. It snarled its horrid, echoing grating sound, feeding on her doubt. But it came no closer.

"Cuk cuk cuk."

Up close, Arianwyn could see its jagged mouth pulsate as it called. She looked away, frightened.

The darkness pressed in farther around her, the shadows flowing like waves rushing at the shore. What was she doing? She had no chance against this creature—she would never be able to stop it. Tears ran down her cheeks, mingling with the rain. She steadied herself, regained her balance, glared up at the night ghast. *Fight it. Control the glyph.* But still, the gloom continued to press toward her.

How is it so cold? she wondered. And it wasn't just the cold, it was the dark sense of nothingness that washed against her every few seconds.

She peered through her hazy vision at the night ghast, but it was as motionless as before, its voided face like marble—as if it was watching, waiting for her to fail. Gimma's still form lay to the right, just out of reach. *Why doesn't she get up?*

She had been so stupid, she could see it now. What was she trying to prove? She had no idea what she was supposed to do next, and the spell was taking control again. Better just to let the darkness consume her. Perhaps it wouldn't be so bad. Gentle and quiet.

The night ghast hissed, a sound like "yessss," as though it had read her thoughts. A darting black tongue emerged from its void of a mouth, tracing around its jagged lips.

"NO!" A strangled sob flew from her mouth, but the shadows swirled around her, closer and closer, like a vortex.

"You should let the shadows take you. I can feel your doubt, little girl. I can smell your fear. I can hear your loneliness!" The voice was cold and bitter. Arianwyn wasn't sure if it was the night ghast or the shadows or her own doubt that was speaking to her.

It was true: Of course she was afraid. She had always been afraid. And she didn't know if this spell would work; nobody did. It was a risk—a huge risk that seemed to be failing. And she was alone, here, face-to-face with the night ghast and these endless twisting shades. She glanced down at her hands and noticed that the darkness curled around her fingers . . . *Or do the shadows come from me?* she wondered.

She detected a movement at her side; a warm hand slipped into her own and held tight. She glanced down and saw Estar beside her.

"You are not alone." He smiled. "You have never been alone; look!"

She raised her eyes back beyond the night ghast and the shadows, and saw Miss Delafield and Salle, even Mayor Belcher, their faces scared but hope lighting their eyes. And farther back, Lull was lit by Grandmother's protection spell and she could see all the people lining the walls. She felt them willing her on.

Smiling, warm, and loving faces. Like stars, like beacons of hope.

Then she knew with certainty that the shadows were not from the spell.

They *were* from her.

The darkness was her own doubt, her own fear, and her own loneliness. To control the glyph, she had to control *them*.

She squeezed Estar's hand and then turned back to the night ghast.

"ENOUGH!" Arianwyn shouted through the darkness, and her voice was a triumphant roar. The shadows paused.

The doubt she had felt was slipping away; she could hear the shouts and calls of her friends. She was no longer alone. And she looked at the night ghast, her jaw clenched. She was no longer afraid of it. She was no longer afraid of her own abilities.

Arianwyn screwed her eyes up tight and thought of sipping hot chocolate in the Blue Ox with Salle; she could hear laughter and feel the warmth of the fire, and just for a second the shadows seemed to recede.

She thought of Colin and his piles of papers, his faith in her, she heard his gentle laughter.

She felt the warmth of Estar's hand wrapped around hers.

She thought of her grandmother and a million happy times spent together and the words of her song: ". . . deep within our true light shines and keeps us safe in darker times."

Suddenly everything shifted.

The dark mist curling from her fingers was changing, lightening, glowing. Estar's hand slipped from her own as she started to rise from the damp ground of the meadow, until she hovered several yards in the air. The shadows and now the light swirled around her.

They were under her command!

Arianwyn raised her arms toward the night ghast, the shadows and light surging forward. Surrounding it, covering it.

There was a pause, as though the Great Wood held its breath. The night ghast, wrapped in shadow, struggled against the power of the spell. Only its head and that hideous mouth moved, twisted this way and that, fighting its own panic as it was consumed.

Then, all of sudden, light ripped from deep within the creature. Arianwyn raised her hand to shield her eyes. Blinding light fractured it, splitting its body into a million tiny fragments. A triumphant shredding noise filled the air, as if the sky was ripping in two.

After a few moments tiny wisps of light were the only reminder that anything had been there at all, and then these too drifted away in the wind and rain.

It felt to Arianwyn as if she had been holding her breath all this time. As the spell receded, the shadows became just normal shadows and the magical light dimmed away. She let out a long slow breath and felt herself float back to the ground. She saw Estar trying to pull Gimma clear of the tangle of tree and hex. She was horribly still.

Now a roaring sound filled her ears—was it the storm? Or some new terror awaiting them? She turned to see the people of Lull waving and cheering and calling out with delight as they raced across the meadow.

She had done it; she had really done it. She'd controlled the shadow glyph at last; there was nothing to be afraid of now. But then she remembered Gimma.

She tried to move forward, to help Estar, but she suddenly felt so tired and her legs couldn't hold her up any longer. She tumbled to the damp, muddy, churned-up ground of the meadow and everything went dark.

Some theories exist that the secondary and cardinal glyphs used by the modern witches of the Four Kingdoms were formed from fragments of an archaic and long-forgotten language.

It is possible that the glyphs we now know so well are reductions or contractions of more complex and intricate spell formations, though no evidence of these "other spells" has ever been found.

CHAPTER FORTY

THE STAR

Arianwyn stood at the edge of the Great Wood. A long yellow-and-black cord stretched from tree trunk to tree trunk as far as she could see. Every few yards a warning sign hung from it.

Out of bounds by Order of the Civil Witchcraft Authority.
NO ENTRY!

"Won't we get in trouble, Wyn?" Salle asked anxiously, glancing around for the hundredth time since they had left town.

"We're not doing anything wrong," Arianwyn replied. "We're not going into the wood."

"That's just me!" Estar said, smiling at Salle and Arianwyn.

"But is it safe?" Salle sounded genuinely scared.

Arianwyn reached out and squeezed her hand tightly. "It's fine, Salle. I'll keep you safe and then we'll head straight back to town, I promise."

Salle was unusually anxious and Arianwyn didn't know why. It was a beautiful late summer's day. The sky above was a hot blue, empty of clouds. The air was heavy and still. A little farther along from where they stood was a gap in the thick never-ending line of the wood. It was a charred, blackened scar, the reminder of the evening two weeks before when Arianwyn had faced the night ghast, and triumphed.

Gimma had not fared so well. She had been bundled off to Kingsport the very next day to be tended by the best physicians.

"Well, I shall say my good-byes," Estar said, interrupting Arianwyn's somber moment. "You will be okay without me, Arianwyn Gribble?" he asked.

"Are you sure you want to go back? You said it wasn't safe for you in Erraldur."

Estar looked off through the trees. The sound of birdsong and leaves rustling filled the silence.

"I promised someone, someone very important, that I would go back there. They risked much to help me. And they may know more about those unknown glyphs and the book that held the page originally."

Arianwyn remembered what Miss Delafield had told her: How trying to use the shadow glyph had driven her sister crazy. "The shadow glyph . . . why was I able to control it, but Effie wasn't? Will I be able to control others?"

Estar chuckled and moved toward the trees. "I think you've had enough of mysterious glyphs for now, Arianwyn Gribble. I shall tell you more one day."

"So you will come back?" Salle asked.

"Of course, now that I have dear friends to welcome me here!" He reached out and patted Salle's hand.

Arianwyn, unsure what to say, glanced back across to the town. She could feel tears forming as she contemplated saying good-bye to Estar. "We all owe you so many thanks," she said, her voice catching.

"Yes, Mr. Estar. Without you, the night ghast would have—" Salle shuddered.

"Just 'Estar,' please. And it was all Arianwyn's work, really." His usually bright yellow eyes looked rather dim and watery.

"Well, I had best be going." He reached out a long elegant hand to Arianwyn. "I wish you well, Arianwyn Gribble. I knew you were a great witch the moment I laid eyes on you."

Arianwyn pulled the small blue creature into a tight embrace and let her tears flow freely as she said, "Thank you, Estar. Thank you!"

"Now, now. That's enough of that!" He patted her gently and then stepped away, making a few shuffling half steps toward the tree line, toward the Great Wood, toward Erraldur and home.

"Take care!" Arianwyn called.

"Good-bye, Mr. Estar!" Salle shouted.

The small blue feyling moved beyond the first trees of the Great Wood, slipping beneath the cord. He turned, raised a hand briefly, and then he was rising a few yards into the air. A brilliant blue light surrounded him in an azure aura.

After a few seconds it was too bright to see anything through it. Arianwyn could feel the strong pull of magic from Estar. There was a shimmering flash: once, twice. The blue light pulsed and there was a loud popping sound. And then he was gone.

Arianwyn wiped away a tear and sighed.

"Are you okay?" Salle asked. She frowned at Arianwyn, looking anxiously at her.

"I'm fine, Salle. I'm just tired. Miss Delafield said it would take a while to get over using the shadow glyph."

Salle continued to frown.

"I really am fine! Come on, let's go back to the Spellorium and have some tea. I made cake!"

Salle smiled, and they wandered back through the long grass and bright flowers in the meadow. Lull stood before them, safe behind its high ancient walls.

"Have you heard anything about how Gimma is?" Salle asked.

"Nothing," Arianwyn said. "Miss Delafield tried calling her parents but they wouldn't speak to her. I think she's going to be in tons of trouble with the CWA." Arianwyn didn't like the idea of Gimma being in trouble with the CWA in any way, shape, or form, even if she had brought most of it on herself. She hadn't deserved to be attacked by the night ghast, though.

They crossed the bridge in silence and passed through the East Gate into town, which seemed strangely quiet.

"I've asked Miss Delafield if it would be okay to take some vacation to go and visit Grandmother in Kingsport," Arianwyn said as they wandered from Old Town Road into the town square. "Want to come along?"

Salle paused and stared at Arianwyn. "Really? Really, Wyn?" She jumped on the spot. "I've always wanted to visit Kingsport; all those theaters!"

"Is that a yes?" Arianwyn asked.

"Absolutely yes!" Salle said, pulling Arianwyn into a clumsy but heartfelt hug.

The town square was quieter than usual as well, although there did seem to be a lot of people gathered in Kettle Lane as Arianwyn and Salle turned into the narrow twisting street.

"What on earth is going on?" Arianwyn asked, standing on her tiptoes and trying to see over the heads in front of them.

Salle stayed quiet but beamed. Just then an old lady noticed Arianwyn; she nudged her neighbor and they both grinned broadly and started to clap.

A ripple of applause ran through the crowd in Kettle Lane and the people parted, forming a narrow path toward the Spellorium.

"What's all this?" Arianwyn asked. Salle simply took her hand and led her along the lane as the applause rang out around them.

As the Spellorium drew nearer, Arianwyn could see Miss Delafield, her leg encased in a plaster cast and a large bruise still blooming across her cheek and around her left eye, and Mayor Belcher standing by the storefront. Miss Delafield beamed broadly and joined in with the applause.

"Ladies and gentlemen," Mayor Belcher called, bringing the applause to a close. "We are here today to celebrate and give thanks for *our* witch, Arianwyn Gribble."

Arianwyn stopped dead in her tracks. Had she heard right? She blushed and shifted from foot to foot and then glared at Salle. "You knew about this?" She grimaced. Salle smiled.

The mayor continued, "As you are all aware, Miss Gribble recently saved the entire town from a night ghast. She did this without any thought for her own safety or well-being and demonstrated a huge amount of courage."

"Hear hear!" somebody called from the crowd, and there was another outbreak of applause. Arianwyn couldn't believe her ears! She didn't know where to look.

"And so I wish to offer her the freedom of the town in recognition of her dutiful and heroic service, in the face of great adversity." Mayor Belcher stepped forward and extended a hand to Arianwyn.

Unsure exactly how to respond, Arianwyn grasped it. "I'm so sorry about Gimma, Mayor Belcher," she said softly.

"Please don't trouble yourself, and besides, I am the one who should apologize. I fear I was blinded by my love for my niece; Miss Gribble . . . can you forgive me?"

Arianwyn smiled. "Of course!"

The mayor smiled and then rather unexpectedly caught Arianwyn up in a massive hug. The crowd of townspeople cheered loudly.

"And now I shall hand over to Miss Delafield, who has

another honor to confer on Miss Gribble." After more applause, Miss Delafield, resplendent in her uniform, hobbled forward on a walking stick—the white cast thumped loudly as she moved. In her free hand she carried a small velvet box.

It looked very familiar indeed.

"Miss Gribble recently undertook her reevaluation," Miss Delafield said loudly, "and has proved to be a singularly powerful witch. It gives me the greatest of pleasures, on behalf of the Civil Witchcraft Authority, to announce that her apprenticeship is at an end and from today she is a fully qualified witch!'"

Arianwyn couldn't believe her ears. She watched in stunned silence as Miss Delafield flipped the box open and there, nestled among the black velvet, was a bright, silver, five-pointed star.

Miss Delafield reached forward and took away the bronze moon brooch and pinned the shining star to Arianwyn's blouse in its place. Arianwyn felt her cheeks warm as the crowd erupted into loud cheers and shouting.

"Congratulations!" Miss Delafield beamed. "I am so proud of you, and so grateful to you as well. And I'm sorry for not believing you." She caught Arianwyn up in a tight embrace and when they broke apart Arianwyn was sure there were tears on Miss Delafield's cheeks.

The lane rang with the sound of cheering, clapping, and the stamping of feet. And then came calls for a speech. Unsure what to say, Arianwyn stood on the steps of the

Spellorium and looked out at the sea of smiling faces before her.

For a second she didn't think she could say anything at all. And then she said, "Thank you all so very much. I feel very honored to have all your support—"

She was just about to thank Miss Delafield and the mayor when a small but urgent voice called out, "Where's the witch, then?"

The crowd parted this way and that as Cyril Myddleton came forward. He had a ball tucked under his arm; his clothes were in their usual disarray. His encounter with the night ghast was clearly long forgotten and no signs of lasting damage remained. Arianwyn smiled warmly, relieved.

"Miss Witch!" he called cheerfully, oblivious of the crowd around him or the gravity of the occasion.

"What seems to be the matter?" Arianwyn asked.

"Me mam says you're to come straightaway please, miss."

Arianwyn went cold. But with all eyes on her, she asked brightly, "And what seems to be the problem?"

"We got ourselves some more of them snotlling things, miss!" the boy said urgently. Arianwyn couldn't help but smile.

"Do you want me to come with you to help, this time?" Miss Delafield asked quietly, coming to stand beside her.

Arianwyn considered for a moment and then said, "No, thank you!"

There was a loud cheer from the crowd and Arianwyn set off, following Cyril along Kettle Lane. People reached out to pat her shoulder or back as she dashed past. She glanced back at Mayor Belcher and Miss Delafield. They both beamed proudly and waved at their new fully fledged witch.

Arianwyn felt her own smile spread across her face and she lifted a hand to wave back.

She felt at home, complete and whole.

— GLOSSARY OF GLYPHS —

 Årdra is the fire glyph. Its strength is immense, as is its ability to destroy at the hands of an inexperienced witch. It also contains properties for light and protection.

 Briå, the air glyph, is summoned for spells that require delicacy. It is used in broomcraft and for transformation. Its defensive properties are limited but can be wielded by a witch with high skill.

 For spells of strength and protection it is best to use Erte, the earth glyph. Strong and resourceful, it is the easiest of the glyphs to summon but the most difficult to master.

 Aluna is the water glyph, useful for spells of healing and for those skilled in the arts of divination. Like water, it can appear weak but has a hidden strength.

 L'ier is the banishing glyph and contains at its heart a sliver of dark magic, for it summons a small rift, opening a portal from the human world to the void to which a dark spirit is returned.

 Oru is the simplest glyph to summon and creates a light spell orb. It is usually the glyph and spell a witch would first learn, before the age of five.

═ ACKNOWLEDGMENTS ═

I have been so lucky to have so much love and support whilst writing this book and many careful hands to guide me along the way.

Julia Williams, who said I should "just get on and do it!" and kindly read some very early chapters—thank you for setting me off on this most amazing of adventures!

Imogen Cooper, Vanessa Harbour, and the amazing team of editors and writers at the Golden Egg Academy who helped to encourage and nurture my little tale and gave me confidence to go on and on and on! What you are doing is a rare and wonderful thing and I feel lucky to be part of your golden-gang, you gorgeous people!

Bella Pearson, my wonderful GEA mentor—your love of my story, faith in me, kindness, and friendship have been more than I could ask for—to have the opportunity to work with you was just amazing.

Early readers Katy Kwa, Emma Greenwood, Kay Vallely, Andrew Wright, Sue Eves, Anthony Burt, Anne Marie Stone, and Fiona Noble—thank you all for your thoughtful feedback, encouragement, and friendship.

To the wonderful, warm community of children's writers out there in the world—you have been nothing but friendly and supportive, thank you for being lovely!

Kate Shaw—the most awesome agent—you are wise, brilliant, and have THE best laugh in the world!

Vashti Hardy and Lorraine Gregory (Moo and Queenie!), your friendship has been the most wonderful thing to come out of this (aside from the awesome book, obviously!). Thanks for keeping me calm, cheering me on, and making me laugh on a daily basis!

I have been so lucky that Barry Cunningham (and his hat!) were both suitably "charmed" by *The Apprentice Witch* and that we have found a home with Chicken House. I'm truly honored and humbled to be amongst the list of the wonderful authors you have published.

To all the marvelous Chicken House team, but especially Rachel Hickman, Jazz Bartlett, Laura Smythe, Laura Myers, and Elinor Bagenal—golly gosh but you are all just AMAZING and I love working with you all.

My wonderful, wonderful editors, Kesia Lupo and Rachel Leyshon, you are stars and have made the book so much more with thoughtful guidance and the gentlest of nudges! You are now officially honorary witches and two of my favorite people ever!

Thank you Leo Nickolls for your fantastic illustrations for the cover—it bristles with magic and mystery and you got Bob in there as well—bravo!

And now I have a wonderful American editor as well! Thank YOU Nick Thomas (my transatlantic pen-pal!) for your thoughtful work in bringing Arianwyn safely across the waves and to a whole new world of readers. Arianwyn and I have felt entirely safe in your hands!

To all my friends and family—thank you for not thinking I had gone totally round the bend for embarking on this and for being proud and promising to all buy LOTS of copies!

To Julian, for never doubting that this would happen, for buying the dishwasher, and for being at my side every day and through everything.

And lastly to you—the reader of this book—you have brought the story to life with your imagination and it now belongs to you! Also, you're very dedicated to read this far!

Keep reading for a sneak
peek at the sequel to
The Apprentice Witch

CHAPTER ONE

BREAKFAST

The kitchen was littered with the remains of breakfast. Plates and bowls were discarded on the table, eggshells sat cracked and empty in their cups, crusts of toast lay abandoned on plates. The table-cloth was sprinkled with crumbs and smeared here and there with rich orange marmalade, butter, or bright raspberry jam. The radio burbled in the background.

Arianwyn took a sip from her cup of tea, looking up from the charm recipe she had been working on to gaze out through the window across the rooftops of Kingsport. Ribbons of smoke snaked high into the bright, cool sky. The leaves of a nearby tree were beginning to fade dusty and pale, and the air through the open window had the crisp, cool feeling of autumn.

She felt wonderfully relaxed. She really had needed a vacation after all the goings-on back in Lull over the summer.

Salle, her best friend in the whole world, gave a squeal of excitement and thrust a crumpled newspaper into her face. "Look! There's going to be a parade from the palace this afternoon." She beamed. "Can we go, Wyn? Please?" she asked, her eyes wide, lashes fluttering.

"But don't you have an audition today?" Arianwyn asked. This would be Salle's fourth audition since they had arrived a week and a half ago. She had her heart set on becoming a great actress.

"Oh, I did." Salle smiled and glanced away for a moment. "But it's a silly part, boring, hardly any lines—I'd much rather go and see the king, wouldn't you? *Pleeeeease*, Arianwyn?"

Arianwyn laughed. "I suppose so. We could go to the Museum of Hylund too; it's just around the corner from the Royal Palace."

Salle nodded enthusiastically, stuffing the last piece of toast into her mouth and beaming again. "I still need to visit Leighton & Dennison's to get Aunt Grace a present," she said.

It was Salle's first visit to Kingsport and they had been making the most of it. They'd explored the city on foot and by bus, visited parks, galleries, and the harbor market—and, in between, they'd hurried to theaters all over the capital in hopes of Salle finally securing her first part in a proper play, show, or revue. She really didn't seem to mind what it was at this point, as long as it was in a real theater.

From out in the hallway, they heard the front door of the apartment open quietly, followed by the clatter of shoes being kicked off in the hall and the sound of keys being dropped into the bowl that stood on the hall table.

"Girls?" Arianwyn's grandmother called. "Are you still home?"

"In here!" Salle called cheerfully, spraying a few more crumbs across the table. Grandmother appeared at the door. She leaned on the frame and yawned.

"Late meeting?" Arianwyn asked.

"Or early, I'm not entirely sure!" Grandmother replied as she dropped into her armchair next to the kitchen fireplace. She sighed contentedly, stretching her legs out and resting her head back against the seat. "I had no idea when I agreed to rejoin the Council of Elders that there would be quite so many meetings."

"I guess there's a lot going on at the moment with the war. Is there still a shortage of trained witches?" Salle asked.

Grandmother nodded wearily.

The war against the Urisians in the northern kingdom of Veersland and the increasing magical activity across the Four Kingdoms in the last few years required skilled witches. There just didn't seem to be enough of them.

"I'll make you some fresh tea," Arianwyn said, getting to her feet. She moved quickly across the kitchen. "Do you want some breakfast as well?" she asked, putting the kettle back on the stove and then arranging a cup and saucer ready for the tea.

"Well, actually, I think it's nearly lunchtime. What on earth have you girls been doing all morning? You're still in your dressing gowns!" Grandmother chuckled.

"We're planning to go and see the parade at the palace and then maybe go to the museum," Salle said brightly.

"That does sound very lovely," Grandmother said, closing her eyes for just a moment.

"Why don't you come with us?" Salle asked. "Have the day off?"

"If only." Grandmother sighed. "But I've got reports to read." She reached for her bag, which bulged with folders and papers. "And I've got to meet with some members of the Royal Senate. Why the High Elder asked me, I have no idea, as the last thing I want to be doing is dealing with a load of politicians. I can't be doing with all their bluster and nonsense."

"Perhaps that's why she asked *you*, then." Arianwyn handed her the cup of tea.

Grandmother rolled her eyes and groaned, but she smiled as she settled back into her seat and sipped gently on the tea.

"We should go and get ready—we don't want to miss the parade," Salle said as she darted out of the kitchen. Arianwyn scooped up some of the breakfast things and carried them to the sink.

"I can sort those things out for you. Off you go and get ready." Grandmother smiled.

Arianwyn skipped to the door and then paused, her hand held on the frame.

"Everything okay?" Grandmother asked, the teacup hovering near her lips.

"I . . ." The question had been gnawing at the back of Arianwyn's mind since they arrived in Kingsport. "I wanted to know what had happened about the . . ." She felt a chill just thinking about the night ghast they had encountered in Lull. She didn't dare to say the words, worried that this most terrible of dark spirits might suddenly appear before them in all its horrifying darkness.

Grandmother sighed and placed the teacup carefully down. "The night ghast?" she said, rising to her feet. She was tall, her long silver hair pinned tidily away. She put her hand on Arianwyn's shoulder. "I keep telling you there's nothing to worry about. The council has reviewed all the reports. Mine, yours, Mayor Belcher's, even the Alverston girl's—"

"Gimma?" Arianwyn asked. A name that she also hadn't dared say for weeks.

Grandmother smiled. "That's all done now, all behind you. You don't need to be worrying about anything, Arianwyn. You did everything you could. There is no blame."

Arianwyn smiled, Grandmother's words soothing the worry. She always knew how to make things right again. Then Salle came barreling along the hallway, pulling on her jacket and at the same time fixing a hair clip into place. "Hurry up, Wyn, or we'll be late . . . unless you're planning on going to the royal parade like that?"

Arianwyn smiled and did a quick spin on the spot, flapping her dressing gown around her like a cloak. "But I hear it's all the rage in Highbridge!" she laughed, her dark thoughts briefly chased away.

Salle and Arianwyn hurried along the sidewalk. The streets were packed with people waving small paper flags and jostling toward the palace.

"Hylund flags! Two for a shilling!" a man called from the street corner. He held a bunch of flags tight in his hand like a bouquet of flowers. "Flags, ladies?" he called as Salle and Arianwyn approached.

"No thank you!" Arianwyn called. Salle looked crestfallen. "You don't want to miss the parade, do you?" Arianwyn asked, dragging Salle along as she gazed forlornly back at the flag seller.

They turned off the main street and onto a smaller, quieter avenue full of dazzling white Highbridge houses, each identical to the last, finished with clipped hedges and high metal railings, with ebony front doors and gleaming brass handles. "We can cut down to the Royal Circle this way," Arianwyn explained, recalling so many trips with her grandmother to look at the palace or visit the nearby parks.

The sidewalks in Highbridge were spotlessly clean— not even the first few scatterings of autumn leaves littered the paving stones. They passed a pristine nanny pushing a vast stroller with huge silver wheels that flashed in the warm afternoon sun.

"Well, it's certainly the swankiest bit of Kingsport, isn't it?" Salle said, twirling on the spot just as an impeccably dressed woman emerged from her front yard. Salle's clumsy pirouette forced the lady to dodge aside, almost tumbling into her neatly trimmed hedge. She muttered something under her breath in a biting, crisp Highbridge accent.

"Sorry!" Arianwyn offered quickly, but the woman only glared at them both and carried on without another word, a bit of hedge stuck to her bottom.

"Snob!" Salle called, with no effort to lower her voice, then imitating the woman's very stiff upright walk farther down the street.

Arianwyn chuckled and ran to catch her up. Just ahead, the avenue widened, the buildings curving off to the left and right, opening onto the Royal Crescent, which was already packed with people. As they passed the last house, they were swept giggling into the crowd like paper boats on a river.

CHAPTER TWO

A GLIMPSE OF THE KING

Arianwyn reached for Salle's hand as she was pulled forward by the overenthusiastic spectators. Her fingers tightened around Salle's and they held on tight.

"Wow—this is mad!" Salle laughed. "I LOVE it!"

They clung to each other and were jostled along with the flow of the crowd, everyone calling and cheering merrily.

"Don't let go," Arianwyn shouted. "Or we'll never find each other again!"

Salle nodded. They were suddenly and miraculously shoved to the edge of the sidewalk, and the scene of the parade opened wide before them. The Royal Crescent stood at the heart of Kingsport, the actual "crescent" being a huge oval park that had once been a rose garden for the palace but was now a public space full of trees, fountains, and brightly colored flowers. A broad road circled the park. Usually clogged with Kingsport traffic, today it was empty of cars and buses and swept spotlessly clean. The sidewalks were stuffed full of well-wishers, all kept in place behind strings of bright bunting and a line of soldiers and policemen. It was a sea of fluttering flags, bright camera flashes, and smiles.

"Oh, Wyn, this is amazing!" Salle beamed.

"I think we'd get a better view from farther up." Arianwyn gestured ahead of them.

"My goodness, that's the Royal Palace!" Salle said, tugging on Arianwyn's coat and dragging her along. "I didn't know we'd get so close. Aunt Grace would love this."

Soon, the flowing crowd of people became an immovable wall. "Will this do?" Arianwyn asked. If she stood on tiptoes and wobbled slightly to the right, she could just see the broad steps that led up to the palace gates.

Salle smiled.

"Oh, and here," Arianwyn said, reaching into her satchel. "I didn't think we could do without these!" She pulled out two small Hylund paper flags. She handed one to Salle and gave her own a little wave.

"Oh, Wyn! Thank you!" Salle grinned in delight and swished

her flag this way and that with more enthusiasm than Arianwyn had thought physically possible. From the steps of the palace came the blasting sound of trumpets, which brought a sudden hush to the crowd. "I can see the king!" Salle squealed, tugging at Arianwyn's coat sleeve. "Look. *Look!*"

A figure appeared, walking steadily down the steps of the palace, flanked by courtiers in shining top hats and long flapping tailcoats, or elegant dresses and hats that looked like very fancy cakes. The king waved gently, and the crowd responded with a loud cheer that became a roar. There was a small surge forward, and as Arianwyn tried to stay upright, she stood on someone's foot.

"Oh my word!" Salle gaped, her eyes wide. Then in a mock cheery voice she said, "Goodness, look who it is." She nudged Arianwyn hard in the ribs.

"Sorry," Arianwyn said, looking quickly up and coming face-to-face with Gimma Alverston. "Oh, heavens!"

"Arianwyn?" Gimma's perfect blonde hair, impeccably styled, was swept over one shoulder in a tumble of white gold. Her eyes, usually bright blue, looked dull and red-rimmed, and her skin was pale, as though she had been shut up inside for too long. The effect on anyone else would have been awful, but it just seemed to make Gimma more beautiful than ever.

"Gimma?" Arianwyn asked, thinking for a moment she was hallucinating. But no. She tugged at the sleeve of her thrift store dress. It was too short for her long arms, her wrists sticking out inelegantly. Gimma's was perfect, pristine white—handmade in the best fashion houses in Kingsport, of that you could be certain.

"What are *you* doing here?" Gimma asked, taking the smallest but most definite step away from them.

"Salle wanted to see the parade," Arianwyn explained. Half of Kingsport was here—what an odd question!

"Exciting, isn't it?" Salle said, fixing Gimma with a hard glare and flicked her flag back and forth.

"If you like that sort of thing," Gimma said, stifling a

little yawn and studying her hands. She was wearing pink suede gloves, despite the warm afternoon.

"Well, I think it's amazing!" Salle said, undeterred, waving her flag twice as fast. "It's nearly as good as the Flaxsham parade in the summer, don't you think?"

Gimma's head snapped around. She glowered at Salle. The Flaxsham witches' parade had been a massive disaster, thanks to Gimma.

"Anyway," Arianwyn said brightly, trying to change the subject, "what brings you here, Gimma?"

"Oh, my father's in the parade with some of the Royal Senate." Gimma flicked her hand as though she wasn't really bothered.

Just then, a lady and her small daughter edged their way carefully to the front of the crowd beside Gimma. The daughter was busily eating a bright pink ice cream. The mother smiled at the three girls and then pointed across the wide street. "Can you see Papa?" A soldier nearby blushed and briefly raised a hand in greeting.

"Been doing anything interesting with your stay, then?" Gimma asked, but she only sounded bored.

"Salle's been for some auditions, haven't you?" Arianwyn said.

Salle nodded, but didn't look at Gimma; her flag-flapping became rather less enthusiastic.

"Oh . . ." Gimma replied, flicking her hair back across her shoulder. "Of course you probably know that I'm on probation, pending further investigation or something like that," she added, as though it was quite an everyday sort of thing to open a rift and let a night ghast through from the void, placing a whole town at risk. "And I have to go back to dreary old Lull. To retrain with dotty old Delafield and . . . oh, *you*, Arianwyn."

Arianwyn nearly choked. Someone was having a great deal of fun at her expense, it would seem. "What? Is that a . . . good idea?" she asked carefully, trying not to sound unkind.

"Precisely what my mother said," Gimma answered. "But the director was having none of it, so back to Lull it is. Wretched little place!"

Arianwyn looked at Salle, who rolled her eyes. Near the palace, the royal party were finally seated in several carriages, which were now moving slowly away. At the head of the parade, a pair of guards sat astride two huge white horses. The horses held their heads as though the parade was for them alone.

"Are you ready to wave your flag?" Salle asked the small girl, who smiled up at her shyly. She handed her ice cream to her mother and flicked her flag this way and that.

"You can do better than that!" the girl's mother encouraged her, and Salle gave her flag a sudden crazy swoosh and whooped with delight.

The girl giggled and tried to match Salle's movement. But she was a little too haphazard. As the girl moved her flag back and forth, she knocked her mother's hand. The pink ice cream flicked from the sugar cone and splodged onto Gimma's pristine white dress before sliding to the ground, leaving a gooey pink trail.

"Watch it! You clumsy idiots!" Gimma roared. She spun around, towering over the small child and the mother, who both shrank back a little. The girl burst into tears.

Arianwyn rushed forward. "Gimma, it's just a little bit of—"

"I'm so sorry. I didn't mean to—" The mother tried to apologize.

"Oh, be quiet, you fool!" Gimma spat.

"Gimma!" Arianwyn gasped. She turned to the mother. "I am so sorry, she's—" Arianwyn started to apologize on Gimma's behalf, but what could she say? *She's not usually like this*? That wasn't entirely the truth. But even so, this seemed more than usually unkind, even for Gimma Alverston.

The mother looked quickly at the three girls, grabbed up her daughter and her basket, and hurried away into the crowd as fast as she could.

"What was all that about?" Arianwyn asked, turning to Gimma.

Gimma, pale and blinking, gazed up at Arianwyn as though she had just woken from a dream. "I . . ." she faltered.

"Do you want us to help you home?" Salle asked, stepping forward and reaching out a hand toward Gimma.

"Just boggin well leave me alone!" Gimma snapped. She pulled away from Arianwyn and turned, crashing into a gentleman behind her.

"Watch it, love!" he said merrily, but shrank back when Gimma glowered at him.

"Gimma!" Arianwyn called.

She turned and her eyes suddenly looked dark and blurry, locking with Arianwyn's for a second. She looked quite unlike herself. Her gloved hand came up to brush her hair from her face, and then she was swallowed up in the mass of people.

Gone.

...nwyn faces the toughest spell
...r witching career . . . Can she
...eally see it through alone?

A WITCH ALONE

JAMES NICOL